I0665855

Breaking the Best Friend Code

Breaking the Best Friend Code

ROMANCE IN RIDGEVIEW ❦ BOOK 1

Amy Green

Breaking the Best Friend Code
Book 1 in the Romance in Ridgeview Series

Cover and interior design by Alt 19 Creative

To those who have ever felt
unseen or unworthy of love.
This one is for you.

THE
Jacobsons

Dan Norah

Danny | Ben | Matt | Amelia "Millie" | Jake | Drew | Maeley

THE

Winters

Jack 💔 Helen

Mark   Jonathan   Rosalyn "Rosie"

CONTENT WARNINGS

Reading is a very personal experience and what may trigger some won't trigger others. Before you read this book please be aware of some subjects that are contained.

- Parental divorce (past)
- Parental abandonment (past)
- Talks of anxiety and depression
- Possible parental infidelity (past)
- Talks of parental manipulation
- Projectile footwear
- Negative feelings towards a fictional character who happens to be vegan (This in no way represents the authors thoughts and feelings.)

Two truths and a lie.

1. My name is Amelia Jacobson, but I prefer to be called Millie. If someone calls me Amelia, I'm either in trouble or they don't know me. Or it's my grandmother.
2. Music and theater have been a big part of my life, and I'm good at them, but it's too much pressure to be the best. Not to mention all those eyes on you all the time. I much prefer books.
3. I have never lied to or hidden anything from my best friend ever.

I COME FROM a large family, the middle child of seven and the first girl. With that many older brothers, I guess it's to be expected that I would have a crush on at least one of their friends over the years, but why did it have to be Mark?

Mark Winters is best friends with my second brother, Ben. Ben is the brother I have the most complicated relationship with. It's not that I don't love my brother. I do. It's just . . . Ben is a lot to handle. He has to be the center of attention. When things don't go the way he plans, he has a hard time adjusting. He's also very territorial. When something is his, he has a hard time sharing. You'd think being the second of seven would cure him of that, but nope. It might have made it worse. If I had to guess, I think growing up in the shadow of our oldest brother, Danny, was a lot for him. Danny was the star athlete, valedictorian, and prom king who married his high school sweetheart. Being only fourteen months younger meant Ben was compared to Danny in everything that he did, so he went out of his way to prove he was not only as good as Danny but better.

If Mark being Ben's best friend wasn't complicated enough, Mark is also the older brother to my best friend. Jonathan and I have been inseparable since birth. Since our mothers have been best friends since they were six, our families already did everything together; by the time we came along, it was written in the stars that we would be best friends. At least, that's what Helen, Jonathan and Mark's mom, always says. She is a hopeless romantic who always has a book or movie recommendation at the ready. My parents have always fostered my love of books, but my deep love affair with literature definitely is a product of my conversations with Helen.

Jonathan inherited his love of the dramatics from Helen, and it's another thing that we have shared for most of our lives. At twelve, we were doing anything and everything that would help us achieve our goals of being stars. More accurately, Jonathan wanted to be Gene Kelly while I just loved performing. I did not, however, love being in front of all those people. Strangers make me nervous.

By the time we were in high school, Jonathan was our student director and choreographer. He would still perform, but the roles were fewer and further between. I, on the other hand, had somehow made it out of the chorus and into lead roles. My anxiety would get me before every single show. If not for Jonathan's constant presence, I'm not sure I would have made it through.

When we went to different colleges, I went back to my old reliable books. Books never made me be in front of people. Books never gave me anxiety, and if they did, it was only a page turn away to resolve it. Books always have a happy ending, at least the ones I read. Life isn't like that. And if my love life has anything to show, it is that life is nothing like books or a Hallmark movie.

If my life was a Hallmark movie, then the whole reason I haven't been lucky in love is because my perfect match hasn't appeared. Either he is the son of a CEO of some big company and needs to prove himself, or I have to move to a small town and meet him in a coffee shop. There is always my favorite Hallmark fantasy, where Mark moves back home and discovers that not only does he actually believe in relationships, but he's madly in love with me. Magically, our brothers think it's great and everyone is happy. Roll credits.

But life isn't a Hallmark movie. And if it were, I'm more the quirky side character, the best friend who supports her friends with all her being and cheers for all of their successes. Don't get me wrong, I love my life. I have a job that I love and I'm good at. Is it what I've always dreamed of doing? No, but that doesn't mean I don't love it. I don't resent my friends for living out their dreams either. Some of us have main character energy, and some of us have sidekick energy. I'd rather be Robin than Batman anyway.

One thing that will never change, Jonathan is and always will be my best friend. He has been my best friend for as long as I can remember. I would (and have) done anything for him. Through thick and thin, we have each other's backs. We talk about everything. There is no such thing as a secret between us. . . unless you count my crush on this brother. That we don't talk about. In fact, if Jonathan even knew I have harbored that crush over the years, he would lose it. The very idea of me dating his brother goes against one of the biggest rules of our "Best Friend Code" Jonathan wrote up when we were eleven. It's right up there with always pick up your best friend's snacks when you are at the store. (We were eleven, it was a big deal, okay.) It's not like I ever thought one of us falling for the other's siblings was ever a possibility—again, we were eleven. Mark was sixteen. Maeley was five. The odds were that it wouldn't ever be an issue. Or so I thought. Then as I got older, my unrequited crush became a bigger and bigger secret that I hid from my best friend. It's not like I went out of my way to keep this secret. I just didn't know how to bring it up. Especially the older we got. That five-year age gap isn't such a gap now that we are adults. Not that any of it matters anyway. Mark has made it very clear that he doesn't do relationships. And even if he did, it would never be with me.

CHAPTER 1

Millie

I GROAN AS MY alarm goes off. No matter the day of the week, 5:30 is way too early to be getting up, but on a Saturday? It should be illegal. I want nothing more than to roll over and go back to sleep, but I know I have approximately twenty minutes before my roommate, Torrance, comes crashing through my door.

My best friend, Jonathan, and I first met Torrance when we were twelve and made it into the prestigious Ridgeview Youth Theatre. I was terrified. Ridgeview Theatre is highly competitive and sought after. People traveled for miles to be part of the program and from even further to see the productions. Even now, almost fifteen years later, it's a big deal that all three of us made it. We were three of five twelve-year-olds to make the program.

I met Tori the second week of rehearsals and was instantly fascinated. I knew I wanted to be friends with her immediately, but it took some convincing on Jonathan's part. He had been burned by so many of our former so-called friends. Tori won him over in the end, and we've been the three musketeers ever since. It probably helped that she went to a different middle school than we did which meant she didn't know all of the drama that happened after Jonathan's parents divorced. Not that she would have cared. Tori has a way of not caring about what other people think that I admire and envy even after all of these years. When she introduces herself to new people, she is always Torrance; I can count on my hands how many people she has given permission to call her Tori.

"You better be up!" Tori calls through my bedroom door. "If you aren't out here in five minutes, I'm coming in!"

And she would too. I miss the Tori that hated mornings as much as I do. The one who growled at anyone who talked to her before 7:00 am. Now she's up before the sun every morning for a run before work.

I groan again as I look at my clock, but I make myself get out of bed anyway. It's the one day a week that Tori, Jonathan, and I all have off, and we promised we would make the most of it now that we are all back in California. Ridgeview will always be home, but part of what makes it home is having them with me. I just wish we did normal things like going to the mall rather than run.

"Up and at 'em!" Tori bursts through my door. She looks at me still in my pajamas. "You aren't even ready!"

"I was stretching." It's a sorry excuse, and we both know it. I make a show of standing up and grabbing my shorts and tank. There will be no missing me in fluorescent pink and yellow. I'll practically glow in the dark. "Why can't we just drive to the trail? Do we really need to run all the way there?"

Tori huffs. "Because we are running the trail and then

going straight to your parents' house for brunch. This way we won't have to go back to the trail to pick up the car and can come back with Amara since she is meeting us there."

"Fine." I groan again.

When Tori and I head out the door, the sun is still low in the horizon. The breeze from the ocean gives the air a slight chill, though it will get warmer as the sun rises. We start out slow but soon pick up speed. I'm not a runner like Tori, but I can keep up. Mostly. Thankfully we take the shortcut that takes us the back way. We meet Jonathan by the corner of the park that is equal distance from our house and his apartment.

"About time," he jokes. "You took so long to get here, I took a nap."

I glare at him. Then I see that he's leaning against his car, and I turn my glare to Tori. "Jonathan drove! We could have driven!"

She brushes me off without a word. "Should we get going?"

"Can someone tell me again why we have to be up so early?" I complain. "And don't tell me it's because of brunch. That isn't until 10:00, and it is currently 6:15." I make a show of looking at my watch. "I know I'm not as fast as the two of you, but I'm not that slow!"

Jonathan sits back and watches Tori and I go back and forth before finally ending our argument. "If you two are done, I'd really like to get my run started," he says with a smile on his smug didn't-have-to-run-to-the-trail face. He hands each of us a water bottle. "Shall we?" And he starts towards the park's trail.

We run the familiar two miles faster than I would like but slow enough that we are able to talk. Or rather, they can talk. I make the occasional single work comment. Anything more makes my lungs burn. Jonathan tells us about the upcoming school year and the ideas he has planned for his students. When we reach the end of the trail, I'm gasping for air. Between the two miles we just ran and the two miles we ran to get here, I'm wiped. If Tori gets her way, we still have three miles to my parent's place. I contemplate which would be better, to go back down the trail to Jonathan's car or just suck it up and end up at my parents'.

I'm too much of a people pleaser, especially for my best friends, so I know what I will end up doing, but that doesn't stop me from thinking about it.

Jonathan gulps down his water as he wipes the sweat from his forehead. "Any idea what the big announcement is?"

I shake my head. "No idea."

Tori, completely unfazed by the run, laughs. "It's Norah and Helen. They will look for any excuse to celebrate. Remember when we were kids and they threw a party to celebrate Jonathan being named student director of the spring play? Or when Matt got his cast taken off?"

Jonathan and I look at each other and start laughing. Tori isn't wrong. My mom loves to celebrate anything and everything. Nothing is too small. And his mom is the best co-conspirator she could ever ask for. This brunch could literally be about anything.

"MARK'S COMING HOME!" Helen's eyes shine with tears as she squeaks with excitement. With the level of reverence she gives the news, you'd think he had been deployed, not just living in North Carolina the last few years. Jonathan's older brother hasn't been home much since going off to college, even less since law school. Much to Helen's dismay. We all know she took it hard when not only did Mark go away to school but then went into law just like his father. I've never heard Helen say a bad word about Jack, but with everything that happened with the divorce, I'd be shocked if she didn't at least think them sometimes.

I haven't seen Mark much the last few years. I think the last time was at Ben's wedding when we danced. My cheeks heat at the memory. Very few people know about the childhood crush I had, and by very few, I mean Tori. I've never told Jonathan, and I never will. When we were eleven, we watched a movie where the two best friends make a pact to never date each other's siblings so naturally Jonathan said we needed a pact too. At the time I thought it was dumb; I mean, my little sister was six, and Mark was sixteen. He never would have noticed me, so I agreed. I had completely forgotten about the pact until a few years later; he brought it up again when we had friends from school get into a huge fight because one had started dating the other's sister and hadn't told the other about it.

"That's why we have our pact." Jonathan had been so sure, and I didn't want to disappoint him. Jonathan's feelings were more important to me than any unrequited crush I had on his brother, who was all the way in Texas being a big shot college baseball star. Not that I kept track of his stats or anything. (I totally did.)

I look over at Tori and see her watching me with her eyebrow raised. She can read me like one of my books. I try to calm my thudding heart before I look over to Jonathan. If Tori can read me then so will he, only he won't know all the details.

When I finally look over at him, he is staring straight ahead, and his jaw is clenched. The vein in his forehead is throbbing like it does when he's stressed. I put my hand on his shoulder.

"Hey," I soothe. "You, okay?"

"Fine," he says through gritted teeth.

"I'm guessing you didn't know anything about this?"

Jonathan relaxes his jaw and turns to face me. "Why would I? It's not like he ever talks to me."

He might look angry, but I hear the hurt in his voice. Neither Jonathan nor Mark are great at letting people in, but the ones they push away the most are each other.

I know more than most about their parents' divorce, but I still don't know everything. We were six, Mark had just turned twelve. One minute we were celebrating Jonathan and me being in our very first play, and the next their dad, Jack, was whisking Mark off for a birthday trip. Two weeks later Mom and Dad told us that everyone, sans Jack, were moving in with us for a little bit. Mark was different than he was before. Something happened that changed him. And it's more than the announcement of their divorce. Even back then I seemed to be hyper aware of him. If it was a book, you would say it was a defining moment in his character development, but this is real life. I just know that ever since that trip Mark has made it a point to tell everyone that he doesn't do relationships and he will definitely never get married.

The part of my heart that compares all men, real or fictional, to him is equal parts giddy that I will never have to see him married to someone else and sad that even if our complicated family situations allowed for a relationship that he would never dream of thinking of me in that way. Now that Mark is moving back to Ridgeview, I'll just have to be extra careful that when I see him that I guard my heart. I can't allow myself to go down that road again. My crush on Mark does just that, it crushes me. It makes it impossible for me to move on. Thankfully I won't have to see him too often, it will be a few family dinners and the possible run in throughout town. How hard could it be?

CHAPTER 2

Mark

"Y OU SURE YOU know what you're doing?" Todd asks as he carries the last box and places it in the moving truck.

"Not at all," I admit. "But I can't stay here."

Todd nods. He knows all too well the drama that has been my life over the last few years. As much as I wasn't sure about him when we first became roommates, Todd Bishop has been vital to my sanity. I never knew how much I had pushed people away and built-up walls until I was injured and all alone. My baseball career was over before it began with not a friend in a two-hundred-mile radius. Todd was there when no one else was, and I will forever be grateful for him. He also knows when to push me to talk and when I've reached my limit.

"You're not hoping for some Hallmark moment, are you?" Todd smirks.

I roll my eyes. "No."

Todd doesn't even try to hold in his laugh. "You sure? Those hometown romances are your favorite."

I shove him in the arm, but I can't hold back my smile. He loves those stupid movies as much as I do, and we both know it. Even if no one else ever will.

My phone rings. When I see my father's name on the screen, my face drops. Nothing like a call from Jack Winters to dampen the mood. I hit ignore. I'm not ready to deal with him right now.

"Jack?" Todd asks.

I nod.

"Have you told him you're moving back to Ridgeview?"

"Nope."

"He's just going to keep calling."

Probably, but that isn't my issue. My father has meddled in my life for the last time. I will no longer be his puppet. This is me cutting each and every string. As far as I'm concerned, it's over. All the strides I thought we had made in mending our relationship was just a lie. All Jack Winters cares about is himself. And I will not be a pawn in his games.

When Todd's phone rings, he looks down and sees it's my father. "What do you want me to do?"

I shrug. It isn't my call what Todd does, but I know he will have my back. He won't tell Jack anything I'm not ready to tell him myself.

Todd hits ignore. "I'll probably regret that." He looks up at me. "You sure you don't want me to come with you? It's a long drive to California."

"Are you changing your mind about moving with me?"

He laughs. "Hardly. I already followed you from Texas, I'm not following you to California. Besides, I have this thing called a job." His phone rings again. "At least I do for now."

The annoyance in his voice is evident. I hate that he's going to get dragged into my family drama even more than he already has. There's nowhere to hide when he works for my stepmother's family. If Dad wants information and Todd doesn't answer his phone, then in-person visits will no doubt follow.

I'll owe Todd forever for this.

A FEW MONTHS after my baseball injury, I got a call from my dad. It was the first interaction we had had in years. At first, I didn't want to answer, but I had made my childhood best friend Ben's dad, Dan, a promise that I was going to give Jack a chance. I hadn't kept my word about that, and I didn't like the idea of lying to the only father figure I ever really had. Dan had stepped up in a big way after my parents' divorce. He and Norah not only took our family in, but for the five years we lived with them, Dan made it a point to show up for me and my siblings like he did for his own kids. Even after Mom got her bearings again and we moved into our own place, Dan and Norah were always there to support us in any and everything we did. Big or small, they were there. Something that Jack has never done, even when my parents were still married. He was always bailing on one thing or another, from attending one of my games to going to one of my brother's plays. He was even absent for my baby sister's first birthday. As terrible as it sounds, Dad was as much a part of our lives before the divorce as after.

But I answered the call because I'd promised Dan. Soon that phone call turned into a lunch. As much as I tried to fight it and knew that it was too good to be true, I guess a part of me was still that little boy who wanted his dad to notice him.

After we had lunch, we started texting and emailing on and off. Even with the extra contact it was a shock when I got the invitation to his wedding. He hadn't even mentioned that he was seeing someone, let alone that he was getting married. It was a gut punch all over again. This time it wasn't Mom he had been lying to, it was me.

Now knowing what I know about my father, I'm ashamed of how much I let him control my life. When I lost baseball, I was broken. I had no direction, which is exactly what my father preyed upon. I'd always been a top student and athlete. I had always known I would and could do great things. Now with the one thing I had been working so hard towards being gone I didn't know what to do. I became a shell of my former self. For the first time in my life, I didn't have a goal or a purpose. With a little coaxing and, what I'm sure he'd call guidance, I fell right into his hands. Dad got me a job working for the firm his in-laws did business with. I excelled. He mentioned going to law school. It wasn't what I had ever wanted to do with my life, but my current job wasn't too bad, and I was good at it. Why not? Sure, I'd go to law school. What I didn't know was that as I worked and worked, he was pulling strings behind the scenes the whole time. Now I look back at that time and I don't know what parts I earned due to hard work and what parts were given to me because Jack Winters had made it happen.

Perhaps I'll never know, which stings. I have worked hard, and I've been proud of that hard work. I've even grown to love the law more than I would have ever imagined. It's become part of my identity. Just one more thing that has been taken away from me.

> **ROSIE:** Call Mom! She's driving me nuts!

> **MARK:** What's going on?

> **ROSIE:** She's all worried about you driving, but she doesn't want you to know she's freaking out so she's just calling me nonstop to see if I've heard from you.

> **MARK:** I'll call her.

I DRIVE FOR a couple more hours before stopping for the night. I pick up some dinner and bring it back to my room before I get settled for the night. I text Todd to give him an update on where I am, and then I call Mom. She answers on the second ring.

"Mark? Is that you?" Her voice is laced with worry, but there is also a familiarity that is comforting.

"Hi, Mom." I settle onto my bed as I talk to her. I think it's the first real conversation we've had in a very long time. She catches me up on her upcoming trip that she is taking with some friends. The irony of her not being home when

I get there isn't lost on either of us. I promise her that I will call her as soon as I get into Ridgeview and that we will have dinner when she gets back.

Mom pauses before she hangs up. "You should talk to your brother."

"Jonathan doesn't want to hear from me," I retort. I don't even know what I would talk to him about. My brother and I have never had anything in common. I was all about sports, and he was all about theater. The divorce just divided us more. While we lived with the Jacobsons, it was just easier to fall into a routine of not talking to each other. Then when we moved into our own house, we were so set in our ways that it was hard to go back to how things were before. I don't know, I'm sure I'm the one to blame. It's not like I've been home a lot over the years. I couldn't wait to get out of Ridgeview. Make my own way in the world.

"That's not true. He loves you, Mark," Mom says, her voice thick with emotion.

A heavy weight settles onto my chest, so I do what I do best: avoid any and all emotions. "I've got to go. It's been a long day. Call you again tomorrow."

After a quick goodbye, we hang up.

I need to get my head on straight. I can't afford to have all these emotions. Emotions make you do stupid things, and I've done enough of those to last a lifetime. I need to shut it down now before they get too heavy to ignore. The last thing I need is to toss and turn all night when I have another full day of driving tomorrow.

Sometimes it is hard for me to remember I have nothing to do with my dad's mistakes. When I was twelve, I was dragged into one of my parents' fights. Dad planned a whole birthday trip without talking to Mom about it. We flew to Chicago to go to a few baseball games, but really we spent time with an overly flirty coworker of his. I'd heard my parents argue over whether there was another woman, but after that trip I could confirm it. I wasn't even that surprised by it, to be honest.

Two weeks after we came home, Dad asked Mom for a divorce. He said she was holding him back, that he wanted more in life than to be held down by a wife and kids. And then he pulled the rug out from under us by putting our house up for sale. Mom probably could have fought him on it, but she was too broken up to know how to go head-to-head with her big shot lawyer of an ex-husband. Thankfully, the Jacobsons welcomed us with open arms into their home.

By the time we moved out five years later, things had changed. My mom depended on me. I wasn't just a son or a big brother anymore. She relied on me to get my brother and sister to school, rehearsals, and whatever else they might need when she was at work. It was way too much for a seventeen-year-old to deal with. When it came time for college I just wanted to get out of there, away from all the extra responsibility. I know logically that my parents' issues are on them and not me, I still sometimes have a hard time being around my mom. At first it was because I knew she needed me, and I just wanted to be a kid. Now its more because I know how much she relied of me and needed me and I, just like my dad, abandoned her and hardly looked back. In all the ways that I have made choices that remind her of my father, I hate that this is one of those things. It hangs over me always in the back of my mind.

Moving home is going to bring up a lot of emotions that I really don't want to deal with. And if nothing else, tonight is not the night to try to figure it out. Right now I just need to get get some sleep so I can be alert on the road tomorrow.

CHAPTER 3

Millie

I SIT AT MY desk twirling my pen over my notepad full of doodles. I should be prepping for my meeting, but instead I'm just staring into space. I flip my pen one more time, but this time I'm less coordinated, and it flies out of my hand knocking down two of my picture frames and the entirety of my decorative cup filled with pens. I scramble to pick everything up.

"What's up with you today?" Trina looks at me with concern.

"Nothing, I'm fine," I lie. I'm not fine, but I don't know why.

"You don't seem fine. You seem…distracted."

"I'm not distracted." I'm a little more defensive than necessary, but there is no need for me to be distracted. There's nothing going on in my life outside of work. I go to work. I go home. Wash. Rinse. Repeat. My life is boring.

Trina picks up one of the frames from the floor. "Whoa! Who's the hottie in this one?"

I peek over at the picture in her hands. It's from a hike we had taken the summer after high school graduation. Jonathan and I had raced to the top of the hill, and I tripped, spraining my ankle. Mark and Ben had been further up the trail and came running down when they heard me scream. The picture was taken when we had made it back down. Mark had insisted on carrying me the whole way down on his back even though it was bad for his knee. We had all been laughing at something that Ben had said. It was a rare moment that the four of us shared. It's one of my favorite pictures.

"Meeting in 15 minutes," calls Kimber. Her eyes narrow in on me from her perch in the doorway to our team of desks. I don't know what I ever did for her to dislike me, but boy, does she.

I return my focus back to Trina, still not sure who she is calling a "hottie" and hopeful that it's not Ben, because gross.

"That's my best friend Jonathan." They've met before so that leaves Ben or Mark. "That one is my brother, Ben. He's married now." I look for any sign of disappointment. Nothing.

"Uh, I mean the hottie who's carrying you."

That's what I was afraid of. The only person left. Mister Unattainable himself. The very definition of off-limits. The one moving back home after years of being away. Not that I've thought about that at all since Helen told us three weeks ago. "That's Mark. He's Jonathan's older brother and Ben's best friend."

I try to keep my reaction even. I haven't seen or talked to Mark since Ben's wedding. He's come home a couple of times, but I have conveniently not been around. I've tried to push everything out of my mind about what happened that night, including that dance, but every once in a while, it creeps back in.

"Please tell me you've dated."

"Me and Mark? Date?" I scoff. I fight the color climbing my neck with everything I have. Trina is eyeing me closely, her perfectly sculpted eyebrow quirked. I bark out a laugh. "He thinks of me as his best friend's little sister."

I half expect Trina to call my crap, but she doesn't. "I wish my brother's friends looked half that good. All my brother's friends are trolls."

"They can't be that bad."

"No, they are literally trolls. They get together and play Dungeons and Dragons on the weekends."

"That doesn't mean that they are actual trolls; they just like to play a game where there are trolls."

"Is this the time you tell me that you are a secret D&D player or something?"

"Hardly."

WHEN I FIRST got to college, I had no idea what I wanted to do with my life. I knew I loved music and theater, but I also knew that being in front of people and being constantly scrutinized was my biggest nightmare, especially with Jonathan being so far away. I fell even more in love with books when I took a creative writing class. The ability to create and tell a story was fascinating. I didn't know if I wanted to write books, plays, or something else, but I wanted to write.

After hitting a few bumps along the way, I lost confidence in my ability to put words to the page. After a few too many negative critiques, I found it was just easier to help others follow their dreams. I'm side character energy; it's kind of what we do. We help others find and follow their dreams. Maybe someday it will be my turn, but for now I'm okay with it.

At least that's what I keep telling myself.

My senior year of college when I got an internship at a big publishing house, I felt on top of the world. It was even better when I was offered an entry position after graduation. Two years ago, Sheila Quimby, my then-manager, decided to branch out on her own and start her own independent publishing company. She wanted to focus more on indie writers rather than bigger names. She believes in giving everyone a voice and asked me to join her back in Los Angeles with a job that was more than I could have ever dreamed of having just started my career. It was an added bonus that the job would bring me closer to home. I could move back to Ridgeview and be close to my family.

Quimby Publishing's goal is that we work as a family and do as much in-house as possible. That means that each department works together to make each author feel special and successful from the start of the project through publishing and launching. We do a little bit of everything, from media coverage and launch parties to the more obvious edits and actual publishing. I have loved being able to be part of the process and holding the hands of my authors', people I have grown to truly care for, as we work together to make their dreams a reality.

"Welcome everyone," Sheila says in her smooth southern accent. "I know all y'all are as excited as I am about a lot of our upcoming projects this quarter. How about we get the ball rolling with a little good news minute. It's important that we celebrate each of our accomplishments." She smiles at everyone around the table, "Even those that aren't work related. We are a family after all." Sheila settles into her chair and listens intently to each piece of good news that is shared.

After everyone shares, Shelia sits up straighter in her chair. Now that we've had our "family bonding," she's in business mode.

"Now let's get a status update from each department." She looks to her right, "Stuart, how are things in sports?"

I must have been daydreaming way more than I thought I was because when Sheila calls my name I jump. Maybe Trina is right; I am distracted. I'm off my game today. Which is so unlike me.

I look up to see Shelia's expectant expression. "I'm sorry, Sheila, I must have missed the question."

A brief impatient look crosses her features before it smooths back out. "I asked how things are going with Franklin Davis?"

"The Forest series is really coming along. I think his readers will really like this trilogy as much as if not more than his last. Book one is doing well in sales and really picking up a following. He's been invited to that FanCon that is happening at the end of next month to do a short...as well as a reading to some of the fans. With this new attention he has asked that some of his contract be revised to include appearances and what is to be expected on either end." I give my colleague Stacia an inquisitive look, and I'm grateful she knows what I am asking her and gives me a wordless nod before, I add, "Contract updates have already been sent off for the added revisions and should be back to us to have Franklin sign by the end of business day tomorrow."

"Perfect. Is Miles' firm handling the contract?" Without waiting for a reply, she answers her own question. "Of course they are!"

Another grueling twenty minutes later, the meeting ends, and Stacia and I are free to head back to our part of the office.

The children's department is a little slice of heaven compared to the dull, monochromatic look of the rest of the office. We have bright office chairs that complement the white desks tops, pictures of books we have published cover the walls, and our newly added reading nook was just the final touch needed. It's perfect.

As we cross the threshold of the doorway Trina looks up from her desk, "Troy called while you were in the meeting."

"Is the contract done already?" I ask with excitement. "I wasn't expecting it to be done until tomorrow at the very earliest!"

"Yes, because he loves you and wants to have your children," she chortles.

Rolling my eyes, I reply, "Just the contract is fine."

"You've got to admire how hard he tries, Millie. I mean your contracts get done so much faster than anyone else's ever do. And you get a personalized call. I usually get an email telling me that they are ready for pickup at my convenience." Stacia almost sounds as if she is complaining.

If I could transfer all this extra attention to literally anyone else I would. I mean, it was sweet at first. Troy learned my Starbucks order, sent imported chocolates to the office, he even once ordered a singing gram. It started crossing the line when the pickup lines got more and more suggestive the more I told him I wasn't interested. He went from the sweet guy across the hall, who I only saw as a friend, to the guy who never grew up and still acted like a frat guy real quick. I've become a challenge he must conquer. Well, sorry not sorry, buddy. It ain't ever happening.

"I appreciate the speediness of his attention to work related things. As far as anything else, the only thing that Troy Donaldson is interested in is the fact that I don't fall at his feet. He certainly isn't used to it."

"But he sure does look good trying," Trina swoons.

"Don't be that girl," I fake a gag. "He's a player, and we all know it. And it doesn't matter how he looks while doing anything since I am not and never will be interested. So, if you all will excuse me, I am going to go pick up the contract so that I can do my job."

I stand and start collecting my things I need to take with me. I look up and notice Kimber glowering over at me.

I glance at Stacia and Trina, "What is it with her? Why does she hate me so much?"

Stacia shrugs. "I don't know. You've both been here forever. Maybe you accidentally said something that she took the wrong way?"

"Maybe, but I can't think of anything. We've hardly ever had a conversation. Then all of the sudden she started glaring at me all the time."

"Maybe it has to do with the fact that you've gotten promoted multiple times and she's still a secretary?"

I shrug, "I guess, but wasn't she offered a job in a different department, and she declined? Said she liked being the executive secretary?"

"It's probably the fact that she's had a thing for Troy forever, and all he seems interested in is you," Trina says nonchalantly.

I groan, "Enough about Troy! Anyone who wants him is more than welcome to him. I don't want him!"

With the mention of Troy, I start making my way to the door. If I can get these contracts, then I can call Franklin. Fingers crossed I can get him to actually sign them.

"At least while you are there try and check out the new guy!" Trina yells as I open the door, "Rumor has it he's one hot…"

The door closes behind me before I hear the rest of that sentence. Not that I need to imagine too hard what she yelled. Trina is a lot of things, and I love her, but when she is between relationships, she is almost impossible to keep on track. She has a one-track mind until the next man.

CHAPTER 4

Mark

I'VE ONLY BEEN back in town for two weeks, and between starting a new job and getting settled into my new place, who has the time to be texting or calling anyone? Not that I've tried super hard. I'm fine on my own. A lone wolf, as they say. Not sure who "they" are, but that's not the point.

I've talked with Ben a few times, but his wife isn't exactly my favorite person (nor am I hers, if we're being honest), and after finding out that they are expecting, I haven't really made the effort to find the time to hang out. Which I know sounds terrible. He's my best friend, and I'm not even making an effort to see or talk to him. I just don't need to be reminded of the life I don't have. Not that I want marriage and kids. I don't. I decided a long time ago that marriage and family weren't worth the risk of hurting those you claim to care about. Some might say I'm jaded; I say I'm a realist.

My mom has never been the same since my parents' divorce. She basically went into hibernation while we lived with the Jacobsons. I don't mean that she wasn't a parent, more that she was always sad. She never talked about Dad leaving and would change the subject whenever anyone else ever did. I know she lost a lot in the divorce. We all did. Not only did we have to move out of our house, but a lot of my parents' friends disappeared. I guess you really do learn who your true friends are when things get rough.

I shake the thoughts away. No need to relive the past. It doesn't change anything. I wish I had some work to distract me, but since I've only been here a short time, I'm still in orientation mode. Which sucks. How am I supposed to bury myself in work when there isn't any work to get buried under?

I smile as I see my little sister's name pop up on my phone.

> **ROSIE:** How's the new job going?

> **MARK:** Fine. Still settling in.

> **ROSIE:** Is that receptionist still flirting with you?

> **MARK:** Sure is.

> **ROSIE:** Is she cute?

> **MARK:** She's old enough to be my mother.

> **ROSIE:** Didn't answer the question.

I know she's joking, but I'm not opening my love life (or lack thereof) up for discussion with my little sister. Not now. Not ever.

MARK: Shouldn't you be in class or something?

ROSIE: Canceled. I have a free hour.

MARK: And you spent it annoying me, I'm touched.

ROSIE: Don't think too highly of yourself. I'm also texting Jonathan.

MARK: Ouch, and here I thought I was your favorite brother.

ROSIE: Have you talked to Jonathan since you got back into town?

MARK: We texted last week.

ROSIE: Are you counting the family group text, or did you two actually talk to each other?

MARK: A group message is still talking.

ROSIE: Really? You're going with that?

Before I can respond, another text comes in.

ROSIE: TALK TO JONATHAN

I know a lot of my lack of relationship with Jonathan is my fault. I didn't know how to deal with all the pressures of being the man of the house. Even before Dad left, I always felt that need to shield Jonathan from what was going on. I didn't want him thinking that any of what was going on between our parents was his fault. He was only six. As we got older I felt that undeniable need to be at everything since Dad never would. I would go out of my way to protect my little brother from anything and everything I could, but we didn't talk. Not about the divorce, not about life. Nothing.

After the divorce was final, we moved in with the Jacobsons. It was helpful for my mom, but now that I'm older, I wonder if it was the final straw that broke what little relationship Jonathan and I had. It was easier for me to talk with Ben and Danny and for him to talk to Millie. It just felt more natural. Once we moved into our own place, the damage was done. We had five years of having others to talk to. We were more set in our ways. I always just assumed we would figure it out someday. Someday we would have more in common. Someday we would be as close as the Jacobsons are with each other.

Someday still hasn't happened. When it came time for college, I all but ran away from Ridgeview, hardly going home even on breaks. It's not like I don't love my brother, I do. I just don't know how to show it. I'm not exactly good at talking about my feelings. I'm so proud of all that he has accomplished; I've just never told him so to his face. I've told Mom and Rosie, which is basically like telling him.

"Well, someone is a Grumpy Gus this morning!" says Nancy.

She runs the front desk and has been more than welcoming to the newcomer. After working for such a large firm in Charleston, this small office is going to be an adjustment. I have a feeling Nancy is all about knowing the ins and outs of everyone's lives. I'm not sure how I feel about that. If I learned anything from my last breakup, it's that it makes life so much easier to keep work and home separate.

Natasha was everything I could have wanted. Not only was she gorgeous, but also wicked smart with a work ethic that rivaled my own. We met shortly after she started at Bancroft and Watson as a paralegal. After working on a few cases together, we started having lunch together which soon turned into dinner. Then we were basically living together. If it would have been up to Nat, we would have been; it was one of our biggest arguments. Call me old-fashioned all you want, but the only woman I will ever live with is my wife.

The beginning of the end of our relationship happened when I brought Natasha with me to Ben's wedding. To say it went badly is an understatement. Natasha and I had been growing more and more distant, and we were fighting more and more. We were always working. I had hoped that coming home to Ridgeview would get us back to how it was before work took over our lives. Before Natasha had become so hyper-focused on me making partner. She wanted us to be some sort of power couple. I just wanted to be proud of my work. If I'm going to dedicate my life to something, I want it to mean something. I don't need nor do I want all the recognition.

Over the week we were in Ridgeview, it became more and more evident that not only had we grown apart, but we also no longer wanted the same things. Maybe we never did. Natasha bailed on all of Ben's wedding related activities and didn't even make it to the wedding. It didn't matter how important it was to me that she be there, work always came first. I would always come second to work. It was my parents all over again.

By the time the plane landed back in Charleston from Ben's wedding, the relationship was over, but the drama of it all was just beginning. Monday morning came, and by lunch the entire office knew we had broken up. I could feel eyes on me everywhere I went. I would go into meetings, and whispering would follow me. Natasha did everything in her power to throw any kind of dig my way, including starting to date my office rival, Rick, just to prove that she could. I kept my head down and did my job. Natasha finally saw that I wasn't going to let her get a rise out of me and backed off.

Six months ago, when it came time for them to announce the new partner, it was between me and Rick. Against my better judgment, I went to dinner with my dad who was in town a few days prior to the official announcement and something in the way he told me not to worry about the promotion, that it was as good as mine, made me pause. He had gotten me the promotion. He was still interfering in my life, despite how much I had told him that I didn't want him to do anything. I still hadn't forgiven him for going behind my back and talking with Mr. Watson after my initial interview. Nothing I had worked for and thought I had earned was really mine. It was all a lie.

I got home from dinner and sent my resignation letter. Rick could have Natasha and the promotion. He could have all of Charleston for all I cared. I was done with it all, including my father. I spent the next few weeks deciding my next move. I didn't talk to anyone other than Todd. I didn't answer texts, phone calls, or emails. I was a complete nomad. By the time I told my mom that I was moving back, I had already been back to California a few times. Once to take the California bar, once for my final interview with Miles Lexington, and once to sign all the closing paperwork on my new place. I didn't see a reason for her to get her hopes up if things didn't work out.

The feeling of eyes watching me pulls me out of my thoughts. I look up at Nancy, still focused on me.

"I'm not grumpy," I say far dryer than I intended. "I just got done talking to my sister," I add hoping it makes my tone sound lighter.

If she is bothered by my tone, she doesn't show it. "Older or younger? My older sister used to give me such a hard time! I always had to remind her she wasn't my mother, and we already had one of those."

"Younger. I'm the oldest."

"Just the two of you or are there more?"

"We have a brother that's in the middle."

"Are you close?"

"To my sister. My brother and I are pretty hit and miss." That's the polite way to describe it, at least to a mere stranger.

"You're from around here, aren't you?"

"Yes, ma'am. Born and raised. Went out of state for college and law school. I've visited over the years, but it's actually been a good two since I've been back at all." That is probably way more information than she was looking for. It was definitely more information that I was intending to give.

"Are the rest of your family still here?"

"My mom is. My brother is a high school choir and theater teacher at our alma mater, and my sister is in fashion school a couple hours away."

"Well, I'm sure your mama is happy to have you home again." She gives me a soft smile and turns to go, but turns back around to add, "I'll be at my desk; let me know if you need anything, Sugar."

"Thank you, Nancy," I say with the first genuine smile I've had in days. Nancy was right about one thing; I am a little grumpy today. I don't mean to be. I've just been under this dark cloud for what feels like months. Maybe a little caffeine boost will help shake me out of my lull.

Making my way from my office to the break room down the hall, I run right into Miles Lexington, my boss and owner of Lexington Law, causing him to jostle and spill his freshly poured cup of coffee all over his white shirt and down his pants, ending in a puddle on the floor.

Completely embarrassed and horrified, I struggle to find the words, "Mr. Lexington! I am so sorry! I—"

Mr. Lexington holds his hand up to stop my stammering apology, "Mark! It was an accident, no harm done. And it's Miles."

He is far calmer than anyone who is covered in a scalding liquid should be.

I'm still in panic mode. "I'll clean it up!"

Nancy appears with a mop, "Already on it." She gives me a reassuring smile.

"Then at least let me pay for the dry cleaning," I beg, feeling completely helpless. I need to do something.

Miles holds up his hand to silence me, "Mark, my boy, it's coffee. It spills. Heck, I spilled some on myself just yesterday. I have an extra set of clothes in my office just for this purpose. If I had a dollar for every time I spilled coffee, I would be a very rich man." His eyes twinkle.

How is this man real? My previous bosses would have had my head if this had happened. Paying for dry cleaning would be the least of my worries. I knew how to deal with that. This? I have no idea what to do next. I stand there dumbfounded for what I'm sure is several minutes rather than the actual seconds it is in real time.

"I'm going to have you shadow Troy for the next couple of days so you can get an idea of how we do things around here now that you have settled in a little more. This way you can start meeting some of our clients. We are a small group, so we don't necessarily have individual clients but rather all work together. We also have a mixer of sorts coming up in a couple weeks where you will be able to meet a lot of them."

"Yes, sir." I correct myself, "Miles."

"Did you hear that, Troy?"

Troy pokes his head out of his office like a gopher, "Hear what, now?"

"Mark is going to be shadowing you for the next couple of days. Show him the ropes. Introduce him to clients. You know the drill."

"Sure thing, boss!" Boss? What is this NCIS? Unless Miles is going to Gibbs-slap him, because that I'd pay to see. It's only been a few days, and I already don't like the guy. He might be a great lawyer, but I'm just not sure about the rest. "I have that contract for Quimby that's being picked up, and then shadow away!"

"Quimby! Perfect! They are one of our most prominent clients! Mark definitely needs to meet them."

"Sure thing, boss." Troy's response is much less enthused this time.

As I walk back to my office, I pass by Nancy's desk and whisper, "What's Quimby?"

"Quimby Publishing, they are our floor-mates. We do a lot of work for them since they are such a small publishing house and don't have their own law department. Troy has had his eye on one of the children's editors for months. Truth be told, I think it's probably because she wants nothing to do with him and the poor boy doesn't know what to do with that."

I think I'm going to really like Nancy, and that little bit of gossip makes me laugh. I want to meet this children's book editor because Nancy is right, I don't think Troy is used to rejection, and I respect a woman who doesn't get easily seduced by big muscles and a wannabe smoldering grin.

Twenty minutes later, I'm sitting at my desk with the door ajar when I hear the office door open, and a bright cheerful voice comes through the door. "Good morning, Nancy! How are you doing today?"

"I'm doing good, sweetheart, how about yourself?"

"I'm excited that these contract revisions got done so quickly. I wasn't expecting them until tomorrow!" Her voice is almost in a singsong pattern, and the animations seem oddly familiar. "How are you doing? Your granddaughter had her birthday last week, didn't she?"

That voice! It's so familiar!

The two of them are laughing as Troy comes bounding past my office like a cheetah stalking its prey. Have I mentioned that I don't like this guy?

"Amelia, I thought I heard your beautiful voice. You are looking as foxy as ever this fine Friday." Seriously? Who calls someone foxy in a professional setting? Forget cheetah, Troy is a snake.

"Hi, Troy." The annoyance in her voice is evident though it is polite. "I was just telling Nancy how I wasn't expecting the revisions to be done this quickly. Thank you for getting it done."

"It was my pleasure to be of assistance to you. We should go out and celebrate later, if you know what I mean."

"The contracts are enough."

"Oh, come on. It would be fun." Troy's voice is oozing with what I think he considers charisma. It makes me uncomfortable, and it isn't even directed towards me.

"The answer is no."

"Why, doll face?" Troy Donaldson is single-handedly what gives men a bad rap. Based on how tight he wears his suits so that they show off the obviously long hours he spends at the gym, I'm sure he's one of those creepy lurkers that sit in front of the weightlifting mirror watching themselves as much as they are watching the room behind them just waiting for their next pounce. "Is it because of that boyfriend of yours?"

She has a boyfriend, and he knows about it? What a louse!

I'm about to make my way out to the reception area and put a stop to the cringeworthy exchange when I run into Nancy. Her eyes are wide and knowing. "Aren't you supposed to be shadowing Troy and meeting some of our clients today?"

"I was just on my way out." I make the boy scout symbol with my hand. I'm not sure why; I was never a scout.

"Amelia, since you are here," Nancy interrupts whatever degrading remark Troy was saying next, "Let me introduce you to our new associate. This i-"

"Mark!" The voice I knew I recognized. The woman who has haunted my dreams for the last three years.

"Hey, Millie." It's suddenly hard to speak. I clear my throat. "It's good to see you."

My voice is an octave higher than normal. I clear my throat again. It's not like I didn't know she lived around here, but I certainly wasn't expecting her to be in my new office.

"I heard that you were back in town!" She comes over and pulls me into a hug. I feel heat at every contact point. "Wait," she pulls back, "you're the new guy in the office that has all the women in the building all hot and bothered?"

I feel heat rising up my neck at her words. People are talking about me? That's the last thing I want. That is part of what was so appealing about working in such a small office. Less gossip.

"You two know each other?" Troy breaks in.

"Yes," we say in unison, "we..."

After we look at each other, I motion for her to continue. No need for us to duet the whole answer.

"We grew up together. Our moms are old friends, and we are best friends with each other's brothers." That was a much clearer way of explaining it than I ever could. I'm still in shock that Millie is here. Millie Jacobson. My Millie. Not that she is mine. I clear my throat again.

"Oh, how wonderful!" exclaims Nancy, finding way more humor in this whole situation than is necessary.

Grabbing what I am assuming is the contract she came for, Millie steps forward and takes an envelope from Troy's hand, and I can't help but smirk as I see the stupefied look on his face.

"Thanks again for being so quick on this, Troy." She points to the envelope. "Nancy, let me know how you and Martin like that restaurant. You know how Amara is about food, and she says that it is worth the drive. Mark," her eyes barrel into me, "we will have to do lunch sometime and catch up!"

I just nod like an idiot.

CHAPTER 5

Mark

Ben's Wedding ❧ Three years ago

TAKING ONE LAST look in the mirror before heading to the patio for wedding party photos, I can't help but notice the hollow look in my eyes. There are dark circles forming, and I just look like I feel downtrodden. It's not a complete lie; I'm physically and emotionally spent. This is supposed to be a happy time. I mean, my best friend found the love of his life (his words, not mine). And yet all I can do is think about all that is missing from my life. How selfish am I? I can't even give Ben one day where I'm not thinking about how I feel versus sharing in his joy.

Seeing him so happy and absorbed in Belinda just makes me realize that I have never felt anything close to that for Natasha, my girlfriend of almost two years, or anyone. Ever. And maybe I never will. Maybe Natasha showing her true colors is just what I need to get it into my head that I'm not made for relationships. I tried. I clearly failed. It's like baseball: it had its run, but now it's not part of my life. That's what this is, just another passing phase of my life.

"Mark!" I jerk at the sound of my name being called. "There you are! My mom has been looking all over for you!"

I look over at Millie walking towards me.

I clear my throat., "Sorry." I was I was just overthinking everything that I have ever failed at. "I must have lost track of time."

Concern shadows her face. "Are you okay?"

I stand up straighter. "Yeah. Why wouldn't I be?"

"I don't know." She studies me closer. "You just seem off."

There's a feeling inside me that I can't explain. It's like my heart constricts to her knowing glance and concern.

I just give her my best grin as I scoff it off. "You look ridiculous."

The dresses for the wedding party have been a bit of a sore subject since originally my little sister, Rosie, was designing and making them. In true Belinda fashion, she not only changed her mind but managed to insult Rosie and everyone who had vouched for her in the process. I don't understand fashion at all, but I know my sister would have made something far better than this fluffy peach monstrosity.

Millie's brows crease as if she is going to say something, but then seemingly changes her mind. She shoves me in the arm. "Don't be a jerk."

I swat at her back. "I'm not being a jerk, I'm merely commenting about how much you look like—"

What is it exactly?

"Molting geese?"

I laugh—, no, that's not it. "A shower loofah."

She goes to swat at me again, but this time I'm prepared and I block her, catching her hand, and I feel the zap through my whole body. I drop her hand as if it burned me. There is a charge in the air as we sit staring at each other, neither of us moving. The silence is crackling.

Millie is the one to finally break the silence. "If you don't get out there, then Ben will never forgive me because it will be my fault."

How long have we been sitting here? It's strange how comfortable it all feels.

"Yeah. Right behind you." I motion for her to lead the way out to the gardens. I make sure to stay a few paces behind.

What is going on with me? I have a girlfriend. You don't look at another woman when you are with someone else. I'm not that guy. That's something my dad would do, not me. What am I doing looking at Millie, of all people, like that? But the voice in the back of my head points out that she was looking at me too. There is no way I was imagining that electric charge in the air when our eyes were locked. The logical part of my brain blames my lack of sleep and the fact that Millie noticed that I was off and not myself. Usually I can mask it, but I'm just too preoccupied with everything else going on, and she found me at a low moment. That's all that was. Friendly concern.

When we finally make it to the garden, Millie and I are clearly the last ones to arrive. Everyone is busy getting into position for the next grouping of photographs. It's only 9:00 am, and it's already been a long day. I want to fast forward through all of this so I can have a moment to clear my head.

My phone buzzes in my pocket. I take it out and read Natasha's name on the screen. I don't even have to read the text to know what it's going to say.

> **NATASHA:** Sorry, can't make it to the ceremony. Meet you at the reception later.

I don't even care at this point. Which should tell me more than I care to read into at the moment. There are tons of people around, and my mask is fully in place now. I transition myself into a completely numb state. I know Todd would tell me that this is a sign I need therapy, but who has the time for all of that?

> **MARK:** It's fine. See you then.

Even as I type out the words, I know I'm lying to myself. It isn't fine.

I have a sudden flashback to overhearing my mom say the same thing to my dad when I was a kid. The numbness that I have been trying to hold onto throughout pictures is fading, and the mask is starting to crack. That's when it hits me: I'm not turning into my dad, I'm dating my dad. Natasha is exactly how he has always been. I try to push the thought out of my head and put the mask back into place. I force back all the feelings of abandonment and resentment from childhood, but the nagging feeling stays in the back of my mind throughout the whole ceremony.

As best man, I have a prime view of the entire audience as they watch Ben and Belinda make their vows. I do everything in my power to not look at my mom, the guilt of all my past feelings creeping up my spine. It just serves as a reminder that as much as I fought not wanting to become my father, what I did was turn into my mother. Always bending over backwards to make those around me happy, even at the cost of losing myself in the process. This new self-awareness couldn't have come at a worse time. I'm barely holding it together. Somehow, someway, I make it through and don't miss any of my cues. I even manage to fake a smile the whole time.

When the preacher finally announces Ben and Belinda as man and wife, the crowd stands in applause as they kiss for the first time as a married couple. As they make their way down the aisle, Millie makes eye contact. I try to break it, but I can't seem to will myself to look away. Something keeps drawing me back in. I can't keep away. Even in that peach loofah dress she's beautiful. Not in the same way that Natasha is.. Natasha spends time and money to look as good as she does, while Millie is naturally enchanting. She illuminates the world around her, and she makes everything brighter.

Later that evening during the reception I look over to see Millie sitting alone. I stand up from my seat, next to Ben's brother, Matt, and walk towards her.

When I reach her table I outstretch my hand towards her, "Dance with me?"

Millie looks at my outstretched hand then back up to me.

"Come on, Mills, it's a wedding. It's kind of our thing."

She laughs but takes my hand and stands up. "I wasn't aware we had a thing."

"We've danced at every wedding we have ever both attended. That's a thing."

"So, are there any other things we have that I'm not aware of?"

I scrunch my face as if to think about it, "I'll compile a list and get back to you."

CHAPTER 6

Millie

I CAN'T GET OUT of Lexington fast enough. My heart is racing. Mark is here. Mark Winters is in my building. I knew he was back. I knew I would see him at some point, but I never would have imagined that I would run into him while at work. And of course, he looked incredible. Because why wouldn't he? That would make seeing him for the first time since the wedding too easy.

I try to shake off my nerves before heading back into Quimby. I have to pull myself together if I'm going to make it through the rest of the day. The last thing I need is Trina quizzing me on what the new guy is like. My whole body will give me away, and then I will never hear the end of it. I lean against the wall and stare at the door, not ready to go in, but I can't stay here in the hall. What if Mark comes out of Lexington and finds me just sitting here? I'd look like some kind of stalker. Maybe I'll just give myself ten more seconds, then I have to go back into work.

My time is up. I need to put on my metaphorical big girl pants and just go back into my office. My hand is inches away from the door handle when my phone dings with a notification.

> **JONATHAN:** These teacher in-service speakers are killing me. I'm so bored!

> **MILLIE:** Only a little longer.

> **JONATHAN:** Is this how my students feel during class? Because if so…

> **MILLIE:** Stop it! You're a great teacher. They are lucky to have you!

> **JONATHAN:** Thanks, Mills. Break's almost over. See you tonight.

"JUST PICK A movie already!" Jonathan yells from the kitchen. It's our weekly movie night that we have had pretty much every week since we were kids. Over the years we haven't changed much, only adding Tori and then our roommates when all of us moved back to Ridgeview. Every Friday night we get together and eat copious amounts of food and watch as many movies as we can stand. Or rather, as many as we can agree on.

"I already gave my suggestion!" Tori yells from down the hall.

"We're not watching Pretty in Pink again!" Amara calls back. "We've watched it four times in the last three months."

Tori barrels through the hallway and launches herself onto the couch next to Kiersten. "It's not my fault you don't appreciate good cinema."

Amara tosses a handful of popcorn at Tori, who responds by throwing a pillow. The two of them go back and forth until Kiersten finally has enough and grabs the pillows. Without a word she puts them back on the couch and picks up the remote, choosing a movie.

Amara bails somewhere between movie two or three to go hang out with her boyfriend, Duncan. Then we lose Kiersten around midnight. Jonathan, Tori and I pushed through to the very end topping out at six movies, not quite beating our long-standing record of eight. Still, we out-did ourselves with the copious amounts of junk food we consumed. I was more than happy to oblige when it was suggested somewhere around 2:00 AM that we skip our Saturday morning run.

I finally stagger out of my room around 11:00 AM with my head pounding. With the way I'm feeling, you'd think we partied harder than watching movies and eating an entire five-pound bag of gummy worms.

"Are you just getting up?" Amara asks as I enter the kitchen. I have a vague memory of her coming home last night, but I have no idea what time.

I muster a nod. "Yeah. We haven't gone that hard on movie night in a long time."

Amara hands me a couple aspirin. "You should probably eat something that has some sort of nutritional value."

I sit and wait for the rest of the lecture, but she doesn't continue. Amara is the most health conscious of all the roommates, but I guess that's to be expected when your parents are some of the top medical professionals in their respective specialties in the country who didn't allow any refined sugar in the house when you were growing up. It didn't help that she also studied nutrition when we were getting our undergrads. Over the years, Amara has become our resident foodie and has very strong opinions on what makes good food. If Amara likes the food from an establishment, then it's bound to be excellent.

I roll my eyes at her as I go to the fridge and grab the eggs. "Yes, Mom."

Amara laughs and swats at my butt.

"About time you got up!" I hear Tori say from behind me. I turn to see her in her running clothes guzzling water. "I've already gone for my run and had a full workout and you're just getting up?" Tori wipes at the sweat beading her hairline.

"How do you have the energy for all that?" I gape at her. We didn't head to bed until well after 4:00. Here I was thinking I was doing pretty good getting up at 11:00, and she's already had a full day of exercise?

Tori shrugs as she grabs an apple and heads down the hall towards her room, passing Kiersten.

Kiersten turns and watches Tori disappear into their shared room before facing us. "She's not sleeping again."

"Again?"

"Not more than a few hours at a time. I haven't seen her this bad in a long time. Any idea what's going on? She usually talks to me, but she hasn't said anything." Kiersten is our mother hen, and she and Tori have a special bond that I used to envy. I used to be the person that Tori told everything to, but as much as things have stayed the same since we were kids, they have also changed. I know I don't tell her everything like I used to. Not that I don't want to talk to her about it; it's more that our lives aren't as synced as they used to be.

"Duncan said he ran into her at one of the bars he plays at a few weeks ago. Do we think she's partying again?" Amara asks.

"He did?" I ask, trying and failing to hide my concern. Tori has always been more of a partier than Jonathan or I ever were. When we were in high school, she would occasionally hang out with a few members of the theater tech crew that were in a rougher crowd, but if Jonathan or I weren't around, she didn't usually stay long. We had more fun doing our own thing than trying to fit in with others.

In college things changed. We all got busy doing our own things, and it took a while for Tori to find her place. Then add that she stayed pretty much year round working and going to school, and she made friends with people that I never met. Not that she ever did any hard partying, but she would stay out late and hang out with people that I never felt fully comfortable around. Tori would just tell me I was too sensitive and sheltered. She would invite me to come along, but I was too chicken to see just how right she was about me. I liked my predictable and sheltered bubble. It was safe there. Why rock the boat?

I send a quick text to Jonathan to see if he has any idea what is going on with Tori and make a mental note to pick up some double chocolate brownie fudge ice cream on the way home. I might not be her go-to person to talk to about everything anymore, but I still know the way to get her to open up is through her stomach.

WITH SCHOOL STARTING next week, I know this will be one of the last chances that Jonathan and I will get to spend time together in a long time. Those first weeks of school are super busy for him as he gets all of his choir ensembles organized and gains a feel for what productions would be the best fit for this year's theater students. As has become our little tradition, the weekend before the new school year, Jonathan and I take a whole day and do all of our favorite things. We go to lunch, get all dressed up, and then go into the city to see a stage production. It isn't as fancy as it once was when Jonathan lived in New York, but living back in Ridgeview makes it more special. It's home.

"I'm glad we're doing this." Jonathan says as we sit down at our table. "This past week of inservice meetings has been torture."

I smile at my best friend. "Of course. It's tradition."

A tradition that I wouldn't trade for the world. Back when we were growing up we would go see these productions and dream of one day being up there, but now I'm just glad to be able to enjoy the show. There was a time not that long ago when Jonathan's dream was still to be on the stage, but after years of living like a nomad, he decided teaching was the life that he wanted, and I'm so glad he did. Those were long years, living in different parts of the country, hardly being able to spend any time together. I guess that's part of growing up—you don't get to live near your best friends anymore—but I much prefer this. Ridgeview wouldn't fully be home if Jonathan wasn't here with me.

We spend the rest of lunch talking about the upcoming school year and some of the students he's excited to work with again. Over the last two years he's put his heart and soul into this program, and it shows. He really does want the best for these students.

"What about you? What have you been working on? Anything exciting?"

Now would be the perfect time to mention that I ran into Mark at work. That he not only works in my building, but that he works for the law office we do a lot or business with. Something holds me back, though, the memory of how Jonathan tensed up when Helen told us the news. Something shifted in Jonathan that night and I haven't been able to figure it out. I also know my best friend well enough to know not to push it. He'll talk about it when he's ready.

"Nothing too exciting. I have a couple authors getting ready for a FanCon coming up." I like that Jonathan is interested in my work, I know it was hard for him to understand why I walked away from theater, but I'm grateful he's been so supportive in my choices to go into writing and then into editing. Nothing compares to the support of your best friend, and I'm glad that we've been able to keep that after all these years.

CHAPTER 7

Mark

THE REST OF Friday went by in a bit of a blur. I tolerated any time I had to spend shadowing Troy as best I could. Since that whole thing with Millie, he had been about as thrilled as I was with the whole situation. But he shouldn't worry because as soon as I can be let loose on my own, we will spend very little time together. I can tell that he is a decent enough lawyer and does his job well, but I'm better. For better or for worse, my competitive nature has been activated.

Old habits die hard, and I, as usual, am one of the last to leave the office.

"Any plans for the weekend?" Nancy asks me as we make our way to the door.

"Nothing too exciting. Just grocery shopping and watching whatever game is playing."

"A handsome man like you shouldn't be stuck at home all weekend. Save that for the old married folks!"

I chuckle. "Not really my thing. And most of my buddies from growing up have either moved away or are all settled down with their own families." I sigh. "Besides, I'm still getting settled into my place. I still have boxes to unpack. Not everything has found its home yet. I still need some furniture as well, so I'll probably do that tomorrow. Is that exciting enough for you?"

"No, but it's a start. And if today is any indication, I don't think you will be single for long." She waggles her eyebrows at me.

I have no idea what she is talking about. What about today would make her think I wouldn't be single for long?

"I've known Millie Girl since Quimby opened, and I have never seen her so animated. She was positively glowing when she saw you."

I try to brush the comment off. "Millie is always animated. I used to call her a live action cartoon character."

Nancy smiles. "She is definitely a breath of fresh air. It's such a shame she is single."

I furrow my brows. "Single?"

I know Troy mentioned a boyfriend in his verbal assault earlier today.

Nancy chuckles. "Oh, she's single." She leans in as if to make sure we aren't overheard even though we are completely alone. "We just tell Troy she has a boyfriend. It's kind of like how he calls her Amelia."

"I was wondering about that. She's always been just Millie."

"I think we both know there is nothing Just Millie about Millie Jacobson."

Don't I know it. And I'm not sure what to do with all of this information that I just got. Millie is single. In all the times we have seen each other over the years, we've never both been single. There's always been a protective barrier. It's a lot easier to ignore any pull I have felt towards her when there is no way to reciprocate. What is it about her that gets under my skin so much? Is it because she should be the very definition of off-limits? Ben would flip out if I dated his little sister. Jon would probably never talk to me again. Not that he talks to me much as it is.

I used to think that the deal to never date one another's siblings Ben and I made in eighth grade was dumb. I mean, we were five years older than his sister and ten years older than mine. Not a chance of it happening. But now? Now I kind of regret the lack of foresight thirteen-year-old Mark had. Not that I could have ever foreseen a building attraction towards Millie Jacobson. She was always Ben's little sister and Jon's best friend. Until she wasn't.

The rules are completely different now.

I say goodnight to Nancy and head the rest of the way to my car. I have a lot of thoughts to digest tonight.

> **TODD:** You're still going to say you aren't living in a Hallmark movie?

> **MARK:** Shut up. I'm not living in a Hallmark movie.

> **TODD:** Are you sure? The woman you've had a not-so-subtle thing for just shows up at your new office and tells you that you should get together. This totally has Hallmark written all over it.

> **MARK:** Aren't you the one who told me not to move home to have a Hallmark moment?

> **TODD:** What can I say, there was a marathon on last night, and I couldn't not watch it.

I laugh. Todd might have a gruff exterior, but that giant goofball is a softy. And apparently an even bigger romantic than I thought he was.

> **MARK:** You watched without me? How dare you.

> **TODD:** You moved away. It's fair game. If it makes you feel better, I didn't come up with any subplots or alternative endings.

> **MARK:** You know, that really does make me feel better.

> **TODD:** But seriously, you're really not going to do anything? She's single. You're single. You haven't stopped thinking about her since you and She Who Must Not Be Named broke up. Hallmark or not, I still think you should at least go to lunch with her. If after that you don't want to ask her out then let it go.

> **MARK:** I can't ask her out.

> **TODD:** Can't or won't? Those are two very different issues. You can't live in fear forever, man.

I know Todd has a point and he means well, but I don't really want to dwell on what all that loaded statement really means.

> **MARK:** Will you stop shrinking me? I'm not one of your patients.

> **TODD:** Of course not. I don't have my degree yet.

> **TODD:** And you'd never be able to afford me.

I'M A GROWN man in my thirties, but you'd never guess it by the contents of my shopping cart. I still live off of frozen, overly-processed food like I did in college. It's during my great frozen pizza debate that I hear my name being called from the opposite end of the aisle.

"Mark? Is that you?" A voice I would recognize anywhere.

I look up and smile at Norah Jacobson. "Hi, Norah."

She parks her cart next to mine and pulls me into a hug. "Welcome home! How are you settling in?"

"It's taking a bit, but I'm starting to feel more settled into my place. And I started work a few days ago so that's helped."

"I know you've been busy, so I will forgive you for not stopping by the house yet."

I know she doesn't mean to make me feel guilty, but I do. I have been avoiding going over there. Not really sure why, I've always loved being at the Jacobsons. I think it was my way of avoiding Millie, but now that I've seen her there aren't any more excuses.

"I ran into Millie today," I tell her, just needing to say something.

"Oh, did you?"

"Apparently we work in the same office building." I'm kicking myself for bringing this up. I know that look on her face, and its trouble. She's starting to plot something. I try to change the subject. "How have you and Dan been?"

"We are doing well, thank you for asking. Dan retired last year, and so we have done some traveling, but nothing major. I want to be around for the kids and grandkids." She looks into the sparse items in my cart. I can almost calculate how long it will take for her next statement's delivery. "You can't be living on all of this junk! Please tell me you aren't living off of frozen and processed meals!"

I laugh inwardly at how familiar and predictable Norah is. I could lie and tell her that these are just backups, but who am I kidding? If I'm not eating out, then I'm eating all of this so-called junk.

"I won't stand for it! You are coming to dinner tomorrow night at our house! Your mother would be horrified if she found out that I knew about this and didn't feed you!"

I can't resist messing with her just a little. "Good thing she is out of the country for the next couple of weeks then, isn't it?"

The look on Norah's face is everything. She swats my arm then gives it a squeeze. "Tomorrow, 7:00."

"I'll be there." I comply knowing there is no use in arguing, plus I haven't had a Norah Jacobson home cooked meal in years. "Do you need me to bring anything?"

I know the answer, but my mother would be more upset if she found out I was rude than she would be to find out I was getting a majority of my groceries from the freezer aisle. I learned all my culinary prowess from her after all.

"Just your handsome self." I haven't been called handsome so many times in one day in a very long time. I'm starting to feel like I'm in grade school and it's picture day. "I'm sure you have seen Ben, and you have already seen Millie, but the rest of the family will be so happy to see you! And Jonathan will be there, of course. I'm still trying to convince Rosie that she needs to come."

"It's quite the drive for her, and she is in the middle of midterms." I have no idea if you even have midterms when studying fashion, but it seems like a plausible enough excuse. I also know that if Norah wants to get Rosie there enough, she will get her there. Even if it takes convincing Dan to go up and pick her up. If it's what she wants, he will make it happen.

I say goodbye to Norah, and I finish my shopping, processed food and all.

The next day I text Ben to check in.

> **MARK:** Hey man, what time are you getting to your parents' house tonight?

> **BEN:** Norah caught you already? She's really stepping up her game.

> **MARK:** Ran into her at the grocery store last night. Think my cart about gave her a heart attack.

> **BEN:** Let me guess, you were in the frozen food aisle.

> **MARK:** You know me well.

I smile at the ease that comes when talking with Ben. Then I feel guilty for not making more of an effort to see him since I've been back. We've texted and tried to make plans, but it just hasn't happened. He has his own life and family now.

> **BEN:** That I do.

> **BEN:** Belinda hasn't been feeling well so I will probably only make an appearance.

> **BEN:** Probably right at 7.

> **MARK:** Leaving me alone in the lions' den, huh?

> **BEN:** Hey, what do you want me to do, abandon my pregnant wife in her dire need?

I roll my eyes. And there it is. The real reason why I haven't seen Ben since I've been back. Belinda is anything but helpless, but she has Ben wrapped around her finger, and he will do anything and everything she says. It's like how his parents are and yet so different. Norah isn't manipulative; she is fully capable and independent. No one knows that more than Dan. He just wants to be the one who helps her dreams become a reality. I don't understand the spell Belinda has Ben under. It's gotten worse the longer they have been together. I've tried everything to get along with her, and it's better than it used to be. At least I don't think she is Maleficent anymore. I still don't like her, but she's tolerable. At least in small doses. It also doesn't necessarily mean I want to spend time with her. Or earn her wrath for hanging out with Ben when he would otherwise be with her.

DRIVING UP TO the Jacobson home feels strange after so many years away. It also feels the most at home I have felt since being back. The whole drive had me swimming in memories. I pass the field where Dan taught us how to drive—in a golf cart, because no one would have been dumb enough to give us keys to an automobile right away. It's also where he taught all of us older boys how to throw and catch a baseball then watched us as we practiced on weekends and during breaks from school.

The road curves bringing me to the area that becomes Santa's Village every December, turning all thoughts and memories back to Millie. I can't get what Nancy said out of my head.

"I've never seen her so animated."

"She was glowing."

What do I do with that? Up until yesterday, the last time I saw her, I was holding her in my arms as we danced at Ben's wedding. If I hadn't still technically been with Natasha, I might have kissed her. There was definitely a charge between us that day. Even in that ridiculous dress Belinda made her wear, she took my breath away. She noticed that I wasn't myself despite having put my mask in place. Millie has always noticed things about me that no one else does. She also has a way of getting me to open up.

I jump when there is a knock on my car window. I'm on such autopilot it didn't even register that I had parked. I look up to see Ben waiting expectantly.

"About time!"

"Benny Boy!" I can't resist using the childhood nickname he hates. I get out of my car and give him a hug. "Good to see you, man! How is Belinda feeling?"

It's a bit of a relief that I don't have to see her tonight.

"Pregnancy is rough! Do you know what all the female body has to go through?"

"I remember enough from health that you can stop that sentence right there." Ben has never had a filter, and I really don't have any need to ever know anything about Belinda and her changing body.

"What are you two weirdos doing out here?" Millie is walking up the path followed by my brother and Torrance running to catch up. Jon gives me the slightest of head nods then he and Torrance go into the house. Millie hangs back a little longer. "You do know you can come into the house. Aren't you two cold?"

I'm about to agree with her when Ben and his inces-sant need to argue launches his verbal charge. "Look who's talking. It's 40 degrees out, and you're wearing leggings, flip flops, and a sweater that doesn't even cover your shoulders. Maybe if you wore more substantial clothing you wouldn't be so cold."

Now that he mentions it, her clothing is all I can focus on. I have to admit, I don't mind what I'm seeing. There is something different about how she looks this evening versus how she looked yesterday when I saw her in the office. I have to stop myself as my eyes start drifting. Nope. Don't do it. Do not check Millie out with Ben standing right here. Just get through tonight and then go home. It's a simple task. The look that Millie is giving me tells me she noticed me looking at her. She doesn't seem to mind.

Oh, boy, am I in trouble.

NORAH PULLED OUT all the stops tonight. She made all of my favorite things. If it was anyone else, I'd swear they were trying to make up for all the dinners I'd missed over the years, but since it's Norah, I know she is just wanting to make me feel welcomed. And I do. A little overstimulated, but welcomed.

In typical Jacobson fashion, the whole family was at the door to greet me the moment I walked in. From a failed prank attempt by Jake and Drew to Matt putting me in a head lock after giving me a big hug, it's as it always has been. Except it's not.

Danny is married. He and Ashleigh are expecting baby number three. Their twin girls run all over the place with Matt's daughter. Jake and Drew are graduating from college. Maeley is home from school for the weekend. Then there's Millie.

She's hardly looked at me all night. I caught her eye a time or two, and she gave me a smile and a wave, but then she went right back to talking to Jon and Torrance. I have to force myself not to watch her as she laughs at something my brother said. I have a sudden jolt of jealousy towards my little brother, which is ridiculous. They're friends. If something was ever going to happen between them, it would have by now. Wouldn't it? Not that it matters to me. It shouldn't matter to me. Oh, but it does.

Bottom of the 9th, my arm is sore. I'm tired. I don't want to look at Coach, I know he'll ask if I want out. If I want him to bring in the closing pitcher. I'm this close to pitching a no-hitter, I'm not giving up now. I take another breath and glance up into the stands.

The entire Jacobson-Winters Clan is in jerseys and face paint with our numbers plastered everywhere. Pretty sure I saw poster cutouts of our faces at some point. Jon and Millie had got the entire crowd hyped up during the 7th inning stretch and haven't stopped except to shout onto the field. Millie is currently trying to get everyone to sing "Sweet Caroline" with her. It's sort of adorable. I'm sure Ben is beyond annoyed, which I'm sure is probably a prominent reason for her doing it.

I turn to look at Danny over on first base. He nods telling me I've got this. Somewhere behind me in left field I know Ben has my back. One more breath and I windup for my pitch with laser focus.

It's all a blur as the crowd goes completely bananas. I did it. I'm still in shock as I get tackled to the ground by my team. Coach pulls me up and pulls me into a hug. With tThe biggest grin on his face, he shouts, "I knew you could do it!"

"Thanks Coach!" At the end of last season I thought he was crazy. I've been playing third base since t-ball, but he needed a new pitcher on varsity and insisted I was the man for the job. We trained all summer and all pre-season getting me ready. "Thanks for believing in me." And I mean it. No one has ever believed in me more than Coach.

A new swell of cheers comes from the stands and I don't even have to look to know who it is. I laugh as I look up to see Millie scream- singing her new theme song for me. It's been her new thing this season to give each of us a new theme song each game. Something about how, "Everyone deserves theme music. It makes them special." I notice that she also selected my number to wear this week.

Somewhere behind me I hear Danny and Ben joking and laughing about Millie. I don't pay them any mind; I think it's kind of cute how excited she is.

Later that night as a crowd of girls surround me and Ben, all I want is to go home, but Ben is loving all the attention. When asked which of the girls I'm interested in, I give Ben a death glare. None of them, and he knows it. I know if I was ever to actually have an interest in someone Ben would step down, but I'm not.

"What, are you waiting for Millie to grow up or something?" Ben jests. "Because I think she'd be totally cool with that." He

laughs. I know he thinks it's funny now, but I also know that if circumstances were different, he'd totally freak out. Good thing Millie is five years younger than us and odds are in his favor of never having to deal with that.

CHAPTER 8

Millie

FAMILY DINNERS HAVE been a staple for as long as I can remember. We always had dinner together growing up, but Jacobson Family Dinners were an event. They were one day a week that my brothers didn't have practice or games, and I didn't have a rehearsal or show. As we got older and moved out of the house, the dinners where we were all there became fewer and further between. When I moved back home, it was the first time in years that all of us children lived close enough to be at dinner each week. It's something that we all make an effort to attend. For one, we know how important it is to Mom to have that one dinner with all of us, but I know it's something we all love as well. At least I know I do. I love being able to see my brothers and sister on a weekly basis. We might talk almost everyday in our group chat, but being in the same room is completely different.

Most weeks Jonathan and my roommates come with me after our weekly dance class at the gym, but this week it's only Tori and Jonathan. Amara has plans with Duncan, who no matter how many times he has been invited has yet to come with us, and Kiersten has been studying for a big test she has coming up and wanted to take advantage of a quiet house. Not that I can blame her on that one; living with three other people can get pretty loud at times.

"I'm pretty sure Missy was trying to kill us this week," Tori huffs out.

Jonathan hands each of us a bottle of water. "It wasn't that bad."

He's not even out of breath. I guess there was a time when I wouldn't have been either, but those days of being able to dance and sing at the same time for hours on end are long past.

I take a long drink from my water bottle before I finish packing up my stuff. "She did seem to be a little more intense than usual."

We grab our stuff and head out to Tori's jeep. It's cool out, but after working up such a sweat driving with the windows down blasting our favorite tunes feels amazing.

As we drive towards my parents' house, it's clear that we are the last to arrive. Tori parks, and as we head towards the house, we run into Ben and Mark talking beside what I assume is Mark's car. I know I just saw him when I ran into him at Lexington, but that doesn't stop me from noticing how much more filled out and muscular he looks now. Our eyes meet, and I'm pretty sure I catch Mark checking me out. It's kind of a great feeling, but it's a short-lived one as I feel my brother's glower. Nothing like the presence of your big brother to throw a bucket of ice water on a moment. After a less than pleasant exchange with Ben, I head inside.

The rest of the evening I'm all too aware of Mark's presence. I try to ignore the feeling, but it's always there in the back of my mind. He's only been back in town for a couple weeks, he's already infiltrated my office building, and now he's at my parents' house. I knew I'd see him, but I really wasn't prepared for how I was going to feel. It's going to be a lot harder than I originally thought to keep those old feelings in check.

I PULL UP to the drive-through window to pick up my usual Monday order: two iced coffees, one hot chocolate, a peppermint tea, and two dozen donuts (of various flavors). Once I get the drinks and boxes secure, I make my way across town to meet up with Ashleigh and the girls for our traditional Monday morning breakfast.

I park my car in the driveway and start gathering everything to bring inside. I'm about to dump all the contents on the front porch when Danny opens the door and saves the drinks from crash-landing into the azalea bush.

"Whoa! Do you think you have enough stuff here?" His amusement is evident though I know he's not at all surprised. I am our mother's daughter through and through.

"It's Monday," I say as if that explains everything. Danny just laughs as he takes the breakfast contents and heads inside.

I race into the kitchen to put down all my bags as I hear running feet speeding in my direction.

"Aunt Millie!" Danny and Ashleigh's twins chant in unison as Austyn flings herself into my arms and Ashtyn grabs my legs. It's a miracle that we don't all come toppling down. "What did you bring us, what did you bring us?!"

They have hardly taken a breath, making it hard for me to answer them. I just laugh as they continue to berate me with questions. Ashleigh waddles her way into the kitchen holding her swollen belly, a bemused look on her face. "Girls! Give your aunt room to breathe!"

I wrap them both in one last hug before I whisper, "Go look in the bags."

I smile as they race over to the table to scavenge through the bags for their treats.

"You spoil them." Ashleigh tries to sound annoyed, but I see the smile she's trying to hide.

"Being the favorite aunt is a lot of work!" I mock protest.

A series of "OHHH WOW!", "This is the best day ever!" and "DONUTS?!" is yelled from the kitchen counter as Ashleigh and I make our way over to the living room sofa.

I grin at her as she sighs and rolls her eyes at me. "Donuts, really? More sugar is the last thing they need."

"It's Monday," I shrug. "Don't worry, I brought you one too."

"You really didn't have to."

"And I got your peppermint tea."

"Bless you." Ashleigh shifts her weight and places her feet up on the coffee table.

"And how is baby Adalyn doing today?" I rub my hand along her stomach and stop when I feel little kicks greeting me.

"It's Anistyn now. She's good. Been kicking me in the ribs since 4 AM, but she is healthy and active."

"She'll fit right in!" My brother says as he comes into the room, kisses his wife, and then continues to tie the knot in his tie.

"Getting a bit of a late start today, aren't you, Danny? I didn't think I'd see you this morning."

"My morning client canceled so I thought I'd stay home and spend some time with my girls." Danny leans down and kisses Ashleigh again.

"Daddy! Daddy! Daddy! Come look! Come look!"

Danny goes into the kitchen to investigate what all the excitement is about.

"If you weren't expecting me, then why did you get my coffee order?" He calls.

"Because you're always late on Mondays," I call back.

I turn back to Ashleigh. "Anistyn, huh?"

"Yeah. I think. I don't know. Maybe? Why? Do you like Adalyn better? Or do we go in a different direction altogether?"

"You do know you can just wait until she gets here, right? See what fits her." I see the stressed look pass over Ashleigh's features. "Whatever you pick will be perfect."

"I know, but I like being prepared. Last time it was all about being new parents. Not to mention the fact there were two of them. This time we will be outnumbered and have three, three and under. It's a lot to try and prepare for."

"How can I help?"

Ashleigh's eyes twinkle, and there is something about the look she is giving me that I don't like. "Oh, you can help by telling me all the details of your life."

I scrunch up my face in confusion. "What are you talking about? You already know all the details of my life. There are no details. I have no life."

"Uh, whatever it is that's going on between you and Mark!" She says it like it's the most obvious thing in the world.

"There's nothing going on between me and Mark Winters." I try to keep my voice even, which is in complete contradiction to what my heart rate is doing.

Ashleigh looks at me in disbelief, "Oh, please. I realize the last time I was single I was fifteen, and I'm an old married woman now, but I have eyes, Millie. There was definitely something going on on Saturday at dinner."

"What are we talking about?" Danny comes in with his mouth full of donut and his iced coffee in hand.

"Nothing!" I say as Ashleigh says, "Dinner on Saturday." Danny nods.

"What's with the nod? Nothing happened at dinner!" I'm getting defensive, but nothing happened. It was a Jacobson Family Dinner as usual. Sure, it was the first one that Mark had been to in years, but that was it. Nothing out of the ordinary happened. Okay, so he might have checked me out, but that was it. Nothing else.

"There was a vibe," Ashleigh explains.

"There was nothing to vibe."

Danny puts his arm around Ashleigh as he sits behind her on the arm of the sofa. "There was totally a vibe."

"What vibe? There was no vibe." What are they even referring to? Nothing happened.

"You and Mark." Danny is being way too casual about this.

"Nothing is going on! I ran into Mark at work on Friday. Mom invited him to dinner, and he came. End of story." I'm ranting now but come on. I'm totally being tag-teamed right now, and this whole thing is coming out of left field. "Mark and I didn't even talk to each other at dinner."

"Exactly," Ashleigh says as she stretches her arms and leans forward while my brother starts rubbing her back. She looks back over at me, "You two were completely ignoring each other."

"So because we were ignoring each other there must be something going on and there was a vibe?"

Danny takes a long drink from his straw. "You and Mark have always had this kind of connection. You just get each other. You always talk. You're one of the few people who can get him to open up." He takes another drink. "The fact that you wouldn't even look at each other says that there is something going on, even if neither of you will admit it. Besides, I'm pretty sure I saw him watching you a time or two."

"Not to mention the last time both of you were in town at the same time was at Ben and Belinda's wedding, and you two got pretty cozy on the dance floor." Ashleigh gives me a smug look. She's lucky she's pregnant.

There is so much to digest right now, but I circle back to what Danny said, "Wait, you said 'even if neither of you will admit to it.' Danny, please tell me you haven't said anything to Mark about this."

Silence.

"Danny," I warn. "Tell me you haven't said anything about this to anyone outside of this house."

Still nothing.

"Danny! I can't believe you! This is so embarrassing!" My cheeks are blazing, and my heart is racing.

He shrugs. "It's my brotherly duty to make sure only guys with the best of intentions come near my little sister." He flashes his devilish grin. "Besides, why does it matter? If there isn't anything going on?"

I bury my face in my hands. I can't believe this is happening. I'm going to kill Danny for this. Ashleigh too, as soon as that baby is born.

Danny gets up, "Well, this has been fun. I'm going to head into the office now."

One last kiss to Ashleigh and he's out the door.

Pure mortification settles over me. How am I ever supposed to look Mark in the eye again? I'm going to have to work with him. Danny went too far. This is so embarrassing! Older brothers are the WORST!

I don't stay too long after Danny leaves. I'm still beyond embarrassed and Ashleigh isn't helping things. Sometimes I feel so lucky that my brother married one of my favorite humans on the planet. Today is not one of those days. Today I wish Ashleigh didn't know how to read me like a book since she's been in my life since I was ten. She's seen me at all my levels of awkwardness and twitterpation when it comes to guys. I never told her about my crush on Mark, but I'd be surprised if she hadn't at least suspected over the years. Which just makes this whole situation even worse!

No sooner am I in my car to leave, then my phone buzzes with a notification from another one of my brothers. They're just coming at me in droves this morning.

MATT: Are you sure you don't mind watching Maddie tonight?

MILLIE: I love watching Maddie. Besides I've been telling you to go on this date for weeks now.

MATT: It's not a date!

MILLIE: Then what is it?

MATT: A work function.

MILLIE: A work function where the two of you will be alone, you made reservations, and you will not be discussing work at all.

MILLIE: At least you shouldn't be.

MILLIE: Matt, don't you dare talk about work to this woman all night, do you hear me?!

MATT: Fine, it's a date, but it's not that big of a deal.

MILLIE: Not a big deal?! Do you remember when your last date was?

MATT: It hasn't been that long

MILLIE: 5 years! That's a long time! You haven't gone on a date since Maddie was born. This is a huge deal!

MILLIE: Go have a good time, and don't worry about me and Maddie. I won't let her stay up a minute past midnight, promise.

MATT: I won't be out that late

MILLIE: I'm just saying if you want to see how things go for longer than dinner I am available for as long as you need.

MATT: Quit suggesting what you're suggesting, Millie, it's a first date.

MILLIE: I'm not suggesting anything. Any suggestive thought that passed through your head was all your own. And even if I did suggest anything, which I didn't, you and Jennifer have been in this dance for months now.

MILLIE: Now if you'll excuse me, some of us actually have work to do. See you tonight.

MATT: Thank you. You're the best.

Of all my brothers, I'm probably the closest with Matt, and not just in age. Matt is the brother who will do anything for you with no judgment. Not that my other brothers are super judgmental. Well, Ben can be. We all fill our roles.

Danny is the oldest and, I would say, the wisest. He will help and support you in anything you need, but he also is going to give you advice whether you want to hear it or not.

Ben is the bulldozer who is going to share his opinion about anything and everything in your life, and you just have to take whatever he says with a grain of salt. He's not going to sugarcoat anything he says. Ben is no-nonsense and straightforward. His opinions have only become more abrasive the longer he and Belinda have been together.

Jake and Drew are the troublemakers and jokesters of the family. No family gathering is safe if both of them are home at the same time. They'll never take things too far, but they are going to get as close to the line as they can without crossing it. It will be interesting to see how things change once they grow up some more and get into actual relationships. It's going to take some special women to tame those two.

Maeley and I are the most similar in our temperaments, though my siblings would argue that I'm the most stubborn. To which I usually stick out my tongue. I would also argue that Maeley has the most grace and poise. Nothing rattles her. She always fights for what she wants. She's definitely main character energy.

Then there's Matt, who has the most patience of anyone I have ever met. Even when life gets hard, he is still there for everyone else. When his ex bailed, leaving only a single page letter, he never batted an eye. He just picked up and made a life for him and his daughter. When I was having a hard time at school and almost quit, he found a way to fly out to Texas to spend the weekend with me. It didn't matter that he was still in school, working full time, and suddenly a single father. He was still there for me like he always had been.

Babysitting my niece, whom I adore, is the least I can do for the brother who literally drops anything he has going on to be there for me. And if that babysitting happens to be because he's finally going on his first date since his terrible ex broke his heart, all the better.

I PULL INTO the parking garage at work Tuesday morning, the lack of sleep hitting me hard, but it's worth it knowing that my brother had a good time on his date. I get out of my car and head to the passenger side where I have a large box that is filled to the brim with potential manuscripts to go through with my team today.

"Millie! Hey, let me help you with that!" I hear Mark say as he grabs the box, I was struggling to get it out of the car. Did it gain weight on the drive here? I got it in the car just fine this morning.

"I got it!" I snap way more forcefully than intended.

He jumps back a step or two but doesn't let go of the box.

"Sorry," I say, struggling to meet his eyes. "Asking for and accepting help aren't exactly my biggest strengths."

"You are a Jacobson, stubborn as they come." It annoys me more than it should that he thinks he knows me so well. If I focus on the growing annoyance I feel, then I can't dwell on that ridiculous conversation with Danny and Ashleigh yesterday. I still can't tell if Danny was telling the truth about talking with Mark, and I'm not about to go ask. If Danny did in fact say something, I don't want to be the one to bring it up, and if he didn't, I don't want to embarrass myself by saying something. Brothers are the worst!

"I know I shouldn't be offended right now, but..." I shove his arm and try to glare at him. "Thank you and all that jazz," I say in my best monotone voice.

Mark isn't even trying to hide his amusement. He is full-on laughing. Deep, guttural laughs. I can't help but start laughing too. I'm sure we look like two lunatics laughing so hard there are tears streaming down our faces. At least down my face—I'm still not ready to make full eye contact yet. Thank goodness for waterproof makeup.

"Thank you for the help. I'm sorry I was so rude. I didn't get much sleep last night, and I'm not my usual self."

"You weren't rude."

"Yes, I was."

"Are you seriously arguing with me about whether I thought you were rude or not?" He's teasing me, and I'm too sleep deprived to not take it for what it is. I'm grumpy and annoyed.

As we walk towards the office building, I know I'm being huffy. The silence is awkward. Mark must feel the same need as I do. We speak at the same time.

"So..."

"You go first," I say bashfully.

I hate that I'm being so ridiculous. Sure, I've had a massive crush on him over the years. Am I pretty sure he almost kissed me that Christmas five years ago? Yeah, pretty sure. Was there some insane amount of chemistry going on during Ben's wedding festivities? Pretty sure there was an electrical current that could run an entire continent. But that was all years ago. He's back in town permanently now. We will have to work together from time to time. We are adults. I am an adult. I am no longer that lovesick teenager who daydreams about the day that Mark Winters finally sees that I'm more than just Ben's little sister or Jonathan's best friend. But then I look at him, and he's just standing there being all attractive and unattainable, and I go right back into old habits. He's always been hot, but when did he get so solid?

Yeah, I said it, Mark is attractive, but it doesn't mean anything. There are lots of attractive men in the world. Movie and television sets are full of them. So what if he perfected the soap opera hair and has perfectly straight white teeth? And that dimple and crinkle in his nose that peeks out when he smiles. And clearly, he still likes physical activity because his body shows it. And—Do not think about Mark Winters doing anything with his body, Millie. This is not the time nor the place to be thinking any such things. Especially about Mark Winters. And now that I have said his name 12,000 times in my head and haven't actually said a single word to the living, breathing human being next to me in several minutes. I'm sure he thinks I'm insane.

"Millie, are you okay?"

"Yeah!" I squeak. I actually squeaked. Kill me now. "Why wouldn't I be okay?" I all but fall over, tripping over my feet as I trip over my words.

"I asked if you'd be up for going to lunch today and you didn't say anything."

"Tacos."

"Tacos?"

"Lunch would be good," I croak out, my throat suddenly very dry. "It's Tuesday, which means Taco Tuesday." I can't even create full sentences. Don't worry, ladies and gentlemen, I have an English degree. "Have you had Loco Tacos yet?" Why am I asking follow up questions? End. The. Misery.

"What is Loco Taco?" He's starting to snicker at me again.

Okay, how long is this elevator? When did we get into the elevator, anyway? Is it hot in here? It feels really hot in here. Am I having a stroke? How do you know if you're having a stroke? Is that when you smell toast? Because I think I smell toast. Stroke aside, answer the gorgeous Adonis—man—human—male human—oh for goodness sake! "A taco truck that parks a couple blocks away on Tuesdays. It has the best carne asada taco you'll ever taste."

"Sounds good. When do you usually have lunch? Would 12:15 work for you?"

"Sure," I croak again. Come on, we are almost to the door, just a few more feet Millie, you can do it. "Well, this is me!" It comes out way louder and more abrupt than necessary. It's not like he doesn't know where I work. Can I just go crawl under a rock now?

"Anywhere specific you would like me to put this box?" Crap. I completely forgot about that. It's the whole reason this humiliating exchange started. Mental note: buy a rolling bag to carry any future heavy loads. I look up and make eye contact with Mark and see him expecting an answer. I'm really rocking this human interaction thing today.

I sigh. "On my desk, if you don't mind."

"Just lead the way."

As I open the door, I can feel all the eyes on us. Mark's appearance has been the talk of the office gossip ring this past week. I never mentioned that I had seen him last week when I was at Lexington, nor did I mention that I knew him. With any luck Trina isn't in yet because she is sure to recognize him from the picture on my desk. The picture! Crap! What is Mark going to think about me having a FRAMED PICTURE of him on my desk? Panic Mode: Activated.

If Mark notices all the gawking eyes on him, he doesn't show it. Dang, ladies, it's just a man, a very attractive man—Stop it, Millie! We're not going down that rabbit hole again this morning. Repeat after me: This is Mark. You do not find Mark Winters attractive. You do not notice how his muscles have filled out and that he clearly still frequents the gym. You do not notice that his deep brown eyes have little flecks of yellow in them around the iris. Nope. You don't notice any of that. And you certainly are not remembering how it felt when his hand was on your waist as you danced the night away at the wedding reception. Or how he so carefully wiped the tears away after your jerk of a boyfriend decided that he didn't want to be your boyfriend anymore. Nope. Not thinking about any of that.

I suddenly find myself sailing through the air as I trip on a pushed-up corner of the rug and start flailing my body in order to not fall. I fail. Miserably.

"Millie! Are you okay!" Mark is at my side in an instant helping me up. I can't take anymore of this annoyingly embarrassing day. I shove my flaming face in my hands. Trying to recover any amount of dignity I may have left—let's be honest, there isn't a shred left—I say in the most calm and cool voice I can muster, "I'm fine." I'm so not fine. "Just give me a second."

I finally will myself to look into Mark's face. He's smiling. He's lucky it's genuine and not at all mocking, or I would probably punch him in his too perfect and smug face. "Here, let me help you up."

"Thanks." I take his outstretched hand and pull myself up. "I'm sure you have more important things to do other than saving damsels in distress." Shut up, Millie. JUST. STOP. TALKING. Forever. You're mute now. This is my vow of silence. Which no one will hear me make because I am now silent.

"If you're sure." There is a hint of amusement mixed with genuine concern. "I'll just see you at lunch then."

I just nod. I'm as silent as a monk.

"Oh, and Mills," he says, and I look back at him. "You might want to stay away from caffeine today."

And with a wink he turns and leaves. A WINK! I collapse into my chair in utter disbelief. Could I have been any more awkward today? And he had the audacity to laugh his sexy laugh and wink at me! What a jerk!

CHAPTER 9

Millie

Christmas ❧ Five Years ago

J WALK OUT OF the room and slam the door behind me. I don't want to go back to that full room of people. Everyone will know about Denham soon enough. I don't need them to read it on my face. I need to get out of this house. It's suddenly suffocating.

I grab my coat and try to slip out the front door as quickly and quietly as possible. I don't know where I'm going; I just start walking. This whole week has been one big let down. From Denham refusing to participate in any of my family's traditions right down to the fact that my favorite time of year is being ruined. I love that my family goes crazy for Christmas. I love that my dad and brothers build a whole village the week before, just so the neighborhood and community can have a little holiday magic. But this year? This year Denham has made sure that I'm as grouchy about Christmas as he is. Even with everything else that has happened, THAT is what I'm most upset about. Sure, it sucks that we just broke up and that "friend" he's going to meet up with, I'm pretty sure, isn't "just a friend". But to ruin Christmas?! That's just... that's just a lot of not nice words that I don't say. Maybe later when I tell Tori what happened she can fill in the blanks. She'd be more than happy to be of assistance.

I walk until I get to Santa's Village and then make a left and head to Santa's chair. Maybe there's some magic left in it to give me some answers, but when I get there, I'm not alone.

"What are you doing here?"

Mark jumps. "Hey! I didn't know anyone else was out here."

"I just needed to get out of there."

He nods then scoots over and gestures to the spot next to him. I hesitate for a moment before taking a seat. We sit in silence. It's the first peace I have felt in days.

"Denham and I broke up." I don't know why I'm telling him. I can't even look him in the eye. I just look up towards the sky, close my eyes, and feel the wind.

He nudges me with his shoulder, so I finally make myself look at him. "I'm so sorry, Mills." I can't read his expression, but I know his words are sincere. "You deserve better."

My eyes start to brim with tears again. Concern blankets his features.

"Oh, Mills, I didn't mean to upset you!"

I laugh through my now traitorous tears. "You didn't. You're just about the fourth person today to tell me that."

"We just want the best for you. Are you sure I didn't upset you? May I?"

My whole body freezes as his hand lifts to my face and his thumb gently wipes the tears on my cheek. His eyes are so intense on mine I couldn't look away if I wanted to. I've lost track of how long we've been sitting here. Time has frozen to this moment.

Mark moves like he's going to say something, but then stops himself and clears his throat. "We should probably get back in there."

I suck in a breath. "Yeah. They've probably realized we're missing. No need to send out a search party."

Mark stands and offers me his hand pulling me up. I don't want him to let it go, but I know he will. My hand misses his as soon as it's gone.

CHAPTER 10

Mark

I'M PRETTY SURE Millie is avoiding me. That's the only explanation I can come up with. I haven't seen her since we had lunch last week. She didn't come to dinner at the Jacobsons' on Saturday, some excuse about having to work. Maybe she did have work, but it still feels like she is avoiding me. We work in the same building, on the same floor. My firm has done multiple contracts for her publisher this past week. Odds are that we would run into one another at least once.

I thought we had a nice time at lunch, at least I did. We spent the whole time catching up on what the other had been up to the last couple of years. A lot was left unsaid, but I can't blame her for not bringing up the last few times we've seen each other. It's not like I was going to. What's the point in talking about the past. It's in the past. Here and now, we are two adults who have known each other since the day she was born. Two people who might have had some insane levels of chemistry brewing between them at some point, but again, that was in the past. No need to dwell on things that can't be changed.

As much as I have come to the conclusion that under any other circumstances, I would pursue Millie, I can't. It's just too complicated. Ben and Jonathan aside, there is just too much history there. If any relationship were to develop and it went wrong, it would completely divide our families. I don't want Millie to be a distraction. She can't be a distraction. Unfortunately for me, not seeing her is proving to be an even bigger distraction.

"You bringing anyone to the mixer tonight?" Nancy pops her head into my office.

"I wasn't planning on it." Panic starts to set in. Was there some sort of date requirement I wasn't aware of? "Do I need to?"

I didn't even think that I would need a date for this thing tonight. Sure, at Bancroft and Watson it wasn't exactly required, but it was expected. I didn't think too much about it until Natasha and I broke up. Then I usually just dragged Todd with me, and we would leave as soon as I made sure I was seen by enough people to prove I had been there. Lexington is night and day different from Bancroft and Watson; they wouldn't make me have a date for this thing, would they? I mean, I'm a grown adult. A very single grown adult as my mother likes to point out. Often.

"Not at all. I'm sure there will be plenty of buzz about your handsome face from all the women at the event tonight. Married and single," she says this way too mischievously. With a wink, she's out the door as quickly and quietly as she popped in.

"Nancy, what did you do?" I call after her, not liking the

strange feeling that she was setting me up for some sort of Bachelor moment. I have no interest in handing out any roses in the near or distant future.

I walk out of my office to face a completely unfazed Nancy. Amusement twinkles in her eyes.

"I didn't do anything, but, honey, you'd have to be blind not to notice how good-looking you are. You're lucky I'm an old married woman." She's toying with me now. "Or rather my husband should be grateful I'm a happily married old woman," she laughs.

As much as I try to resist, I can't. I head back into my office when I hear her mutter, "This will work nicely."

I turn back and eye her. "What will work nicely?"

She looks up at me with all the innocence of a fox. "Oh, nothing. Don't you worry your pretty little head."

"Nancy," I say warningly, "what are you playing at?"

She keeps the innocent act in place. "I don't play games, honey." I resign myself and turn and walk back to my office. My steps falter slightly when I hear, "I win them."

I don't know what Nancy thinks she's planning, but I would bet that it has something to do with Millie. She has talked up Millie every chance that she can, permitting Troy is not in earshot. I almost welcomed his smug presence when I had to shadow him on client calls and meetings if it meant not having to be constantly reminded how amazing Millie is. I am highly aware. I am also very aware, thanks to Nancy, that Millie hasn't dated anyone seriously since she's been at Quimby. I also become more and more aware of how off-limits she should be by the guilty feeling I have each time I get a message from Ben when I've been thinking about Millie.

I NEVER SHOULD have let Rosie talk me into this navy suit. It is far more form-fitting than I would ever choose. I feel like one of the Jonas Brothers or One Direction. The annoyance that I even know who those people are bothers me even more than the restrictive material that is currently suffocating my body. And how did she ever talk me into a bright pink tie?

Walking into the hotel ballroom, I'm not sure what I was expecting from this mixer, but it wasn't something of this scale. Miles majorly undersold how much business Lexington does in this town. This ballroom is filled with hundreds of people representing the various clientele that we work with.

I saw Nancy, and a man who I assume is her husband, from across the room when I first came in. I've also talked with a few people I've met so far, but for the most part I've stayed to myself. Which is fine by me. My social battery is lowering by the minute, and I'm counting down until it would be socially acceptable to leave. I feel so awkward talking to strangers. I keep reminding myself that eventually these clients won't be strangers and I won't feel so uncomfortable, but in the meantime, I have built in small breaks where I mostly people-watch. My current source of entertainment is watching Troy schmooze and hit on every presumably single woman in the room. It's almost painful to watch. I'm not sure which is worse, the total flops or the near successes. It's impressive and yet sickening all at the same time. It's like watching Barney Stinson at work.

"Looking good, Winters."

I recognize her voice even before I turn around. My breath catches as I struggle to not let my eyes roam. Millie has her auburn hair down with soft curls that bounce around her face and shoulders, hitting just above her clavicle. Her dark blue dress fits her perfectly and stops just above her knee. It's hard to not follow the lines of her toned bare legs. It's suddenly very warm in here, and I try to loosen my tie without being obvious. I am absolutely not noticing how sculpted she is in all the right places or how those heels only add to the flawless, classic beauty that Amelia Jean Jacobson is.

"Hey, Millie," I gulp. "Just getting here?" Get it together, Mark, it's just Millie. You have talked to Millie a thousand times. Yeah, and after the last time she started avoiding me.

"Yeah." It shouldn't give me so much comfort noticing how awkward she also feels. "I had to make an appearance at my parents' house, you know, after missing last week."

"So…are you avoiding me?" I blurt.

Millie's eyes go wide, but she tries to recover. "Why would I be avoiding you?"

"That's what I've been trying to figure out."

"Well, I'm not, so there isn't anything to figure out."

"I just haven't seen you since we went to lunch and since we work in the same building—on the same floor—I just figured I'd at least see you from a distance, and I haven't."

"Work has been really busy lately."

My confidence is building as I watch her squirm under my attention. "You're lying."

"I am not!" Millie squeaks.

I bite my lip in order to stop the smirk.

Millie shoves me. "Jerk."

I release my smirk and shove her back. This is better. This is the most natural we have been since I ran into her. "You ignore me, and I'm the jerk? How does that work?"

"Because," she tucks a strand of hair behind her ear, a nervous tick she's had since we were kids. "Because it just does."

I square my shoulders and ask again, "So, why are you avoiding me?"

Millie squirms under my gaze.

"I might have been avoiding you," she looks at me bashfully, "a little."

"Why?" I almost whisper.

"Because it's you."

Now I'm really confused. "You're avoiding me because I'm me? How does that even make sense?"

Millie throws up her arms, "It doesn't! And I know it doesn't, it's just... it's just so complicated."

Complicated. I'm really starting to hate that word.

"What's complicated about tacos?" I know she isn't talking about lunch; I know she is thinking about every single little complication that I have also considered.

"Tacos that I didn't mention to Jonathan. Or Ben for that matter. And I know you didn't either because I would have heard about it from one or both of them by now."

She's right. I haven't said anything to anyone about us going to lunch.

"It's none of their business with whom and when we consume tacos." I know that isn't the reason why neither of us have said anything, but I want her to say it. I want her to admit to feeling this connection between us.

Her old defense mechanism starts kicking in. She is getting more and more defensive and annoyed. "You might not care what they think, but you're not the one they are going to bombard with questions and accusations. Any information in the hands of those two, no matter how innocent, will go over like a grenade in a china shop."

"That's quite the visual."

She rolls her eyes.

I know the next words I say will make or break this whole situation. "Last time I checked, we were both adults. I think we can choose who we want to spend time with."

"I know." Her eyes are saying more than her words ever could. I know she feels this connection. I know she's as conflicted as I am about the whole situation. I also know that if anything were to happen between us, she would get the worst of it from our brothers. Jonathan would be furious with me, but I don't know if he would ever forgive her. Ben would make it his life mission to forever play the martyr at any family function.

I say the only thing that I can that can keep her in my life and still in the parameters of safety. "But you would still feel more comfortable if we were just friends."

She nods. It's not a win by any means, but at least it's better than her avoiding me.

"I was about to head to the bar, want anything?"

"A cranberry seltzer with a twist of lime, oh, and can you please make sure they don't put any vodka in that? Actually, would it just be easier for me to go? I tend to make orders a little complicated."

I laugh. "That's not complicated. I think the bartender and I can handle it."

"My apologies. Some of us haven't been going to functions with the Charleston elite."

"You grew up in the same gated community and went to the same country club functions that I did." I nudge her with my arm, partly to give her a hard time and partly because I crave that electrical current each time we touch. "Hate to break it to you, but you grew up as one of the elite."

Millie rolls her eyes then grabs me by the shoulders and turns me away from her. "If you're going to get drinks, then go get drinks. If not, then I'll go myself."

I turn my head to look over my shoulder as I start to walk away, "As you wish." I wink at her.

She's shaking her head, but she's smiling, and it's my favorite thing that has happened all night.

I return with our drinks, and we pass the time people-watching, mostly sitting in silence. Occasionally Millie points out people that she knows, but mostly we are watching awkward flirting and failed passes. By now, most of the married couples have left for the night, leaving a rough-looking crowd who are all a few too many drinks in to be making any sort of responsible decisions.

Millie points towards the bar. "Look at that couple."

I look over and see a man who is presumably in his

mid-to-late fifties with a scantily clad woman clinging onto him who has to be at least 25 years his junior.

"Is that really what men want?" Millie says, almost disgusted. "There isn't a part of her that is real."

I'm a little taken back. Millie is usually the first person to rally other women and is certainly not the type to look for anything negative to say. "I'm sensing some hostility."

"It's not hostility," she states matter-of-factly. "It's just, whatever happened to admiring someone for their mind over their body?"

"Can't both be admired?"

She scoffs, "Not in my experience. It's all talk. Sure, you say you want someone who is real and has a mind of her own, but as soon as some bare-legged Barbie doll in a short skirt comes walking by then it's goodbye reliable and hello fake bake bimbo."

I instantly remember that idiot boyfriend she had a few years ago. The one that had her in tears after they broke up. The one that left two days before Christmas to go on some vacation with another woman. Even the thought of the pain he put her through makes me want to hunt him down and pummel him to the ground.

"You're giving me judgy face."

I take a drink while I decide my next words. "I'm not judging."

"Yes, you are," she argues. "But I can't expect someone who dated Corporate Barbie to understand."

The disdain in her eyes makes the green around the iris blaze, overpowering the blue.

I take my napkin and wave it in surrender. "I didn't mean to start a war."

Her eyes soften. "I'm sorry. That wasn't fair."

"No, it wasn't," I agreed. "But I will admit, Natasha wasn't my best decision."

Though I will defend myself on one point: it wasn't all about her looks for me.

"That's her name! I just called her Evil Elsa."

I snort, and I start coughing, choking on my drink.

Millie purses her lips trying not to laugh.

"Have to admit, that is a new one."

"Maybe to you, but trust me, the rest of us had plenty of names for her."

"Of course you did! And what about you with what's-his-name, Jeans Boy!" I mock.

Millie is the one to choke this time. "Denham?"

"That's what I said."

She hiccups.

"How about a truce? I think we've both had some bad judgment in the past."

"Fair." Millie wipes her eyes. "But admit it, Natasha was way worse than Denham was. She bailed on your best friend's wedding."

"Oh, because that is so much worse than breaking up with you at your parents house days before Christmas and then going on vacation with a friend—a female friend."

"At least my family liked Denham," she argues.

I scoff, "No, they didn't! They hated him!"

"They were nothing but polite!"

"Which should have been the first sign!" Why are we even arguing about this?

I need a change in subject, but I also need to clear my head. All of this arguing about nothing mixed with the close proximity is making me want to end this in a much different way than friends would.

Before I can say anything, Millie breaks the silence. "Why did you move back? From what I heard, you were kind of a big deal at the firm where you worked."

Her question shouldn't take me by surprise, but it does. I don't want to talk about this. Not here. Not now. If there were someone I would want to talk to, it would be Millie, but I just can't right now.

"Sorry. That was too much. You don't have to answer," Millie splutters. "I was just being nosy."

"No—I mean—I want to answer, I do. I just don't really know the answer."

"You don't know why you moved back? Or you haven't over-thought it enough to be able to formulate the answer?"

I really didn't need her making herself even more desirable and yet here she is. Showing how much she gets me, even when I don't say anything she gets me.

"Care for another drink?" Not the smoothest of transitions, but who's keeping score at this point.

Millie thinks about it for a minute then agrees.

The bar was much busier this time around, and it takes me a while to get our drinks and make my way back to our table. I see Troy slithering towards her with a glint in his eye I don't like. He's a python ready to strike.

"Amelia! You made it!" He shouts his greeting as if he's a frat boy hosting a party. Have I mentioned how much I despise this guy?

"Hi, Troy."

"How about we make good use of this music and dance?" He says this while getting way too close and way too handsy.

Millie pushes him away. "Troy, you're drunk."

"I'm not drunk! Come on, baby, lets dance," Troy slurs while he grabs at her again and begins to dance, but she's not having any part of it and neither am I. I step between them, intercepting his next attempt at groping her.

"Dude! What's your deal?" Troy yells.

My blood is boiling, and my heart is racing so hard I hear it in my ears. It takes everything in me not to deck him right in the middle of the dance floor.

"Pretty sure she said no," I sneer through gritted teeth.

"Well, why don't we ask her?" Even in his drunken state he's challenging me, and I'm about to take the bait. Movement behind me catches me off guard, and I turn to see Millie bolting for the far doors of the ballroom.

I don't even look back at Troy; he doesn't matter. I take off after her, just leaving him in a wobbly fighter's stance.

"Millie! Millie, stop!" Millie's steps halt, and she is breathing heavily. As she turns to face me, her eyes are dark with fury. "Millie, what's wrong?"

"What's wrong?" Her whole body is rigid. "You! You are what's wrong!"

"How am I wrong? Troy was messing with you, and I stopped him!"

"I was taking care of it!"

"And then I did so you didn't have to." I'm not sure why she is so mad. All I did was help her.

"That's not your place! I didn't need help. I didn't ask you to help. I was taking care of it!" She takes a big breath in and slowly lets it out. "I've been dealing with Troy and men just like him for years. I know how to take care of myself! I'm not this damsel in distress that's just waiting for a big strong man to come and save me!"

Ice floods my veins as I think of Troy or any man acting like that around her. "I'm sorry I got overprotective."

"You were impulsive and possessive! You're MIA for years and then after one night of going down memory lane, suddenly you're here to solve all my problems?" I've never seen Millie so infuriated. "Guess what, Mark, I don't need your help! And I don't want it! You have no claim on me."

She's right, I don't have any claim to her. I don't have a chance to respond before I'm suddenly being pelted in the head by a pink stiletto heel. She threw her shoe at me!

"Did you really just throw your shoe at me?"

"You're treating me like a child anyway!" She goes to throw her other shoe at me, but as I try to deflect it from hitting my face, I inadvertently get hit square in the chest. I had forgotten just how good her aim was. Still recovering from the shoe raid, I'm a bit dazed as I see her making her way to the parking garage barefoot.

"Millie! Wait!"

No response.

I watch as she moves through the doors to the garage and disappears, leaving me standing in the hallway of the hotel holding two pink stilettos. I'm perplexed about what just happened. One thing is for sure, that isn't how friends react.

It's the bottom of the 9th, all bases are loaded. I'm about to make the biggest play of my life.

CHAPTER 11

Millie

I'M SO FURIOUS at Mark right now! Who does he think he is? He's been back in town for like thirty seconds, and he thinks he can just step in and fight my battles? I'm not some helpless little girl anymore! I'm not the eleven-year-old who was getting bullied and made fun of for having a boy best friend and doing theater. I'm not that girl anymore. I haven't been her in a long time. Why is it so hard for Mark to see that I've grown up? That I'm capable of making my own decisions and defending myself?

And to add to everything, I lost Tori's shoes that she let me borrow. Okay, so I didn't lose them. I threw them. At Mark's head. But he deserved it!

Am I being childish? Probably, but I don't care. I don't need Mark swooping in to save the day. He's not my knight in shining armor. That daydream ended long ago. This is real life and not some fairytale. No Prince Charming is coming to slay the dragon and save the princess. What's worse, the whole night, once we got past the awkwardness, was perfect. If it would have been a date, it would have been perfect. If I hadn't been in love with him since I was twelve, I would be now. But then he had to go and ruin it by stepping in where he wasn't needed. It was like I was a child who couldn't take care of herself all over again. All those old insecurities resurfaced. All the feelings of never being enough. Everything reminded me that I'm not a main character. Main characters stand up for themselves.

I am in no condition to drive, but I also need out of this hotel garage. At this rate I'll end up sitting here all night and run out of gas. Then Mark will show up to save the day. Because that's just how my life goes. Everything is good, and then suddenly something happens that brings Mark Winters back into my life. It's like some magnetic pull that draws me in. I'm a moth headed straight into the light about to get the life zapped out of me.

My phone buzzes in my hand, and I all but shriek as I throw it. It takes me a moment to find where it landed. Under my passenger seat. Just wonderful. I move the jackets and sweaters (I should probably clean my car out) so I can grab it.

> **TORI:** How's tonight going?

> **TORI:** It's boring without me, isn't it?

> **MILLIE:** Not all of it.

> **TORI:** Ooo, gossip! Yay! I do love a good story. Especially if I'm in no way involved.

How does she do that? I can't even blame it on my face giving it away when it's in print.

> **MILLIE:** There might have been a bit of people watching.

> **TORI:** Boring. I need the juicy stuff. People being caught in an affair, someone getting exposed for being a rotten thief and stealing all the clients, corporate espionage.

I roll my eyes as I type.

> **MILLIE:** That's it, no more Gossip Girl

> **TORI:** You know you love me, XOXO

I can't help but laugh. Which is calming me down.

> **MILLIE:** Fine. There might have been a thing with Troy.

> **TORI:** The lawyer guy who always hits on you?

> **MILLIE:** The very one.

> **TORI:** Thing? Like you hooked up?!

> **MILLIE:** Eww!

TORI: Sorry, you said "thing"

MILLIE: He was drunk and got way too handsy.

TORI: I really hope you kicked him where it counts, but that's more my style than yours.

MILLIE: No. I didn't kick him (as much as I wanted to). But that's not even the whole thing.

TORI: How close are you to the house? I need visuals!

MILLIE: I'll be there in about twenty minutes.

TORI: More than enough time to make some popcorn!

By the time I got home, Tori had not only popped enough popcorn to feed an army but gathered Kiersten and Amara into our small living room. I barely have a chance to close the door before Tori pounces on me for more information.

"So? What happened with Troy?" Her dark green eyes are glinting. One thing about Tori, she lives for drama. She loves it. Unless it involves her, then she bolts faster than a cheetah trying to outrun a gazelle. She probably could outrun a gazelle with as much running she does.

"I'm assuming when everyone was summoned you gave the background?" I motion to Kiersten and Amara.

"Duh. I am a professional."

"Just making sure. Okay," I settle into my spot, because I might as well be comfortable. We're going to be here awhile. "Troy came up to me and was extra frat boy-esque and so obviously drunk."

"How is that even allowed at a professional event?" Amara breaks in.

"Shh!" hisses Tori. "It's really not that uncommon. Especially for corporate parties."

"But shouldn't it be less for a small company like Lexington? I mean, how big was this thing anyway?" Kiersten weighs in.

"Can Millie please finish this story?! My popcorn is getting cold!"

I hold back a laugh. I also like torturing her a little, so I take my time giving lots of dramatic and unnecessary pauses as I recount all the failed flirting from Troy and how I turned him down to dance. By the time I get to Mark busting in, I am in full theatrical reenactment mode. When I finish, there is silence.

"So, you threw your shoes at Mark?" Amara summarizes, clearly stunned.

"You threw them at his head? Like at the same time or one at a time?" Kiersten asks.

"And they say I'm the impulsive one of the group," Tori says as she sits back on the couch.

"He deserved it!" I object.

"Wasn't he just trying to help?" Usually I love how optimistic Kiersten is and how she always looks for the good in every situation, but right now it's annoying. She's supposed to be agreeing with me. She's supposed to give me validation. Is throwing a shoe the mature and rational reaction to anything? That's not the point! The point is that Mark had no right to step in like that!

"I know what he did would seem nice on the surface, but it's the reasoning behind his actions. He still thinks of me as a helpless little girl!" I protest.

"I can see how that would be frustrating." Kiersten starts rubbing circles on my back to help me relax. "I still don't see how that made you mad enough to throw a shoe at his head."

"Because she's madly in love with him." My face heats as I turn and glare at Amara. She just shrugs. "What? You never talk about anyone with as much annoyance or admiration as you do Mark. It's been like that since college."

"Oh, it's been longer than that." I turn my glare on Tori and throw my pillow at her, knocking her bowl of popcorn and spilling it everywhere. Good. I'm not even going to help clean it up.

Who am I kidding, yes, I will.

"Wait." Sudden realization dawns on Tori's face. "Didn't you borrow my perfect, just right, bubble gum pink heels tonight?"

I give her a sheepish look; I was really hoping she didn't remember that tonight. "I'll replace them, I swear!"

Amara dismisses Tori's comment. "Shoes aside, I'm still confused about one thing."

"What?" I try to run though all the night's details. Did I forget something?

"Why was Mark even there?"

"That's an excellent point!" Tori interjects. "Why was Mark Winters at this corporate event that you were attending?"

"I told you guys that he worked at the law firm in my building." I knew I hadn't, but maybe I could get away with this teensy-weeny little lie.

Nope. Not even a little bit.

"No, as far as we knew, the one and only time you have seen Mark Winters since he has been back in town is last weekend at your parents' house." Tori's eyes narrow in on me intensely. I swear she could be a human lie detector. She must be terrifying at work.

More ice cream and junk food than I will ever admit to eating in one sitting later, I finally finish telling them about running into Mark at work on his first day and the awkward run-in in the parking garage. I talked about going to lunch. I tell them about avoiding him at my parents' house and every day since. I tell them everything except for the part of the night when we talked about why tacos are complicated. That part seems too intimate to share.

I know deep down in my gut that neither of us were talking about tacos. I know he was insinuating what I have always wished he would, but I also meant what I said about it being complicated. I've always known, but since Ben's wedding, it's been even more obvious. I hardly saw Jonathan at the reception, but I saw his reaction to me dancing with Mark. I had brushed it aside and told him it meant nothing.

How was I supposed to know that 24 hours later Mark would be single again? I overthought the events of that night for weeks. Was I part of the reason they broke up? Who broke up with whom? Did he have feelings for me and break it off? Did she think there was something between us like Denham had? I had so many questions and no way to get answers. I had wanted Mark to want me for so long that I had to finally make myself give it up. It was a childhood fantasy. It would never be a reality. I needed to stop wishing for things to magically work out.

Needing a change in subject and all eyes off of me, I grab the remote and turned the TV on. Thankfully I find a Gilmore Girls marathon, and we are quickly off the subject of me and Mark and having a healthy debate on which of Rory's boyfriends were the best. (Though the answer is obvious). The debate only stops when a trailer for the newest Marvel movie comes on, and we switch to arguing over which Hollywood Chris is best. (Evans, obviously.)

We all head to bed far too late. I'm going to hate the consequences in the morning, but that's Future Millie's problem. Tonight I am just going to go to sleep and try not to overthink every single move I've made or word I have said in the last 24 hours.

I'm about to turn off my light when Kiersten sticks her head in.

"For the record, I think there is something else to the whole Mark situation."

I'm so tired, but it still catches me off guard. "What do you mean?"

She comes the rest of the way in the room and closes the door behind her. I scoot over on my bed making room for her next to me.

"From everything I've seen and heard over the last eight years, it's that you have always kind of had a," she pauses, "complicated relationship with Mark."

There's that word again.

"You have obviously liked him for years but don't talk about it because of your brothers and Jonathan. I mean, I grew up with an older brother, I get it. Then add in all the things that have happened the last few years, and there is a whole new level of complicated."

"What do you mean?" I never gave too many details about anything that happened between me and Mark the last few times we had been home at the same time. I knew Jonathan would freak out, so I didn't tell anyone. It was safer that way.

"I think more happened that Christmas than you told us. Something happened to make you not want to go back home the next year."

I know exactly what she is referring to. It's a memory that lives rent free in my head.

"I didn't go the next year because it was right after your accident."

She puts her hand on my knee, "And I love you for it, but you didn't want to go home long before that. If you would have, then you would have already been in California when my accident happened. You were still in Texas, Mills. You were avoiding something."

I blink at her. Was I really that transparent? And if I was, why has no one called my bluff up until tonight?

"The next time you were both in Ridgeview was for Ben's wedding."

I nod.

"Something happened on that trip. You sent text after text complaining about how horrible Mark's girlfriend was and how he deserved so much better, but when you got back and found out that they had broken up, you were silent. You've hardly mentioned him since. Then you run into him and don't tell us about it. You're avoiding him."

"Are you sure you're not in school to become a therapist? Because I think you'd be really good at it." I groan into my pillow. "It still doesn't explain why he did what he did tonight."

"It kind of sounds like he was jealous."

"Jealous? Why would Mark be jealous of Troy? I clearly wasn't interested."

"Maybe it's more like he's jealous of how Troy has the freedom to hit on you. You really think you're the only one who has thought about how a relationship between the two of you would immediately involve your entire families?"

I hadn't thought about that. I had always thought that I was the only one with this unrequited crush and that those moments that meant so much to me were just flukes on his part. I never let myself think that maybe, just maybe, he was struggling in the same ways that I was. If anything ever did develop between us, there would be no hiding it. It would be public knowledge, and family involvement would be full throttle. That's a lot of pressure. Pressure that wouldn't be present in any other relationship.

There has to be a way that I can keep things friendly with Mark and not develop feelings. Or rather resurrect feelings. Avoiding him isn't working; if anything, it is adding to the suspicion. Danny and Ashleigh made that very clear when they pointed it out as a sign that something was going on. I'm just not sure what will work.

By Monday morning, I've recognized a few things.

Fact: I can't keep avoiding Mark. No matter how much I wish I could. It's time to put on my metaphorical big girl pants and be the independent grown up I keep accusing everyone of not treating me as. Guess I'm just as guilty in that aspect as everyone else is.

Fact: I lost my cool on Saturday night. I threw shoes at the man, for heaven's sake. That's about as embarrassing as it gets. And that's including all the things I did to get his attention when we were kids. No need to relive all those moments. And there are a lot of them.

Fact: I'm trying to get Mark's attention. But I need to do the opposite. I do not want the attention of Mark Winters. Maybe if I say it enough, I'll start to believe it.

"You look extra nice today." I look up at my brother as he picks up his Monday usual off the counter.

"I have a meeting today." I do, but I also may have to pick up a contract at Lexington on the way back from that meeting. Just because I don't want Mark's attention doesn't mean I don't want to make him at least do a double take. Besides, who said it was for Mark? Maybe I've had a change of heart about Troy and—I can't even finish that thought without igniting my gag reflexes.

"A meeting, huh?" Danny eyes me.

"What?" I try to muster the most innocent face I can. So what if I put in some extra time getting ready this morning?

"That's an awful lot of leg to be showing for a meeting."

I'd try to deflect, but Danny will just read into it, so I remain silent.

"Be nice," Ashleigh playfully elbows him in the ribs. "I think you look great. What I wouldn't give to be able to wear that outfit right now. But," she rubs her belly, "outfits like that don't go hand in hand with motherhood."

"Outfits like that made you a mother," Danny mutters.

This time I elbow him in the ribs, but I'm not as gentle as his wife was.

"You make it sound like I'm wearing something super revealing. They're shorts." My brightly colored floral shorts hit my legs mid-thigh, and I paired them with a complimentary tank with a French tuck to show off the slight bedazzle of my white and gold belt that ties into the lightweight cardigan sweater. I look professional, yet young and carefree. But not too young. Because that would be the opposite of what I'm trying to convey. I am a sophisticated adult who can take care of herself.

As soon as Danny closes the door behind him, Ashleigh turns her full attention on me. "Okay, so why are you really dressed up? Because I'm not buying this meeting story."

I roll my eyes.

"Don't roll your eyes at me. I have three younger sisters and twins who are three going on thirteen. I'm immune."

I groan. "Fine. I have to pick up some contracts at the law office that we work with."

Ashleigh's eyes are glinting. "And?"

"And I want to make sure I look nice when I go in to get the contracts."

"And?"

"And nothing. That's it. I got up this morning and made an extra effort to make sure I looked my absolute best so that one of the lawyers would notice me."

"The lawyer is Mark, right? Just making sure I've got all the pieces."

"Yes," I sigh. "The lawyer is Mark."

"I knew it! I knew there was something going on there!"

"There's nothing going on!"

"But you want there to be." She's not asking me.

"No, I don't!" I protest.

Ashleigh gives me a sideways glance. "Then why do you want him to notice you?"

"Because he still thinks of me as a little kid, and I'm not. He needs to understand that I am a grown woman who can make her own decisions."

"So you want him to notice you but not notice you?"

"Precisely!"

"Girl, you've got it bad!"

CHAPTER 12

Mark

I'M SITTING AT my desk staring at those stupid pink shoes. I should just man up and take them across the hall. It's early enough she might not even be in yet. I could just put them on her desk. Wouldn't even have to say a word. Just returning these shoes you projected at my face. Then we wouldn't have to be awkward when we see each other again. IF we ever see each other again. I'm pretty sure Millie is a professional avoider. If she doesn't want to see me, she's not going to see me.

"You seemed to be having a good time on Saturday." Nancy gives me an approving look.

Saturday night had been better than I had expected it to be. Until it wasn't. I still don't understand what I did wrong. I have two pink shoes sitting in my office that are proof that I did something. When I told Rosie about what happened (the CliffsNotes version—I don't need her thinking I have feelings for Millie. I most certainly do not. Mostly.), it was a good thing that she was two hours away because if she could, she would have thrown more shoes at me. When I asked what I did wrong, she didn't make any more sense than Millie had. I still have no idea what I did.

"It was fine. I never got a chance to come over and say hi. Did you and your husband have a good time?"

"We did." Nancy smiles. "We usually just make an appearance. My Marty isn't much for big parties. He gets all nervous around people he doesn't know, but he goes for me."

"Marty sounds like my kind of man."

"Oh! You two would get along splendidly! We will have to have you over for dinner sometime!"

I smile at her enthusiasm.

"I did see you and our girl getting awfully cozy over at a table." Nancy winks at me.

"We weren't cozy," I protest. "It was just drinks between friends."

"Umm-hmm."

"It was! We needed to clear the air, and then we people watched."

"Honey, I may be old enough to be your mother, but I'm not that out of touch with reality. You two couldn't take your eyes off of each other. Three different women came walking past your table, and you didn't even notice them."

I try to think back. "No one came by our table all night."

"If you say so." Nancy winks again.

"There is nothing going on there. There never will be. Millie made that very clear." Might as well tell her the truth since she seems to have a sixth sense about my feelings.

"You sound disappointed."

I shrug. "I don't know. Her reasons make sense."

Nancy motions for me to continue.

"I mean, our families are super close. Me and her brother. Millie and my brother."

"Excuses."

I guffaw. "It's not an excuse. Ben and Jonathan are two of the biggest…"

I don't even know how I want to finish that statement. Ben is my best friend, but he is also one of the most selfish people I have ever known. On more than one occasion I have questioned why his opinion matters to me so much. But Ben is also one of the few people who has always had my back over the years. He never saw me as anything other than me. A lot of things changed after my dad left us. A lot of so-called friends disappeared, but Ben never left. Don't I owe that same level of loyalty?

When it comes to Jonathan? Well, I don't actually know how my brother would react to me dating his best friend. He and I barely know each other anymore. I'm not sure I've ever really known my brother. Part of me resents how different his experience with the divorce was. Another part of me is scared to know if he resents me for how much I tried to take on and take over, especially once we moved out of the Jacobson's. I never meant to try and replace our dad, but in hindsight I'm starting to think that is exactly what I did. Not knowing how Jon would react is far more terrifying than knowing how terribly Ben would react.

"So, what I'm hearing is the two of you obviously have a connection and feelings for one another, but you're both afraid of how your family would react."

"I can't answer for both of us, but yes."

"You mean to tell me that your families and so-called

best friends would rather you be miserable than with the person you want to be with?"

"I—I wouldn't go that far."

"So if you told your mother that you wanted to date Millie, she would...what?"

"Be thrilled beyond belief." I think. Either that or she would go into why relationships never last. It's hard to tell where Mom is going to land on the subject of love. Not that I even know what love is.

"And her mother?"

"Would most likely start planning the wedding before we even went out on a date."

"So the real problem is that you're both too afraid of your supposed best friends?"

"I wouldn't say I'm afraid of Ben."

"But you are afraid of your brother?"

"No?" I hesitate.

"Is that a question or an answer?"

"Are you sure you never went to law school? You would have put some of my professors through the wringer."

Nancy pats my arm gently. "No law school, just the school of life," she grins broadly, "and raising two of the most stubborn children you'll ever meet."

I nod.

"Can I leave you with one more piece of advice? Then I'll step away. Promise."

"Sure."

"Don't let fear of what all could go wrong stop you from something that could go all the right ways. If your friend, or brother, can't be happy for you, then that's on them."

"But what happens if they can't deal with it? What then? We can't just walk away from family."

"The only people who can decide if you and Millie are a good fit are you and Millie. They might be mad initially, but if they really care about you, then they will see what you see in each other, and it will be enough."

"How do I convince Millie of that?"

"Prove to her that you care. Show her how you feel. Millie loves deeply and completely, but that girl is more guarded than Buckingham Palace. She needs to know that you're always going to be there no matter what."

"So what do I do?"

"Be her friend. Show up for her. Do things for her. Be in her corner. Love her for her. Once you prove that, well, she'll be so in love with you that nothing else will matter."

I don't even flinch when Nancy says the L- word. It's not a word I typically keep in my vernacular. I'm not even sure what it means. I used to think my parents loved each other. I loved baseball. Do I love Millie? Am I in love with Millie? I don't know, but Nancy is right, the decision is mine and Millie's to make. I guess now the only thing to decide is how I am going to convince Millie that it's a decision worth making.

I'M FINALLY IN the groove of things and working on a contract for one of our new clients when my phone rings. I don't even look to see who it is before I answer.

"Mark Winters."

"What are you doing Saturday?"

I silently groan. Why didn't I look at the caller ID? I don't have time for Ben right now.

"Ben, I'm at work. Can I call you back later?"

"This won't take long. What about Saturday?"

I'm not caffeinated enough to deal with him today, at least not right now, so I stall.

"Nick Klinefeld asked me to come by sometime to see his team this year. I figure their game on Saturday would be as good as any."

"Nick Klinefeld? Why would he call you about that? It's not like we were friends with him."

"You weren't friends with him. Hate to break it to you, but I wasn't monogamous in our friendship."

"That doesn't matter, the game is what? In the afternoon, right? So you're free Saturday night?"

"My mom just got back into town; I was planning to go see her, but why don't you just tell me why you called and stop all the fake pleasantries?"

"You make me sound so shallow and self-centered."

He said it, not me.

"Come out on a double date with me and Belinda!"

"No."

"But you haven't heard who we want to set you up with."

"It doesn't matter. The answer is no."

"You haven't been on a date with anyone since you've been back to town, and here I am with the perfect excuse to not only go on a date with someone but also get to hang out with me. It's a win-win."

I'm not sure he really understands what a win-win situation would be, because any double date that involves Ben—or worse, Belinda—will not be a good time. He will dominate all conversations, and she will complain about everything or at the very least act as if she is above anything and everyone.

"Fine." I resign myself. "Who are you attempting to set me up with? Not that I'm saying yes." It better not be any of Belinda's college roommates, because every single one of those women has been worse than the previous. I didn't even know that was possible. "Do you even remember the last blind date you tried to set me up on?"

"So you ended up getting a few stitches. It was a simple misunderstanding."

Misunderstanding? He was joking, right? The woman was insane. She had come into town to visit Belinda one time when I had been home visiting. Belinda thought it would be a fantastic idea to set "Karen" (I've blocked any recollection of her real name) and me up on a date. I had initially declined, but Ben, wanting to keep his new wife happy, had somehow talked me into it. It was the worst. We hadn't been at the restaurant twenty minutes when "Karen" accused me of flirting with the waitress and threw a candlestick at my head. It hit me right above my eye, and next thing I knew all I was seeing was red.

"Thirty-two! I had to have thirty-two stitches! All I did was ask for a wine list, and I ended up with thirty-two stitches! The answer is no! No more blind dates. No more set-ups at all."

"Come on, it's Belinda's cousin."

"No! You and Belinda are the worst matchmakers."

"It's just one date. Besides, I already said yes."

"Ben!"

"What? It made Belinda so happy. Someday you'll understand. Someday you'll meet that special person, and all you will want is to make her happy."

Images of Millie flash through my mind, but I can't dwell on that right now. Right now, I currently have to un-alive her brother.

I groan inwardly as I rake my hand through my hair. I haven't made much of an effort to see Ben since I've been home. It's one night. "This better be the last time. Do you hear me? THE. LAST. TIME. No more after this."

"Hear you loud and clear, buddy."

"I mean it, the very last time. After Saturday, your interference in my dating life is done. Just because I'm back in town doesn't mean I'm your puppet."

"Absolutely."

Yeah, right.

"Be at our place at around 7:00?"

"Won't that interfere with your family dinner?"

"Don't worry about that, it's not like we can't miss them from time to time. Besides, it's family. Belinda's cousin is only in town for the weekend."

I suspect that Ben being so willing to miss out on his family dinner has a lot more to do with Belinda not wanting to go. It's no secret that Belinda isn't the biggest fan of living near the in-laws. Unless things have changed dramatically since their wedding, I'm sure the feelings are mutual. At least with his siblings. They can't stand her. Norah tries, but she's the nicest human on earth, and Ben is her son. Fact about Norah Jacobson: she will put up with a lot for the sake of her children. Even the daughter-in-law from Hades.

Ben hangs up before I can ask for this mysterious en-chantress' name so I guess my fate will have to wait until this weekend. I'd look up my horoscope, but I'm sure it would say, "Outlook not good." Or is that a Magic 8 ball?

CHAPTER 13

Millie

I T HAS TAKEN me all morning, but I have finally summoned the courage to go over to Lexington. I really
need to pick up those contracts. And to apologize for
acting like a child...and throwing shoes. I was really in top
notch shape on Saturday. Good job, Millie.

My resolve and confidence lessen with each step I take.
The hallway seems way longer and yet all too short at the
same time. My body is humming with nerves. I can do
this. I am a strong and independent woman. So what if my
emotions got the better of me last night? I can act rationally.
My hand hovers over the door handle as I have the sudden
realization that Mark might not even be in the office today.
I didn't see his car in the garage earlier. I'm about to bolt
when the door opens.

"Amelia."

I freeze.

I take a deep breath and try to compose myself. "Hi, Troy."

I really don't have the patience for this today.

"I didn't see you at the party the other night," Troy says and I can't tell if he really doesn't remember or if he is pretending that he doesn't. Either way I'm just letting it slide.

"I was there. You must have been busy networking." I don't think he notices the sarcasm in my voice; then again maybe he does since he nods and excuses himself.

Before I can back out further, Nancy sees me in the still open doorway. "Millie! My, don't you look like a burst of fresh air! Oh, to be young again! How nice of you to stop by, do we have a contract for you to pick up?"

"Umm…yes…" I wipe my suddenly very sweaty hands on my shorts. I feel her eyes on me, and I want to faint.

"Oh, and I've been meaning to thank you for that restaurant recommendation! It was wonderful!"

"I'm so glad you and Martin liked it." My voice squeaks. Up until the last three weeks, I had never squeaked in my entire life, and now I have on multiple occasions. This is getting out of hand.

"If you are looking for Mark, he is in his office. Just knock." She gives me a knowing wink. A wink! Nancy just winked at me. What is she up to?

Mark's door is partially open; I sit and watch him for a moment. He has his collar unbuttoned and his sleeves rolled up to his elbows. Even from here I can see the definition in his arms. Why is that so attractive? It's clear he still spends time at the gym. I wonder if he still goes to the batting cages or if that ended when he stopped playing. I'm pretty sure I'm drooling. I'm definitely gawking.

"Knock, knock," I say while actually knocking, each making the other redundant.

"Millie!" He jumps out of his chair. "I—I mean—This is a pleasant surprise."

He awkwardly motions to the chair opposite his.

I sit, noticing my shoes sitting on the end of the desk like a pink billboard sign to remind me why I'm here and why it's so awkward.

I sheepishly pick them up. "Sorry I threw these at you. Not exactly my finest moment." I put them in my bag. They don't really fit, but I'd rather not look at the cause of my demise. "It was immature and childish of me. And I'm sorry."

"It's okay"

"No, it's not. I got mad, and I didn't think. I just acted. As you can tell, impulse control is still a bit of a problem at times."

"I'm sorry I upset you. I really didn't mean to. I was just trying to help."

I open my mouth to, what, argue? Mark stops me.

"I had no right to step in where I wasn't invited. You are more than capable of taking care of yourself." He runs a hand along his well-defined chest. "Your aim alone proves that."

I bark out a laugh. "This whole situation is rather ridiculous."

"It is," Mark smirks. "It's not like I was going to wear them."

I have an image of Mark wearing pink heels, and it's a good thing I wasn't drinking anything because it would have been an epic spit take. "Bubble gum pink not your color of choice?"

"I much prefer Pepto-Bismol pink. Those clash with my suit."

I snort as I try to hold in a laugh. "You picked the only pink thing you could think of, didn't you?"

"Maybe."

My insides flutter. I can spend time with Mark. I want to spend time with him; he makes me laugh. He's taken every curveball I have thrown at him the last couple of weeks, and he still wants to spend time with me. At least he did before I threw shoes at him.

"Do you have plans for lunch?" I blurt. I can't read his expression. Surprised? Pleased? Confused? I'm going to be overanalyzing every movement from now on, aren't I?

"Nope. Do you have any ideas?"

"Why don't you pick? I picked last time."

You can do this, Millie. You can spend time with Mark. You want to spend time with Mark.

"What kind of food were you thinking? Or not wanting? Both are very valid when choosing food."

"It doesn't matter to me." I don't have the brain capacity to choose food right now. The longer he looks at me like that, the longer it's going to take for oxygen to reach my brain. I'm sure I'm completely flushed. I probably match those shoes.

"Oh, no, I'm not falling for that."

"Falling for what?" I am genuinely confused.

"The whole 'it doesn't matter what we eat' thing that women do."

"That's not a thing. At least it's not a me thing. I really don't care where we go. I'm not picky."

"But you are opinionated." He stops me before I can argue. "Don't even deny you are. You are a Jacobson, and the whole lot of you are stubborn and opinionated, especially with food."

I can't argue with that, but I also can't let him win. "I'm not picky or opinionated. I'm particular." I look at him indignantly. "It's different."

"You just have to have the last word, don't you?"

"Not at all." I challenge him to respond. I swear I hear him mutter under his breath, but I can't make out any words.

"We obviously won't come to any decisions just sitting here." I get up and grab my purse, forgetting the added bulk of the shoes. "Do you want to drive or should I?"

"I drive. You navigate."

"Lead the way, Tarzan."

He gives me a wry smile as he leads the way out of the office. As we pass Nancy's desk, there is a twinkle in her eye.

"You two kids have fun!" she calls out after us, and I wonder how much of that conversation she overheard.

We make our way to the parking garage, and as we approach Mark's car, he finally breaks the awkward silence, "Where are we going?"

Is he really refusing to decide?

"I told you. You choose." I'm getting the feeling he enjoys annoying me.

"Just make a decision, Millie." He's getting annoyed. "At least pick a type of food!"

I like this feeling of power.

"Hmm. I don't know...give me some options." His nostrils flair. I'm enjoying this way too much.

"Sandwiches?" I shake my head.

"Do you like pho?"

"Yes, but not today." I can't help myself. His face reddens with irritation. I'm done. For now.

With the most innocent, doe-eyed look I can muster, I say, "I'm sorry. I said I wouldn't be difficult and here I am." Did that just come out breathy? Too much, Millie, pull it back a notch or twelve. I clear my throat. "Have you been to McGills Bar and Grill? They have lots of really great menu options. Which is surprising."

"Lead the way."

OUR WAITER SEATS us in a booth and hands us the menus. This suddenly feels a lot more like a date than tacos ever did. We drove here. To a restaurant. There is a booth involved. Mark is sitting across from me, and our knees keep brushing. I'm vividly aware of every movement as his pant leg rubs against my bare legs. Why did I choose to wear this outfit again?

I pretend to look over the menu as Mark watches me. I blush under his gaze.

"In case I didn't say it earlier, you look incredible today."

My blush deepens, and I nervously brush a loose curl behind my ear.

"Thanks."

"What's good here?" he asks, finally picking up his menu.

"I've never had anything bad here."

He looks up at me surprised. "I wouldn't have taken you as a sports bar girl."

"Why, because I'm a woman?"

"No. You know more about sports than pretty much any

woman I know." Mark clears his throat. "I mean, you got dragged to enough games."

I shrug. "I didn't mind." I catch a glint in his eye telling me he's about to call me out, so I add, "Much."

Mark grins. "Well, you endured it much better than a lot of other women I know."

"You can't judge all of us by, what was her name? Nastia?"

"I would never compare you to Natasha. It wouldn't even be a fair fight."

The blazing look in his eyes tells me more than his words ever could. I would win. In a comparison between me and Icelandic Barbie, Mark Winters would pick me to win. The thought makes the butterflies in my stomach do all sorts of flips. Our eyes are locked as we sit in this electric-charged staring contest. Mark is the one to finally break the silence. "What do you recommend?"

"Can you handle the heat?" I will my eyes not to go wide at what could totally be taken as an innuendo. I choose to roll with it like that's exactly what I meant to say. A smile tugs at his lips.

"I do alright. Don't give me any ghost peppers or anything, but I can handle some heat." His gaze is smoldering. I guess we aren't going to completely ignore my heat comment. I'm suddenly very warm. Is the heater on? I remove my sweater. Then immediately feel goosebumps as his eyes rove over my bare shoulders.

I totally missed what he just said. That knowing smile is tugging at his mouth again. I try to avert my eyes from his mouth, but I can't seem to look away. "You've been here before, so you order for the table. Next time I promise to make all the decisions."

I sit stunned at the promise of another lunch, but I get ahold of myself enough to nod in agreement. It's about the only thing I can do with him looking at me like that.

"How did you find this place?" he asks. "This isn't exactly the kind of place your family would frequent."

"My ex used to come all the time. He and his buddies fancied themselves craft beer experts. They weren't, but I would tag along. Some of the other guys would bring their girlfriends, but I didn't exactly have a lot in common with them so I usually just ordered some food and would either read or watch whatever game was playing."

"So, you'd come with your boyfriend to hang out and then each do your own thing?"

"And people wondered why it didn't last." I laugh.

"How long did it last?"

"Um, a month. Maybe two? Honestly, I don't remember. I haven't really dated anyone seriously since Denham. And we all know how that went." I give a wry smile. "What about you? Any relationships other than the Ice Queen?"

Mark gives a short chuckle. "Not really. I've gone on a few dates here and there. No one worth mentioning. Things with Natasha got pretty nasty when we got back to Charleston so I mostly focused on work."

"I'm sorry. I knew she was terrible, but I had no idea she made things hard for you after you broke up."

"Eh, it was all for the best. She showed her true colors. Eventually she figured out that she wasn't going to get a rise out of me, and she stopped trying to make my life miserable.

It made ending things when I did the best decision of my life. It only took me realizing how much like my dad she was for me to end things." He clears his throat again. "Anyway. Enough about my baggage."

"Do you still talk to your dad?" I didn't mean to ask that question out loud. "Sorry. I don't mean to pry." I wave off the question. "Just ignore me."

"No. It's okay." He pauses. "I stayed in contact with him over the years, much to my mother's chagrin, but once I found out how much of my life he had been interfering with behind my back I cut the strings. At least I'm trying to. He's pretty persistent. I refuse to be his puppet. And the only way I could do that was to leave Charleston, so I quit my job and left."

"And you came back to Ridgeview."

"And I came back to Ridgeview."

"I know your mom is ecstatic to have you home again."

"I find it ironic that she was the one out of town when the prodigal son returned."

I giggle. "Whatever. You've always been the perfect son." Mark scoffs. "Hardly."

"You were always Mister Dependable. Mister Responsible. She would have been lost without you. You have to know that." A shadow falls over his face. What did I say?

Our server, Chad, saves the day as he comes bearing our food. I could have kissed him for saving the inevitable awkwardness that was about to occur. Then again, kissing our server would probably fall under awkward.

We fall into a comfortable silence as we each loaded up our plates. If this had been a date, I might have held back. I remind myself for the thousandth time this isn't a date.

This is just lunch. With the man I spent half of my childhood in love with. Who at times has made me think he feels the same. I need to think about something else.

Anything else.

Come on, brain. Think of a topic. Any topic. Anything at all. Food. Food is a safe topic. We are currently eating food.

"So, what do you think?" I ask.

I caught him mid-bite. He wipes his mouth with his napkin before replying, "Everything I've tried so far has been good."

The rest of lunch goes by in an enjoyable blur. We talked about anything and everything. Mark opened up a little bit more about life in Charleston. I learned a lot about his friend and former roommate, Todd. It sounds like he's been a really good friend to Mark. He deserves that. I know I would be lost if it weren't for my friends.

Other than a conversation that lasts way longer than it needed to about the level of hot sauce I prefer, we had fun. It's not my fault my brothers used to have hot sauce eating contests. And it's not my fault that they were all weak in comparison to my apparently iron stomach. It's definitely not my fault that Mark is evidently a wimp when it comes to spice no matter how much he claimed otherwise.

I enjoyed myself today. I enjoyed spending time with him. I want to spend time with him.

I want him.

CHAPTER 14

Mark

EVEN IF I'M never able to taste things again—holy cow, that hot sauce was HOT—today was worth it. Spending time with Millie is worth any bodily harm that may come my way. There is something between us. I felt it when our eyes locked. I know she felt it. We talked about things that I never talk to anyone about. She's always had this way about her, but there is something more mature about how she goes about it now. Sure, there are still traces of the girl I once knew, but she is all grown up now, and it's time I show her that I've noticed.

I noticed five years ago when I ran into her in Santa's village. Even if that jerk of a boyfriend, she had was too stupid to see what he was giving up. I noticed her. I noticed three years ago when she came looking for me at Ben's wedding. And I'm definitely noticing now. I just need to figure out a way to convince her. She might be the only person on the planet that overthinks more than I do. Right now, my plan is to see her as much as possible. Proximity is everything. It's time I take Nancy's advice and put it into action.

First step: lunch. Every day this week if I can swing it. I did promise to make all the decisions next time we went out. And I am a man of my word.

Saturday rolls around way faster than desired. The day of the illusive blind date has arrived, and to say I'm not excited is a gross understatement. I know anyone will pale in comparison to Millie. Doesn't matter who she is. If she's not Millie, then I don't want her. The more time we spend together, the more evident that fact becomes. I've never felt this way about anyone before. That thought should scare me, but it doesn't. It excites me. Millie brings out something in me that I never knew I could feel. Hope. Hope for a future that I've never allowed myself to hope for.

On my drive to Ben and Belinda's house, I start a list of all the things I would rather be doing. They range from extensive dental work to a colonoscopy to last and definitely least, bar hopping with Troy.

There will be a time when I am going to need to talk about these feelings I have for Millie with Ben (and probably Jonathan), but tonight is not the night. Tonight is about getting through the blind date from the underworld while in the presence of the Mistress of Darkness and her cousin. With that ominous thought, I park my car and head up the driveway. Before I knock on the door, I try to give myself one more pep talk. Maybe Belinda won't be so bad. It's been over a year since I've seen her. Maybe impending motherhood has made her more…what's the word? Pleasant?

Belinda's cousin, Zoey, seems normal enough. I've only seen her from a distance, but there are no noticeable signs of insanity, so that's already better than the last person they tried to set me up with. She's dressed in an overly billowy dress, and her hair is on top of her head in some sort of updo—pretty sure Rosie calls that a top knot or something equally ridiculous. I'm ready to get this night going. The sooner we leave for dinner, the sooner the night can end. No offense to Zoey, but I'm not interested. I will never be interested. Even without my growing attraction to Millie, Zoey isn't my type. Not that I know what my type is. All I know is my cheeks are starting to hurt from this fake smile that is plastered on my face, and I wish we could just get going already.

While Zoey and Belinda finish getting ready, I sit in the living room with Ben.

"Glad you could come buddy!" He's beaming while he claps me on the back. "We don't do this enough."

"I told you this is the last blind date, Ben."

"Give her a chance. She's Belinda's favorite cousin." Oh, goody. Negative ten points for Zoey, not that she had too many to begin with. "But that's not what I was talking about," he continues.

"I've been busy." It's not a lie, I have been, but it's also not the full truth. If I'm honest, I've been avoiding him. I don't want to associate him with Millie any more than necessary. I don't want any thoughts of him to stop me from feeling what I feel when I'm with her. Like right now. I notice how their eyes are the same shape. I've never noticed Ben's eyes a day in my life, but now I see it, and that makes me think of her which makes me feel guilty that I'm going on a date with another woman. Then I feel guilty for not telling him that the real reason I don't want to go on this date is because I want to date his sister. My brain can't handle much more of this.

"There are more important things than work."

I know he means well. Even though we have grown apart, he does still have my back. I resolve to give tonight at least a chance. Not Zoey—she's still not Millie—but I can at least try to give Belinda a chance. She is my best friend's wife.

I smile at him. "You're right, there is. I'm starting to realize that more and more with this move back home."

I'm tempted to tell him more, excluding names for obvious reasons, when Belinda and Zoey come back in the room.

"Mark," Belinda's voice oozes disdain, but before I mentally put her in a witches costume, I remember my mental promise to give her a chance, for Ben, and I let it go.

"This is my cousin, Zoey."

I don't know if I'm supposed to just respond or wave or what, so I go for a handshake. Evidently this is the wrong response. Zoey is yelling something about poor innocent animals and runs out of the room. Belinda is on her heels following after her. Guess I didn't have her at hello.

"What they heck just happened?" I look over at Ben, but by the look on his face, he has no idea either.

Belinda comes back into the room; Ben and I both look at her expectantly.

"Was it something I said?" I ask, knowing that I didn't even say anything other than hello. I'm not even sure I said that much to her.

She gives me her customary look of disgust. "It's your watch."

"What about my watch?" It's nothing fancy; it was my grandfather's. Just a regular analog watch on a simple band.

"It's leather," she says like that explains everything. She studies me then adds incredulously, "She's vegan…"

How was I supposed to know that?

"Okay? I wasn't aware of that."

Belinda's gaze makes my stomach churn. Pretty sure I'm about to be turned into a toad.

"You didn't tell him?" She shifts her focus to Ben. I watch as his six-foot three-inch frame becomes putty in her hands.

"I told him, I'm sure I did." He looks at me, and I shake my head. "I'm sorry, Dumpling."

Dumpling? Add that to the list of things I didn't need to know about Ben and Belinda.

"Look," I break in, "I didn't know. I'll apologize." She eyes me coolly. "And I'll take it off." That seems to satisfy the Evil Queen since she turns to go get Zoey from the other room.

After that whole fiasco, I suggest we take two cars, mostly because I don't want to be in proximity to Belinda for an entire car ride. It's bad enough that I'll have to be at the same table at dinner. I'm overruled by everyone else. They think that two cars is ridiculous and "bad for the environment" so we end up cramming into Belinda's sedan.

I don't know how Ben fits into this tin can comfortably; it is way too tiny for someone as big as he is, and I've got a little more than an inch on him and much more muscle mass. I stifle a laugh as I think about the scene in the old

Doris Day and Rock Hudson movie when he tries to fit into an old sports car. I never fully appreciated that scene until now. I also know my audience well enough to know not to share the comparison. I make a mental note to tell Millie about it next time we talk.

I swear Ben chose a restaurant way on the other side of town because it is taking way too long to get there. I'm also pretty sure my left leg is asleep. I try to talk to Zoey, but even when Belinda doesn't answer for her, I'm bored. So far, I've learned that she's not only a vegan but a raw vegan. I could ask follow-up questions, but I'm pretty sure I'm smart enough to figure it out. Not that I care to. She is also an aura cleansing therapist. Again, I don't ask follow-ups. Once she told me she lived in a yurt at a meditation retreat camp in Oregon, I was done. I go to look at my watch to see if this night had really been as long as it feels but remember I put it in my car back at Ben's house so that I wouldn't lose it after I took it off. Fan-freaking-tastic.

After what feels like an eternity of Ben singing—or rather trying to sing—Billy Joel songs we finally park and start getting out of the car. I'm reminded once again how ridiculous both Ben and I must look getting out of this clown car. The night is cool, but the fresh air feels good after that car ride. Belinda had insisted that she was cold and had the heat blasting. I take a moment to stretch before making my way over to the rest of the group.

"You made sure this place was vegan, didn't you?" Belinda hisses at Ben.

"Yes, Dumpling." I still can't get over that nickname. "It

has a wide variety of options. It's the best of both worlds. Something for everyone."

Her eyes narrow on him. "More than just salads?"

"Yes. I looked at the menu online and even called and checked. They have a full vegetarian and vegan menu. That traveling cooking show you like came here and gave it 5 stars."

With that her face relaxes, and she motions for everyone to follow as she and Ben lead the way into the restaurant.

Have to give Ben credit, this place looks nice. He really did a good job trying to find somewhere that had something for everyone. We are settling into our seats as our waiter comes to give us some menus and take our drink orders. All the insanity from earlier seems to die down, and I'm relieved.

Until Zoey opens up her menu.

If I thought her fit about my watch was insane, the amount of yelling and screaming she does about the slaughtering of innocent animals all for the sake of someone to eat them was a whole different level. She's practically turning this nice establishment into a one-woman PETA protest. Even Belinda is embarrassed.

I can't take anymore; I tell Ben and Belinda to meet us out by the car as I stand up and pick Zoey up. I literally have to carry her out while she has a tantrum like a three-year-old. Actually, I may not know a lot of three-year-olds, but the ones that I do have more control over their emotions and actions than this grown woman. If I wasn't done with Ben and Belinda setting me up on blind dates before, I am now.

As I carry Zoey over my shoulder, she continues to yell rather obscene things to the poor patrons and guests. I carry her out the doors and don't put her down until we are far away from the entrance in fear that she will charge in and continue to make a scene.

Ben and Belinda are already at the car, so I open the door and let Zoey get in. When I close the door, I shake my head, and I can't make myself move to the other side. It is as if I am held by some invisible force to the ground.

What am I doing? I don't want to be here. I don't even say anything; I just turn and walk away. I don't know where I'm going, but it's not back in that car.

Ben yells after me, "Mark! Wait up!"

I don't stop. He has to jog to catch up. "Where are you going?"

"I don't know, but I can't go back there. You can't ask me to do that. That was the most uncalled for, most immature display I have ever seen. And I'm a lawyer. I used to defend juvenile delinquents who had more respect than Zoey just showed. How could you ever think that I would want to spend time with that?" I'm on a roll now, and it's all coming out. "You want to know why we don't spend as much time together?" Stop, Mark. You're going to say something that you regret. I continue, "It's because I can't stand the person that you have become. Where is my friend?" The thing about word vomit is once it starts coming out you can't make it stop. "You used to at least occasionally think about some-one other than yourself. Now if it isn't Belinda or yourself, you don't seem to care. I told you I didn't want to go on this date. Yet here we are because even before you asked me, you had already decided that I was coming. And is it my fault for coming? Yeah. I shouldn't have done that, but I did.

Because you are my friend. Now, you're going to go back to your car, and you are going to take your wife and Zoey back to your house, and I am going to go back into that place of business"—I point to the restaurant—"and apologize."

Ben is stunned and just looks at me. I know I've been harsh and will regret at least some of what I have said tonight. When he still says nothing, I head back towards the car, passing it as I go back into the double doors of the restaurant.

As I leave the manager's office, I apologize yet again for how the evening had played out and promise it will never happen again. I also pay for the drinks we never received and leave a hefty tip. We shake hands, and I leave.

When the cool air hits my face, I finally take a deep breath. I don't think I have taken a full breath all night. I pull out my phone to request an Uber back to my car. As I wait for my ride to arrive my mind is reeling. I don't even know what time it is, but it doesn't matter. Without a second thought, I send Millie a text.

> **MARK:** Hey

I don't have a minute to dwell on how lame that text is when she replies.

> **MILLIE:** Hey back.

> **MARK:** Tell me you're having a better night than I am.

Unless you're out with another guy, then maybe don't tell me. But would she be texting me back if she was with another guy?

> **MILLIE:** Nothing too exciting. Just have some people over for a game/movie night. Aren't you supposed to be on that blind date tonight?

> **MARK:** Dumpster fire. Actually no, that's too nice.

> **MILLIE:** Not your soulmate then?

> **MARK:** Haha. Far from it.

> **MILLIE:** You're a good friend for going.

Guilt hits me. I said some pretty terrible things to Ben tonight. And thought a whole lot worse.

> **MARK:** Far from it. I said some things to Ben tonight that I probably shouldn't have.

> **MILLIE:** I'm sure he deserved it. You'll figure it out. You always do.

> **MARK:** How do you do that?

> **MILLIE:** Do what?

> **MARK:** Say things that make me feel better so quickly?

> **MILLIE:** I don't know. I guess I just know you. I know you wouldn't do anything that would intentionally hurt someone.

> **MARK:** Can I see you tonight?

> **MILLIE:** I have people over.

Before I can type out a response—either to take it all back or beg, I'm really not sure which—my phone dings again.

> **MILLIE:** Come over, it's a bit chaotic at the moment, but we have food coming, and we are going to either play games or watch a movie. We can hang out.

> **MARK:** Send me your address.

I'm startled when a car pulls up next to me. Once I get my bearings and realize that it is my Uber, I climb inside, and we drive towards Ben's house. When we arrive, I think about going up to the door and apologizing to him for the things I said, but the house is dark, and their car isn't in the driveway. I decide it's probably for the best. I will message him tomorrow. I get in my car and put my watch back on as I input Millie's address into my GPS.

CHAPTER 15

Millie

I'M HAVING A mild panic attack. This is fine. Mark and I are friends. Friends hang out. Friends hang out at each other's houses. This is completely normal. I can do this. Stop stressing, Millie, this will be fine. This will be fun. It's not like the two of us are going to be alone; there is a house full of people. Not that we haven't been alone multiple times this week…Or ever…This is completely fine.

I can do this.

After my short little pep talk, I start to calm down. Slightly. I give myself a once over in my mirror and decide that I suddenly need to fix my hair and maybe add a little lip gloss. I am a hostess. I need to look the part. That is all. It has nothing to do with Mark and the fact that he's coming over after having been on a date. With another woman. A date that went badly. I can't help but smile. No! Stop it, Millie. Remember what you said. Just. Friends. NOTHING MORE. Just friends. A friend I wouldn't mind having a whole bunch of benefits with. ARGH! I need out of my head!

From my room I can hear a change in the music playing from the living room, and the volume increases. The perfect distraction. Tori has no doubt kicked Amara's boyfriend, Duncan, off of his DJ equipment and taken over.

"Are we really going to stay in all night?" Tori yells over the now-blaring music. She could turn it back down, but that's not how Tori works. "That's so boring! Work sucked this week! I just want to let loose!"

Kiersten holds her ears as she walks over and turns it down a few decibels. My growing headache silently thanks her. Kiersten turns to face Tori with one of her mothering looks. "It's not boring. It's responsible. Besides, some of us should be studying."

Kiersten's master's program keeps her pretty busy. I'm surprised we even got her out of her room tonight.

"Come on! We're young. We're single. It's not even that late! It's Saturday, for goodness' sake! We should be out doing something fun and crazy!"

"Umm, not all of us are single, Tori," Amara says as she extricates herself from Duncan just long enough to get the words out then returns to their intertwined canoodling. I laugh as Tori rolls her eyes.

For as long as I can remember, Tori has been anti-relationship. She's dated but nothing serious. She likes to keep people at arm's length.

Amara is the very opposite. The moment she met Duncan, they became inseparable. Sometimes opposites attract, and it's a force to be reckoned with. We all know it's just a matter of time before he proposes.

"Where's Jonathan tonight? He'd be on my side!"

"He said he's going to be a bit late. Something about additional practices before the show opens next week."

A flood of relief rushes over me as I hear this. As much as Mark and I are just friends and just hanging out, I still haven't told Jonathan I've even seen Mark other than that Saturday at my parents' house. Guilt settles into my gut. I don't know why I can't talk to him about this. He's my best friend. Mark's his brother. Wouldn't he want us to be happy? Because spending time with Mark makes me happy. I'm tired of trying to deny that. There's this pull towards him that has never been there in the past. I'm drawn to Mark like a magnet. I feel lighter and more myself when I'm with him than I do with anyone else. My best friend would want that for me, wouldn't he? That's what I want for him.

"We can't go out," I say. "I just invited Mark over for game night."

Silence.

"Why are you all looking at me like that?"

"You invited Mark over?" Kiersten asks cautiously.

"Does Jonathan know about this?" Tori asks. I try to ignore the growing pit in my stomach.

"No. I just invited him," I explain. "Mark just moved back to town. He doesn't know too many people anymore. He's had a bad night, and I thought that game night might cheer him up."

That's not a complete lie. He seemed desperate to get away from whatever mess Ben and Belinda concocted for the evening. It was the polite thing to do. Friends cheer each other up when they have a bad day.

Can I see you tonight? His question seared into my brain. Calm down, heart, he didn't say he needed to see me, he just asked if I was available. I can't go reading between the lines. It was a text so there weren't any clues into its inflection or meaning. He could have meant anything by it.

I know I'm lying to myself, but I also don't want to get my hopes up. I've wanted him to want me for so long I'm not sure I'd ever recover from the rejection if he did refuse me.

"Who's Mark?" Duncan asks.

"Babe, remember I told you about the guy that she grew up with that works in the same building? The lawyer."

"I thought that lawyer was a jerk and a total tool?"

"You're thinking of Troy. This is Mark, Jonathan's brother."

"Wait, you have a thing for Jonathan's brother?" Duncan's eyes are now on me and wider than I have ever seen them.

"We're just friends," I retort. I hope no one else heard the squeak that narrowly escaped, "Nothing else. Yes, he works in the same office as me. Yes, he is a lawyer who works with Troy. Yes, he is Jonathan's brother. No, I do not have a thing for him. We are just friends."

My face heats. I hate being the center of attention.

Duncan and Amara share a look. UGH. Couples!

I don't even look at Tori. She is being eerily quiet, and that can only mean one thing: disapproval. And I can't deal with her disapproval. She's the only one who has ever known about my crush on Mark, but even she doesn't know all that has happened the last few years. I definitely haven't told her anything about all the lunches this week. She'd call me out for being a coward for not telling Jonathan. And tell me that I'm a terrible friend for lying to him. She'd be right. I am a lying coward.

Tori finally breaks her silence. "I just texted Jonathan, he's up for going out tonight. Anyone else?" She looks around the room, and when no one responds, she adds, "Whatever. I'm going to go change."

"Well," Amara removes herself from Duncan and the chair they have been sharing, "if Tori and Jonathan are going out tonight then I think we might take off too."

What?! No! This can't happen!

"You can't take off! I can't invite someone to a group hangout and then there be no group hanging out! It's going to look like I asked him over to Netflix and chill!"

"Guess you better watch Hulu then," Duncan jokes.

Panic is setting in again. Breathe. In, two, three. Out, two, three. I'm pacing all over the place. All the thoughts in my head are going around like a tilt-a-whirl, and I can't make heads or tails of them.

"Come on, guys, please? Just give me an hour. Then you can go and do whatever you want with the rest of your night. He's had a long day; I'm sure he's only coming over to be polite." I hold my breath hoping I'm convincing enough to get them to stay.

"I can stay for a little bit," Kiersten says, "but then I need to go study. I have a big test coming up."

"Thank you, Kiersten!" I run over and give her a hug. I cling to her, afraid that if I let go, she will change her mind. This will all be fine. We will play some games or watch a movie. We have food coming. It will be a fun and relaxing night, then Mark will leave. A simple hang out. Nothing to stress about. The doorbell rings. My heart rate speeds up. A moment of sheer panic hits me. Mark. Here. House. Help. Panic. Now. No one moves towards the door. I'm stuck in place. Duncan gets up from the chair he's been occupying to answer the door.

"Pizza's here!" He yells. I take a brief breath of relief. "And there's a guy! Are you Mark?"

I can't hear the rest of what he says. Duncan walks in carrying the food with Mark following behind him.

WOW.

Mark is good-looking, no one can deny that, but Date Mark? Date Mark looks like he stepped out of the pages of GQ with his well fitted jeans and T-shirt that hugs all the right places. Tugging on muscles that have names and uses I don't know , but I do know that Mark has good ones. Very good ones. His hair is tousled like he's raked his hands through it a few too many times tonight. I itch to comb my fingers through it to see if it really is as soft as it looks. Is this how he gets ready for a date he doesn't care about? What does he look like when he cares? Realizing I'm staring, I clear my throat.

"Hey, Mark! You made it!" I squeak.

Internal cringe.

"Thanks for the invite." Mark starts to move towards me.

Tori bounds back into the room with a glint in her eye that is never good. "Mark, fancy seeing you here."

I glare at her from behind his shoulder and mouth, "Be nice!"

She bats her eyes at me, feigning innocence. But her lips curl into a smile that would rival the Grinch's when he decides to steal Christmas from the Who's.

"So, Mark, I hear you've just moved here. Or back?" Duncan breaks the awkward silence. I've never been so grateful for him being a constant in our home than I am at this moment.

"Uh, yeah. Been back a few weeks now." Mark glances at Duncan before shifting his attention back to me.

"Cool."

"Hi! I'm Amara," Amara slides in next to Duncan. "One of Millie's roommates!"

"I'm Kiersten, nice to finally meet you!" Finally? What's with everyone tonight?! I don't need Mark thinking I've been talking about him. Which I haven't. Much.

"Nice to meet all of you as well." Mark walks over to where I've planted myself.

"Hey," his voice is a little husky as he wraps me in a hug. This is new. I can feel his firm muscles through his shirt. Gosh, he smells good. It's intoxicating. What is that? Cedar? Sandalwood? Whatever nature-y scent it is, it's working.

"Hey," I whisper back.

"Are you sure no one else wants to come?" Tori asks.

"No!" A chorus responds.

"Your loss. I'm out!" She's out the door, slamming it behind her.

"I see Torrance is still the same," Mark whispers into my ear. He's still so close. Are we still embracing? I should probably step away. Just a friend would step away. I don't want to, but I reluctantly step away from Mark and his addictive embrace.

"We're going to head out too," Amara says, gesturing to Duncan then dragging him by the arm behind her. There is a glimpse of an apology in his eyes as they pass on their way towards the door.

"I have a test on Monday so I'm going to go study," Kiersten winks at me. She WINKS. The little traitor.

"I thought we were going to play games. Watch a movie?"

"Go ahead." She calls as she disappears down the hallway. There's a, "Have fun!" followed by the sound of her bedroom door closing. That's it. They're all dead to me now. I look up at Mark, who is still standing right next to me. It wouldn't take but a fraction of an inch and I could just—

Nope!

I need to move away from him. Put some distance between this all-too-attractive man and my olfactory system.

"So…" I say looking at Mark not sure what else to say. "Hungry?" I basically yell it in his ear. He takes a step back. I internally groan. Why do I always have to be so awkward around him? "We have plenty of pizza and wings."

Mark just nods as he looks down at me, searching my face for something. I feel each and every searing look deep in my soul. I let out a low breath. Oh, boy. I'm a goner.

"Sorry, everyone bailed. I swear we really were going to have a game and movie night."

"It's okay. You're the one I came to see."

My heart flutters at his words.

"We could still watch a movie or something. It's the least I can do after inviting you over."

"Are you trying to Netflix and chill me? Amelia, I'm shocked!"

My eyes go wide. "No!"

Mark smirks.

I shove him. "Jerk!"

My hand rumbles as he laughs because apparently when I shoved him I never removed my hand, and I'm all but groping his, what are those muscles called? Pectorals? Whatever they are called, they are firm.

And I'm still groping them.

I remove my hand sheepishly. "Sorry."

"Don't be."

I don't dare look into his face. Any more fluttering and I'm going to take flight. Or I'm going to die after my heart explodes out of my chest.

"Doesn't matter to me what we do. Anything is better than that date."

"It couldn't have been that bad."

"No, bad would have been an improvement. Let's just say, there is a restaurant that I will not be showing my face in ever again."

"Okay, now I need details." I never thought I would be spending my evening having Mark act out his entire date. He even does different voices. This is a side of him that I have never seen before even in all the years that I've known him. He is so animated. I think it's my favorite. I don't want the night to end, but it's getting late.

I'll just not mention it until he does.

Mark looks down at his watch, "I didn't realize it was so late." He stands up and puts his hand out to pull me up. We stand there staring at each other. "We should do this again. Maybe actually watch that movie."

There is a sexy gravelly tone to his voice. My breath catches. He's standing so close I can hardly focus on words to formulate a sentence.

"That would be fun," I finally manage to whisper breathily.

I walk him to the door not knowing what to say, but I'm not ready to say goodnight. His lips part as if he's about to say something then changes his mind. Instead, he pulls me into an all-enveloping hug. For a moment I can't tell where I end and he begins. I take in his scent, knowing this is a moment I will be reliving in my mind over and over all night.

"I'll text you."

I think I manage to nod my head.

This man, whom I've known my whole life, the one that I have dreamed of, has the uncanny ability to render me speechless with seemingly very little effort.

CHAPTER 16

Mark

MY HEART IS racing as I walk out to my car. Tonight was... tonight was unexpected. The blind date was even worse than I could have ever imagined, but the night ended better than I could have anticipated.

I wanted to see Millie. I wanted to spend time with her. I was happier than I should ever admit that she invited me over when I asked if I could see her. I won't even pretend to be offended or saddened by the fact that all of her roommates bailed on whatever they had planned as soon as I got there. Pretty sure the blonde one—Kiersten?—winked as she left us alone. She was the wingman I didn't know I needed.

The whole night was perfect. I couldn't stop smiling as she laughed at my retelling of the now infamous Zoey. I even used different voices and acted out the comedy of errors that was the entire evening. I've never done that. Ever. My brother is the dramatic one, not me.

The reminder of Jonathan makes the pit in my stomach grow a little bigger, but I push it aside as I do with everything involving emotions. I don't want anything to taint tonight.

I don't want to ruin anything before it even starts, because something is starting. I can feel it.

Instead, I drive home on cloud nine.

There is no way I'll be able to go to sleep. I'm too hopped up on adrenaline. I have a surge of hope that I haven't felt since finding out I couldn't play baseball anymore. I feel such a strong pull towards Millie. A spark went straight to my heart when she put her hand on my chest to shove me. I think my heart about exploded. What a way to go.

When I get to my condo, I put my keys on the hook and head up the stairs to my room. Just looking at the empty space makes me get all twitchy. I'm not much of a sentimental person, but even I can see that the condo lacks personality. I still have boxes in every corner filled with who knows what. No time like the present, I guess.

I change out of my jeans and t-shirt into a pair of athletic shorts and an old hoodie from college. I look around the bare space. I have no idea where to put this stuff. I'm not even sure what all this "stuff" is. Dad had hired someone to decorate my place in Charleston. Then Natasha had "fixed" it. When I moved out, Todd kept what he wanted, and the rest was packed up. Since I hired movers, I haven't a clue what is in these boxes.

I guess I could ask my mom for help. She's been asking if I need anything. I bark out a laugh when I think about how Nancy would tell me I should ask Millie to help. Then the more I think about it, I realize it wouldn't be such a terrible idea. She used to help Danny and Matt back when they were flipping houses when we were younger. Even if she hasn't done it in a while, she has a great sense of style and color combinations. She pairs pieces of clothing I never would even think of putting together, but somehow on Millie, it always works. It would also let me spend more time with her away from work. Time alone. It even follows the advice Nancy gave me about showing Millie that I value her opinion. The more I think about it, the more I think it's a stroke of genius.

I'll text her about it tomorrow—I look down at my watch—or rather later today. Wow, it really is late. I should really head to bed, but I can't seem to make myself head that way.

On impulse I pull out my phone and text Millie.

> **MARK:** You awake?

I hit send and groan, instantly regretting it. What am I doing sending a text at this time of night? Who sends a "You up?" message at this hour? Nothing good can come from this. Maybe I'll luck out, and she will have her phone on Do Not Disturb so I didn't wake her up.

My phone vibrates in my hand.

> **MILLIE:** Yes.

> **MARK:** Did I wake you up?

I hold my breath.

> **MILLIE:** No. Couldn't sleep.

I have to tread lightly with this next question.

> **MARK:** Not tired or something on your mind?

My heart races as I watch the little bubbles at the bottom.

> **MILLIE:** Both.

> **MARK:** Anything I can help with?

> **MILLIE:** You're probably not the best person to help.

My heart sinks.

> **MILLIE:** You don't typically talk to the person who is causing all the over-thinking to help you figure it out.

A jolt like I've never felt zings throughout my body.

> **MARK:** Or maybe that makes them the best person to talk to about it. Go to breakfast with me?

Dot bubbles. Then they're gone.
The waiting is excruciating.
Dot bubbles. Then nothing.
More waiting.
Dot bubbles. I'm about to send a retraction when a response comes in.

> **MILLIE:** Okay.

MARK: Okay?

MILLIE: Okay.

MILLIE: When?

MARK: Pick you up in 20 minutes?

MILLIE: I'll be ready.

When I pull into Millie's driveway, she's sitting on the front step waiting for me. It's really not fair how good she looks in a simple pair of leggings and an oversized sweater. She has her auburn hair gathered into a long braid that's pulled over one shoulder. I suck in a breath and get out of the car meeting her halfway.

"Hey."

She looks up at me. "Hey."

I pull her into a hug, and she snuggles into me. She smells of coconut and vanilla. Is that soap or some kind of body spray? Whatever it is, I can't get enough. She pulls away and looks up at me. Her eyes are searching for something as she looks into mine. I take another step away, widening the space between us. Not because I want to, but because if I don't, I'm not sure I'll be able to stop myself from kissing her. I'm pretty sure that, no matter how much I think she is feeling the same pull that I am, she's not ready for that. Not yet. When I kiss her, I want her to want me to kiss her. And I want her to kiss me back.

"We should get going." My voice is gravelly.

"Lead the way," she says with a smile. "Where are we going? Pretty sure most places aren't open this early."

I open her door to let her in then race over to my side and start the car up.

"It's a bit of a distance if you're up for it, but it'll be worth it. I promise." I look over and give Millie a smirk. I might have even winked. I'm not really sure anymore. This whole night is turning into some sort of out of body experience. I'm doing and saying things that I have never done in my entire life. I'm finding out what I'm going to do along with Millie.

"I'm up for anything." My eyes drag down to her mouth, but I make myself look away quickly as I put the car into reverse.

"Any music preferences?"

"Driver chooses. Besides, I'm curious about what you listen to. My guess is elevator music." Even in the dim light her eyes sparkle with mischief as she teases me.

"You make me sound like an old man."

"You said it, not me." Her laughter fills the car.

"Oh, you're in for it now!"

"Bring it on, Grandpa."

We settle into an easy jabbing and banter back and forth as we make our way to our breakfast spot. I'm almost sorry when we pull into the parking lot of Old Mabel's Diner.

"Wait here," I say as I run to the other side of the car. "Have you ever been here before?" I ask as I open her car door.

"I've heard of it but never been here. Wasn't this place featured on one of those hidden gem shows on TV a couple years ago?"

"I think so. I don't exactly watch those shows too often."

"I wouldn't expect you to." She nudges me with her whole body. My body sings at the contact.

"You must think I'm super boring."

"I don't think you're boring," Millie says with a more serious tone, making me believe her sincerity.

"You have a funny way of showing it." I return her nudge.

"Truce?" She turns to face me, offering her pinky finger.

"Truce," I agree, accepting her pinky promise.

"How did you find this place?"

"Your dad brought me here back when we were kids."

"My dad?"

"Yeah. It was shortly after we had moved in, and I was having a hard time. He came into my room one morning and told me to get in the car. So I did. We didn't talk the whole way, just sat and listened to the radio, neither one of us said a word until we were sitting in the booth." I pause. "I don't think I've ever told anyone that. I don't think even Ben knows."

"That sounds like my dad," Millie says smiling. "Always looking out for everyone."

"He's a good guy."

"He's the best, but I'm also pretty biased."

Having breakfast with Millie is the most natural thing in the world. We talk about anything and everything. Before we know it, we've been sitting in our booth for a couple hours, and the diner's usual Sunday morning crowd is starting to file in the doors.

"Shall we?" I say motioning toward the door.

"We probably should," Millie agrees as she watches the crowd grow larger. We vacate our booth, and I go to the counter to pay for our meals.

"You up for something else before we head back?" I'm not ready for this to be over. She nods in agreement. Millie heads for the car, but I grab her hand and lead her in the opposite direction. Confused, she gives me an inquisitive look.

"It's just up here," I explain. I'm still holding her hand, but she hasn't pulled away, so I keep going.

"What is?"

"You'll see"

"Or you could just tell me," She coaxes.

"Nope."

"You're no fun."

"So you've said." I give her a sly smile.

"I just don't see why you can't—oh wow!" I watch her as she takes in the view from the outlook. "This is amazing!"

"I told you it was worth it."

"You sure did," she says as she gives my hand a squeeze.

I take a chance and start rubbing circles on her palm with my thumb. She surprises me by intertwining our fingers.

"I found this path a few years after your dad and I first started coming here. Whenever life was getting to be too much, I would get in the car and just drive, and I'd usually end up here."

"It's beautiful." She squeezes my hand again.

"I haven't been back here in a long time." I don't know why, but I feel like I can share everything with Millie. I want to share everything with her. I've never wanted to share my thoughts or feelings with anyone. I hardly share them with myself. This realization should freak me out, but as with everything else, Millie just makes everything make sense, and I want more of that in my life. I need more of that in my life.

I can't take my eyes off of Millie. There is something that is waking up within her soul as she watches the sun rise further up in the sky. Her eyes are bright blue with excitement. Her passion for life is intoxicating, and I crave more of it. I crave more of her. She still has her hand in mine giving it a little squeeze.

She tears her eyes away from the skyline and meets my gaze. "Thank you for bringing me here."

"Thank you for coming." I twirl a loose curl around the forefinger of my free hand and give it a slight tug before placing it behind her ear. A soft pink colors her cheeks as she looks away.

Millie gives my hand a small squeeze.

"We should probably head back. I'm sure everyone has noticed that I'm not home by now. Don't want them to worry." She lightly pulls my arm towards the car.

I nod.

We drive back to her place in a comfortable silence, fingers intertwined. As I pull up to the house she looks at me and speaks for the first time since we got in the car. "Thank you for today. Breakfast was almost as wonderful as that view."

"You're welcome." I hesitate. Then look into her eyes that are now an ocean blue. I could swim in those eyes forever. "Millie…"

There's a moment. All I'd have to do is—

"Do you want to come in?" Millie blurts. Not ready to go back to my empty condo, I agree.

We walk through the door, and Kiersten is sitting on the couch eating a bowl of cereal. She eyes us and then looks down at our hands. "Well, hello…"

"Hey, Kiersten," Millie says nonchalantly.

"And where have you two been so early this morning?" There is amusement in her voice. I like her.

"We went to breakfast."

Kiersten lifts an inquisitive eyebrow.

"It was a bit of a drive. Had an early start," I add.

"Umm-hmm." A smile tugs at the corners of her lips.

Kiersten goes back to her cereal and whatever show she had on. When she finishes, she gets up and washes her dishes. After disappearing down the hallway, she comes back with her book bag and keys.

"I have a study group and then work so I'll see you guys later."

"Okay," says Millie. "Is anyone else up?"

"Not home," Kiersten responds. "Amara and Duncan left shortly before you got here. They have brunch with his parents. And Tori isn't home yet."

Millie's eyes furrow. "What is going on with her lately?"

"She met up with Jonathan last night. She probably just stayed at his place."

"You're probably right." Millie's face relaxes, but her shoulders are still tense.

"You two have fun." Kiersten waggles her eyebrows at us.

"Bye!" Millie shouts as she buries her face in her hands, letting go of mine for the first time since we entered the room.

Millie and I sit on the couch as she starts to channel surf. She finally stops on a movie I don't recognize and curls up with a blanket leaning against me. As we sit, I can feel myself finally relaxing enough that I start to yawn.

The fact that I've been up for close to 30 hours starts to hit me. I strain to keep my eyes open and place my arm on the back of the sofa. Millie leans more into me, and I must have closed my eyes because next thing I know I hear, "What in the actual—What is going on here?!"

Even with my eyes shut, there is no denying that voice. It's my brother.

CHAPTER 17

Millie

A T THE SOUND of Jonathan's voice, I about jump out of my skin. I was full on asleep on my couch, laying on Mark's chest with his arm around me.

"Jonathan! It's not what it looks like!" I exclaim.

"It looks like you're asleep with my brother!" Jonathan fumes.

"Well, technically that's true, but that's not what happened," I try to explain. I look to Mark for back up.

"We fell asleep watching a movie, Jon. That's it." His voice is calm and steady.

"Why were you even on the couch to begin with?!" Jonathan is still breathing fire.

"We went to breakfast," Mark explains.

"Like on a date?" Jonathan's eyes are shooting lasers.

"No!" I protest before Mark can say anything else. "We're just friends that went to breakfast together and then came back and fell asleep watching a movie. It's nothing."

"Is that true?" Jonathan directs this question to Mark.

"Yeah. It's true." I can hear the hurt in Mark's voice. There's so much more than that, but I'm not even sure what's fully going on to even know how to explain it to Jonathan. This could quite possibly be the start of his biggest nightmare come true, and here I am lying about it.

"I should be going," Mark stiffens. "I have work stuff I need to get ready for tomorrow."

Mark gives a halfhearted smile at me, pats his brother on the shoulder, and walks out the door. My eyes are stinging, but I fight back the tears. I can't think straight right now. So much has happened tonight. This whole month really. I don't even know how to begin to process the way my feelings have changed and grown for Mark since I first saw him in Lexington. I never would have thought that my childhood dream could come true. And now after one perfect night, I go and make a mess of it all. Whatever it all is. The look on Mark's face and the sound of his voice will haunt me for weeks. I need sleep. And I need Jonathan to stop staring at me.

"You sure it was nothing?" Jonathan says again. His gaze is baring into me, but he softens when I don't answer him. "Is everything okay, Mills?"

I'm so drained I don't even answer him. I just turn and walk away.

Tori grabs my arm as I pass her. "Mills?"

"I'm tired. I need sleep," I say with all the emotion I can muster. Down the hall and to the left. I somehow manage to get to my room. I don't even remember sitting on my bed, but I know I must have since the next thing I know I'm opening my eyes.

I have no idea what time it is. Or even what day it is. I don't hear anything outside my bedroom door, and it's dark outside. I don't even bother looking at the clock. It doesn't matter anyway. With the way my head is throbbing, I need more sleep. I send a quick email to Sheila and tell her I will be working from home. Then I change into more comfortable clothes and get back into bed. Only this time I don't fall right to sleep.

I keep replaying the whole weekend over and over, from the perfection of Saturday night to the disaster of Sunday morning. Every look, every glance, I analyze it all. When all else fails, I make a pro/con list with all the reasons why Mark and I would and wouldn't work. I'm majorly sleep deprived and anxious, so the list isn't helpful, but that doesn't stop me from making one.

These are the times that I usually rely on Tori and Jonathan to talk me down, but that isn't an option right now. Not when one of the biggest cons on the list is Jonathan. I'd talk to Tori, but I know she'd just tell me to talk to Jonathan. And she'd be right. That is the adult thing to do, but I don't want to be an adult right now.

After tossing and turning for a couple hours, I finally drift into a restless sleep where my subconscious fears and trepidations take root. Weird dream after weird dream. I finally shake it off and am able to get some rest around 5:00. I faintly hear the front door open and close and know it must be Tori going for her morning run. When I wake up, it's almost 11:00; I've slept all morning. I look at my phone, and there are a series of messages from Danny and Ashleigh.

DANNY: Where are you? It's not like you to be late?

DANNY: Missed my iced coffee this morning. JK

DANNY: Okay, seriously, where are you?

DANNY: Hope everything is okay.

ASHLEIGH: Hey, Mills, are you okay? Do you need anything? Danny is really worried.

3 MISSED CALLS: Danny

DANNY: Seriously, what's going on? Where are you?

DANNY: Amelia!

ASHLEIGH: Just text when you have a chance.

ASHLEIGH: Danny's really worried. Text him first.

DANNY: AMELIA JEAN ANSWER YOUR DANG PHONE

MILLIE: Sorry! I slept in and I forgot to charge my phone.

DANNY: You about gave me a heart attack!

MILLIE: Sorry! I didn't mean to worry you.

DANNY: I'm just glad you're okay.

MILLIE: I'm fine. I promise. I just slept in.

MILLIE: Sorry about earlier, cool if I come by?

ASHLEIGH: Come on over. Girls just went down for a nap.

I take a quick inventory of my appearance. I better change. If my brother caught sight of me looking like this, he would pop a gasket. If it was anyone else, I would be annoyed, but not with Danny. He's always just wanted the best for the rest of us siblings. He really is the greatest big brother. Ashleigh is amazing as well. If anyone knows how to help my current predicament, it will be them. And heaven knows I need some perspective. I change into something more outside-world-appropriate and head out the door.

When I get in my car, I send a quick message before pulling out of my driveway.

MILLIE: I'm so sorry about yesterday. Can we talk?

When I pull up to Danny and Ashleigh's, I almost expect Danny's car to be in the driveway, but it's only the van. Ashleigh is sitting on the porch waiting for me as if she knows I need to talk.

"Hey, stranger."

"Hey," I say, defeated. I'm still drained from the lack of sleep and the overwhelming feelings of confusion that have taken over my soul.

Ashleigh gives me a once-over. "You look awful."

From anyone else that would feel like an insult, but I know Ashleigh means well, and frankly, it's true.

"Well, I feel awful."

"I'm just guessing, but Mark?"

I nod.

She motions towards the porch swing, "Come on, tell me all about it."

"SO, HE JUST got up and left?"

I nod. Tears are stinging my eyes. "He looked so hurt, Ash. And now he's not answering my messages. I think I really messed up."

"Maybe he hasn't seen your message yet."

"Maybe? I don't know. I think I really hurt him."

She grabs my hand and gives it a squeeze. It's the straw that breaks the camel's back. It's a deluge of tears. I'm full-on ugly crying. Just call me Tobey McGuire in Spiderman. It ain't pretty.

Ashleigh rubs my back. "Oh, Mills, you really like him."

"Yes," I croak out between sobs. "And—and now I've messed up everything."

"You don't know that."

"You didn't see his face. He was so mad."

"Mark will come around. You'll see."

"No! Not him!"

Her eyes furrow with confusion.

"Jonathan!" I croak. "I've never seen him so mad. I panicked."

"Jonathan will cool off. He can't stay mad at you."

"I don't know. I broke the cardinal rule." I gasp for air. "Then lied about it all while being caught red-handed."

My phone buzzes, and I race to take it out of my pocket.

> **MARK:** Don't worry about it.

"Who is it?" Ashleigh asks.

I show her the screen.

My hands are shaking as I type back.

> **MILLIE:** Can we talk? Please.

> **MARK:** I don't know if that's a good idea.

> **MARK:** You told me the other night that we weren't a good idea. I didn't get why until yesterday.

NO. NO. NO. This isn't what I want!

> **MILLIE:** Don't shut me out. Talk to me.

MILLIE: Please

MARK: What is there to say? You were right. Anything between us is complicated and impacts our entire families. It's not just us. It's our whole family involved from the get-go.

MARK: I can't–I won't–hurt Jon like that.

My heart shatters. How have we gone in such a polar opposite direction than we were headed yesterday? I drop my phone in my lap and start crying all over again.

Ashleigh rubs my back some more. "Give him some time."

I shake my head. "I think he made it perfectly clear where he stands."

She swats the air. "Oh, he doesn't know what he's talking about. I've never seen Mark like this. He's in completely uncharted territory. He's never felt for anyone what he feels for you."

I gape at her. "How would you know?"

"Because last night he looked as miserable as you do." I stare at her. "Did I not mention Mark came over for dinner last night?"

Her eyes dance. What is she talking about, and why has she just let me sit here crying my eyes out when she had information?

I sit up straight.

"No," I say, the tears instantly dried. Now I'm just annoyed at the pregnant woman sitting next to me. "It must have slipped your mind."

"Huh? I could have sworn I mentioned it."

"If you weren't pregnant, I'd pummel you."

She puts her arms around me. "No, you wouldn't."

I lean my head to hers. "No," I agree, "but I'd want to."

She laughs.

"So what do I do?"

"Give him time to sort through his feelings. He was pretty torn up about Jonathan's reaction. I don't think he knew how much he cared about Jonathan's opinion until he saw how upset he was."

"So I just sit and wait?"

"Not forever. Just long enough to give him time to process how he feels. He's having a whole paradigm shift going on right now."

"What am I supposed to do while I wait? I'm not exactly the most patient person."

"Except when it comes to Mark." She gives me a nudge. "You've had feelings for him for too many years to give up on him now. Not right when he's starting to have them back."

I roll my eyes. "Can we please talk about something else? Anything else?"

"Have you heard about the surprise baby shower Belinda is planning for herself?"

"No!" Not that I'm surprised.

We spend the rest of the morning talking about how Belinda refused the baby shower my mother offered to throw her, stating that she and her mother were planning a shower and that Mom's help was not needed.

It's a further reminder of how after my last—and only—serious relationship, I vowed that I would only ever date someone that got along with my family. With a family as close-knit as ours, it's difficult having someone who doesn't want to be a part of the craziness. There are a lot of us, and we are always in each other's business. It's just the nature of large families. This is also a reminder of how if I did date Mark, it would be public knowledge very quickly and hardly private. There would be no hiding it, not that I would want to.

So, if, and it is a really big if at this point, Mark and I did date, we would have to tell our families early on. If word got out that we were together and hadn't told anyone, it would make for a much bigger deal. Not that any of this matters if Mark isn't interested. And based on that last text message, I'm not sure he is anymore.

I'VE MADE A lot of mistakes lately but the decision to stay home wasn't one of them. After coming home from Danny and Ashleigh's, I tried to go through some manuscripts I've been meaning to get through, but I couldn't concentrate for more than a few sentences. I tried binge-watching shows I haven't had time to watch, but it was useless. Everything Ashleigh told me today keeps swimming through my mind. Mark's never felt for anyone like he feels for me? He was miserable. I don't want him to feel miserable. I don't want to feel miserable. I know she said I should give him time, but I can't just sit here waiting for who knows how long. I need to do something. I have to do something. Anything.

I groan as I fall onto my bed and let out a good long scream into my pillow. Not knowing what else to do with all this pent-up energy I head to the kitchen. I open up all the cabinets and the pantry door and just stare. I have no idea what I'm going to make. I just need to create something. I need some sort of control over my current situation.

I start pulling ingredients. Two dozen cupcakes, six batches of cookies, three loaves of bread, and a casserole in the oven later, Kiersten and Tori come home to find me, and our kitchen, covered in flour and sugar.

"You lasted longer than I thought you would, I'll give you that," Tori says, inspecting the cookies before deciding which one to eat first. "What kinds did you make during this round of stress baking?"

"I'm not stress baking!" I snap. "Mint chocolate chip, snickerdoodle, pecan turtle, cookies and cream, s'mores, and a new Hawaiian flavor that I'm not sure about."

"If you made it then it's good." Kiersten comes up behind giving me a hug. I sigh, and the tears start all over again.

"Millie, what's wrong?"

"I'm just so tired."

"Mark?"

"Of course, it's Mark!" Tori's mouth is stuffed to the brim with a cookie, and she swallows with a big gulp. "You know the only time she mega-bakes is when she's upset over a man."

"Hey! Not true!"

"It is too! You first created this recipe after things with D-bag Denham blew up," Tori argues.

"Shh! We don't speak that name! It's like Beetlejuice, or worse, Voldemort!" Kiersten hisses at Tori. I'm not sure if Kiersten's goal was to make me laugh, but at least I'm not crying anymore.

"Okay, so I've been known to stress bake in the past, but it doesn't mean that's what I'm doing now," I protest.

Tori and Kiersten just stare at me and then the countertop bakery that I've created.

I take a deep breath. "Okay. Fine. It's about Mark." I sigh. "Ashleigh says I just need to give him time, but I don't know."

"Big baby," scoffs Tori.

Kiersten slaps Tori in the arm.

"It's a confusing situation for both of you," she reassures me.

Tori rubs her arm. "What else did the wise Ashleigh have to say?"

There is no mistaking her sarcastic tone, but I choose to ignore it.

"That Mark had dinner at their house last night and was absolutely miserable and that she's never seen him like this before." I shrug. "I don't know. He was pretty adamant in his message this afternoon that he doesn't want to hurt Jonathan."

"I just don't think that Jonathan would stand in the way if the two of you wanted to be together," Kiersten says.

"I don't know," Tori interjects. "I've never seen him so mad. He was pretty upset when he left. He hasn't answered any of my messages all day either. Have you tried?"

"No." I hadn't even thought about talking with Jonathan. How terrible of a friend am I? I groan, throwing my head into my hands.

"So what are you going to do? Avoid everyone and bake until you run out of supplies?"

"Maybe? What else am I supposed to do? I can't just sit here and idly wait. I have to do something, or I'm going to go crazy."

"Just go to his house," Tori says while stuffing another cookie into her mouth.

Kiersten's eyes widen. "Jonathan's or Mark's?"

"Mark's. It doesn't matter what Jonathan thinks if Mark doesn't want to go forward," Tori reasons.

"And do what, Tori?!" I'm so tired I can't even try and hide my annoyance.

"Tell him you like him."

"Just like that? What if he doesn't answer the door?"

"If he's home, he'll answer the door."

"You don't know that."

"He'll answer the door, Millie," she says more reassuringly.

"Even so, he could still refuse to talk to me. What then?"

"He's not going to turn you away."

"There's no way for you to know that."

"I saw how he was looking at you Saturday. He's into you." I scoff.

"If he wasn't into you, then he wouldn't be so hurt and upset right now."

"But if he does, which he won't, but if he does," Kiersten cuts in, "you walk away knowing you did everything you could and at least you tried."

"I don't even know where his house is."

"Excuses. Excuses," Tori singsongs.

"I think it's a pretty valid point," Kiersten points out.

"Kiersten, you're supposed to be helping me, not helping her with excuses," Tori says with mild irritation.

"Sorry, but she has a point. She needs to know where to go," Kiersten argues.

Tori rolls her eyes as she pulls out her phone and starts typing away.

"What are you doing?" I'm almost too scared to ask.

"I texted Carson to ask Rosie. She will obviously know where her brother lives."

"Why don't you just text Rosie directly?"

"Because she may or may not still be mad at me from Christmas."

"What happened at..." Kiersten stops mid-sentence. "Never mind. I don't want to know."

"Got the address." Tori passes me the phone. "Thank you, Carson."

I stare at the phone dumbfounded. How did Carson get this so fast? The pros and cons of your best friends' little sisters being best friends. And right now I'm not sure I'm seeing it as a pro. My heart is racing. This is impulsive. This isn't something I would normally do. This is main character energy. This is what Tori would do. I look up to meet Tori and Kiersten's eyes.

"It's up to you, kid." Tori takes her phone back. "Are you willing to take a chance?"

CHAPTER 18

Mark

I'M NOT PROUD of how I've acted the last couple of days. I just—I don't even know. I've never felt so many conflicting emotions all at once. Waking up with Millie in my arms was a more than pleasant surprise. Waking up because my brother was angrily standing over us? Not so pleasant.

Have I talked to him about it? Of course not. What is there to talk about? Millie and I were asleep on her couch. Nothing happened. Did it sting when she said we were only friends? More than I will ever admit. I was playing with fire, and now the harsh reality of that decision has burned me. The only thing to do is to push all those feelings away and hope that they disappear.

I decide to take a drive up the coast to clear my head. The weather is nice out today, and the ocean air blowing in my face as I drive is just the distraction I need. Add this to the pro column for coming home.

While driving down Pacific Coast Highway, my phone dings with a message from Ben. I'm not ready to unpack all of that just yet so I swipe the notification away. I'll read it later, if for no other reason than the annoying red notification circle will drive me crazy. I don't know how people can stand having those. I don't even know what to say to Ben anyway. I know I need to talk to him eventually, but now is not the time. For now it can sit in notification purgatory with dozens of messages from my father.

My phone dings again, and I groan. This time the message is from Danny, and I swipe it open to read it.

> **DANNY:** I know it's last minute and you might have plans, but Ashleigh and I would like to invite you over for dinner tonight.

> **MARK:** No plans. Dinner sounds great. What time?

> **DANNY:** Ash says 6:00, but that really means 7:00 so really just show up anytime.

> **MARK:** You guys home now?

> **DANNY:** Come on by. The girls and I are doing art projects (read: making a mess) while Ash naps.

I laugh as I think about what a sight neat and tidy Danny Jacobson making a mess with art supplies would be. He's always been the clean freak of the Jacobson siblings; maybe it has to do with being the oldest, since I'm the same way when it comes to my siblings. Still the thought puts a smile on my face, which I could definitely use. Besides, what better way to stop thinking about Millie than distracting myself with two crazy and rambunctious three-year-olds.

I MIGHT HAVE overestimated how easy it would be to not think about Millie while at Danny and Ashleigh's. Let's start with the obvious:

1. Danny is Millie's older brother. They look alike. They have very similar personalities. THEY LOOK ALIKE. They might have different hair colors, but there is a Jacobson look and it is strong. And after and entire evening of trying to notice anything else, I can also say with confidence that Danny and Millie might be the two Jacobsons, other than the twins, that look the most alike. Actually, Jake and Drew are fraternal twins so even including them. They have the same mannerisms, speech patterns, similar sense of humor. I've never been so annoyed with Danny as I was while trying to be polite and yet also not think of his female clone.

2. Danny and Ashleigh's twins, Austyn and Ashtyn, ADORE their aunt and talk about her constantly. Apparently, she's the one who got them the art kit they were playing with. She gave them the princess dresses they insisted on wearing at dinner. And she's the one who introduced them to the book series they are now obsessed with. The one they not only wanted read to them after dinner but wanted me to read. When I didn't

do the voices, I was quickly reprimanded on how Aunt Millie would do it. Basically, she's the perfect aunt. Not that I'm surprised by any of this information.

3. Ashleigh Jacobson is a naturally curious person; she has been for as long as I have known her but add in pregnancy to an already stubborn nature and wow. Ash wouldn't let up with the questions! "Are you seeing anyone?" "Why aren't you seeing anyone?" "Would you ever consider dating someone you've known for a long time?" Gee, I wonder who she could possibly be thinking of. She wasn't even trying to be subtle.

I try my best to be in a good mood. I really do. All of these reminders of Millie are just too much. I wanted a relaxing dinner with my friends and their family, and what I got was an even bigger hole in my heart. Not only was it a reminder of what my siblings and I have never had, it's also a reminder of what I will never have of my own. Relationships just don't work out. Not for me, anyway. I'm just not made for relationships. It's in my DNA or something.

I end up leaving Danny and Ashleigh's with more on my mind than when I got there. I want to text Millie or go over there and see her, but when I drive by her house (in a non-creepy stalker-ish way), I see my brother's car in the driveway, and I just keep going. No need to stir that pot more than I already have. I've made my decision. I'm choosing my brother's feelings over my own. Millie is his best friend. I won't make her choose between me and him. I won't let him loose her. I might not be able to have any deep relationships in my life, but that doesn't have to ruin the best relationship he's ever had. Even if they are only friends it still feels like some kind of triangle situation and no. Just no.

AFTER A RESTLESS night of overthinking, all I've managed to do is wallow in the emptiness that is my life. I'm grasping at straws for reasons why Millie and I can't be together. I spent half the night wracking my brain for any clues that there might possibly be something or ever have been something between Jon and Millie. They spend all their time together. They've never had any relationship that didn't last longer than a few months. They have tons of common interests. They support each other 100% even when they don't agree. They would do anything to make the other one happy, even if that meant sacrificing something they wanted. Pretty sure those are all reasons used in in Hallmark movies that I may or may not watch with Todd.

Rationally I know that I'm being ridiculous. Millie and Jon may be best friends, but they are more like siblings. They encourage each other to go on dates and then talk about them extensively. I don't know about you, but if I was harboring a crush on someone, I wouldn't want to hear all the details of their dates with other people. In fact, I know I wouldn't because even the idea of Millie dating someone else makes my stomach do all sorts of crazy things.

There must be a reason why I can't have the only thing I've really wanted in a very long time. I spent the rest of the night thinking of all the reasons why being with Millie is a terrible idea and will never work out because nothing I ever want ever works out. Like I mentioned, I am wallowing.

When Millie's text came in this morning, it took everything I had not to leave the office and go right to her, but I just couldn't. I didn't see any other way to answer. I never meant to hurt her, it hurts me too, but it's better this way. Isn't it? Isn't this what's best for everyone? I mean, sure, it sucks now, but she'll get over it. She'll move on. She'll find someone who deserves her, and she'll totally forget about me. And I'll learn to live with this new level of emptiness.

The longer I sit with this decision the more I hate it. I've typed and erased so many messages to Millie that I've lost track. Even leaving work early and taking out all my frustrations out at the gym didn't ease the empty pit. I want to take back what I said. But we can't do that. The one thing that hasn't changed is the image I have seared in my brain of the look of betrayal in my brother's eyes. He and I might not have a great relationship, but he's still my brother. And Millie's best friend. If it had been Ben who walked in the door, I can't say I wouldn't have done the same thing she did. A moment of panicked decision-making and here we are. Friends. Only, I don't want to be just friends with Millie. If that's all we can be, I'd rather avoid her for the rest of my life because I can't be just friends. How do you put all of that in a text message? You can't.

I try to distract myself and drown my thoughts by channel surfing, finally deciding on a 1986 playoff game. This is what my life has become, watching a basketball game from before I was born. I don't even like basketball.

I turn the TV off, throwing the remote to the opposite side of the couch. I might as well unpack some boxes. I have nothing but time. It doesn't take long to realize that the whole reason why they were still packed is because I don't know where to put any of it. I also remember how I thought about asking Millie to help me. I close the box up and stack it back on the pile. That's a problem for another day. Maybe I should eat something other than a bag of Skittles. I head to the kitchen. Nothing sounds good. A bowl of cereal it is. I'm about to pour another bowl when there is a knock at the door.

I suck in a breath when I see her.

Millie.

"Hi," she says sheepishly.

"Hi."

"Hi."

"Hi." You're a grown man with a vast vocabulary. Use some of it! "What are you doing here?" Maybe not the best choice.

"I made cookies!" She squeaks.

"Okay…?"

Millie shoves a box into my hands. "I made six different kinds. I don't know what you like so I brought some of all of them. You don't have any allergies, do you? I don't remember you having any allergies, but…"

"No allergies." I'm just staring at her. She's here. At my house. With…cookies. "How did you know where I lived?" A look of panic flashes in her eyes. She's about to dart. "Not that I mind! I just…no one has been to my place yet."

She takes a shaky breath before speaking. "Rosie told me...well, sort of...she told me through...I mean, we messaged...and then...ummm, it's a long story?"

Nervous Millie is adorable.

I smile. "Do you want to come in?"

"No!" She coughs. "I mean, no. I just came to bring you cookies."

"Thank you."

"You're welcome...Okay...bye!" She turns and starts walking away.

"Millie, wait!" I start after her, not sure what I'm doing. "Hold up," I grab her arm and turn her around, but she won't look me in the face. "Why did you bring me cookies?"

"I told you. I made a lot, so I thought you'd like some."

"But why did you bring them over? Now?"

"Because cookies are best when they are fresh."

"Cookies are best when they are fresh, and you made a lot of them, so you naturally decided to get my address, something you didn't have, from my sister?"

"Hmm-hmm." She nods.

"Why are you here, Millie?"

She finally looks up at me. "You know why."

"I'm not sure I do." I fold my arms across my chest.

"Yes, you do." Her voice is cracking.

"Just say it then." It comes out almost as a plea.

"I can't," she whispers.

I can't take it any longer. Her big blue eyes, brimming with tears. Seeing her makes it clear to me. Every complication is worth it. Who cares what any brother or best friend thinks? I need this woman in my life. And not as my friend.

My hand slowly moves a piece of hair from her face and puts it behind her ear. My hand cups her face, and I place my forehead on hers.

"I want this. I want us."

"Me too."

My other hand starts tracing circles on her shoulder. Our eyes lock. My lips part. I start to close the gap. Millie yelps and jumps out of my embrace as the sprinklers go off. Of all the times! We are both soaking wet. Millie starts laughing uncontrollably; I start laughing too. Leaning my forehead to hers again, I trace her jaw with my thumb. I pull her into me.

"Come inside, let me get you a towel to dry off."

"It's okay." She pulls away to look up at me. I eye her skeptically. "I really need to get going."

"Fine." I run my hands up and down her arms. "What are you doing tomorrow night?"

"Nothing."

"Dinner? 7:00?" I take her hands in mine, interlocking our fingers.

"Mark Winters, are you asking me out on a date?"

"You bet your cute butt I am."

"See, I knew you were checking out my butt the other day!" Her smile lights up her whole face.

"Yeah, yeah, yeah, you caught me. So what do you say?" I grin back.

"I say, yes." She squeezes my fingers. "I would love to go to dinner with you tomorrow night."

She turns to dashes off to her car, but I pull her back into me giving her a hug and kiss her on the top of the head.

After drying off and changing my clothes, I crash into bed completely exhausted from the last few days but smiling like a fool.

CHAPTER 19

Millie

OH HOW MUCH things can change in 24 hours. Yesterday I was the most miserable I have ever been. Today? Happiest I have ever been.

I know I should have skipped lunch today, especially since I didn't get much work done yesterday, but when Mark texted and asked me, I couldn't say no. I just want to spend all the time I can with him. It came down to being distracted looking at him or being distracted thinking about him. Frankly, I prefer the eye candy.

Mark's phone rings while we sit at our table and wait for our number to be called. I can see from here that it's Jack, but Mark doesn't answer. Mark still hasn't said what made him want to move back to Ridgeview, but I have a sneaking suspicion that in one way or another Jack is behind it. I don't have many memories of the man, and the ones that I do are fuzzy. Of the few things Jonathan has said over the years very few have been positive. But I would find it hard to say anything positive about a man who did nothing but demanded perfection, constantly bailed on promises, and ultimately abandoned his family.

I don't think I've even seen the man since I went with Mark, Jonathan and Rosie to his wedding when I was sixteen. It was the first time I had ever truly seen how much of an effect he had on them. Rosie was a nervous mess, which is the complete opposite of her calm and cool demeanor. She has the least memories of the divorce since she was barely a year old when it happened. I think she only went to the wedding because it was expected she attend.

Jonathan was just less that night. Less animated. Less opinionated. Less vocal. Less him. He sat back subdued, hardly talking to anyone. Jonathan is one of the most extroverted people I know. He can make friends with anyone in a matter of minutes but put him in a country club surrounded by his father's future in-laws and friends, and the overly talkative boy became a mute.

Mark's behavior was the most surprising to me that night. He had been away at school, and we hadn't seen him. It was after his injury and subsequent surgery, and he was just lost. He wasn't the Mark I had grown up knowing. He was more cynical and got angry about little things Jack would say. The Mark I knew would never have called out his dad for leaving like he did, at least not somewhere as public as the man's wedding. Now as an adult I can see how much Mark was hurting. He had lost one of the most constants in his life when he lost baseball, and yet all he had ever wanted was to be noticed by his dad. The man who rather than showing up for his kids chose to put himself first. Even the stories Jack told that night were to put him in a good light, make him look like the doting father he never was.

As I watch Mark ignore another incoming call from Jack, I can still see that hurt little boy who only ever wanted his dad to love him. Who would have done anything for his approval, even if that meant losing himself in the process. I don't know what all happened in Charleston, and I hope Mark will tell me about it someday. But today isn't the day. Today is a day we get to focus on the here and now. A here and now that I really hope is the start of a future.

"Any clues as to what we are doing tonight?"

Mark grins over at me. "Nope. It's a surprise."

"Surprise as in you're not going to tell me or surprise as in you haven't figured it out yet?"

"Just trust me." He laughs and nudges my shoulder.

I nudge him back. "I do trust you. I just need to know what to wear."

That, and although I love planning surprises, I don't like being surprised myself. I like knowing what to expect. I research the menu of restaurants before I go there so I'm not overwhelmed with needing to make decisions on a first date, just as an example. I also like to have the proper footwear. I once went on a date expecting us to go to a sit-down restaurant, and we ended up going paint balling. To say heels were a bad idea is an understatement.

Mark waggles his eyebrows. "Polite society dictates clothing in most situations, but I say you do you."

I all but spit out my food as I try to contain my laugh. "Stop! You're making me blush."

He leans in closer to whisper in my ear. "I like when you blush."

I lightly shove him away. "Behave."

"Fine." I want to wipe that smug look off of his face. At the very least poke him in that devilish dimple. I don't. I muster enough self-control to keep my hands to myself.

"You're not going to give me any hints about tonight, are you?"

"Nope."

"Fine. Ballgown and roller skates it is."

"Just be ready by 7:00, Your Majesty." He mock-bows.

IT'S 6:00 AND I still have no idea what I'm wearing on this date. I've been staring at my closet for the past hour, and I have come to three conclusions:

1. I have a lot of the same colors.
2. I really need to organize my closet better.
3. I don't seem to own any date clothes.

I'm just about to call out for help when Tori and Kiersten poke their heads in.

"How's date prep going?" asks Kiersten.

"Help! I have no idea what to wear, how to do my hair— what shoes do I wear? Dating hasn't always been this complicated, has it?"

"Only when you really like the guy."

"What are you doing anyway?" asks Tori.

The fact that Tori is even here helping me is huge. She's made her feelings about this whole situation very clear. She doesn't approve that I haven't told Jonathan I'm going on a date with Mark. If we're being honest, I don't like that I haven't told him either. If the roles were reversed, I'm not sure I would be as supportive as she is being. I haven't talked to Jonathan since Sunday when he walked in on me and Mark sleeping on the couch. I know I need to; I'm just not sure what to say. We've never had a fight before. At least not to this level. I don't think buying him a Jamba Juice is going to work like it did when we were kids.

"No clue. Mark hasn't told me anything."

Tori rolls her eyes.

"I think it's sweet. He wants to surprise her," Kiersten protests.

"Even players can play sweet."

"Since when has Mark been considered a player? All the stories I've heard from when you guys were growing up makes it seem like Ben dated around and Mark didn't date."

After a few more back and forth comments, I finally break in, "Hi. Remember me? The one you're supposed to be helping get ready?"

Kiersten jumps into action as if she and Tori haven't been going on and on for the last ten minutes. "I have the perfect outfit! I'll be right back!"

Once Kiersten exits the room, I turn to face Tori. "What's your deal tonight?"

"I just think you should tell Jonathan."

"You're the one who, just last night, told me that it doesn't matter what Jonathan thinks. If I want to date Mark, then I should date Mark."

"And I standby that!" She snaps.

"You can't be on both sides! The back and forth is giving me whiplash."

"Have you even talked with Jonathan since Sunday?"

"No," I admit. I haven't had time. Or more accurately, I haven't wanted anything to damper my dream world I've been living in.

"Does this have anything to do with that dumb best friend code you two made up when we were kids?"

I shrug, not able to meet her eyes.

"That's kind of a jerk move, Millie. If you thought he was mad on Sunday, how do you think he's going to react when he finds out that you hid this behind his back? You two have always been nothing but honest with each other and told each other everything. If I wasn't so secure in my role in our friendship, I'd envy the level of understanding you share."

It takes everything in me to force myself to look Tori in the face. "I'm not hiding anything. I just haven't had the chance to tell him yet."

Tori and I are in a complete stare down when Kiersten comes back with the most perfect blue and yellow dress.

"Oh, Kiersten! It's perfect!"

"I figured this with your lace Converse. Dressy and casual all at the same time so you are ready for anything Mark might have planned."

"You're a genius!" I give her a quick hug as I start getting ready.

"MILLIE, MARK IS here," calls Amara.

After one final look in the mirror as I apply my lipgloss, I grab my phone, keys, and jean jacket before heading down the hall. As soon as I enter the living room, I feel Mark's eyes on me giving me a once over. I can't help but blush as his grin deepens showing off his dimple.

"Hey, beautiful." Mark wraps me into a side hug. Gosh, he smells good.

"Hey."

"I brought you these." Mark hands me a bouquet of white daisies, sheepishly he adds, "I wasn't sure what your favorite flower was, but I saw them and thought of you."

Suddenly I'm six years old again and I've just finished my first play. Everyone is surrounding me and Jonathan congratulating us on a great performance when Mark hands me a small bouquet of flowers.

I'm sixteen, and it's my first show without Jonathan or Tori on the stage with me. They're both behind the scenes, and I'm terrified I'll mess everything up. A vase of white daisies is delivered with a card.

> *Good luck tonight, from Texas.*
> *-Mark*

"White daisies are my favorite. They're perfect," I say, shifting to the present and trying not to cry at the thoughtfulness. "I don't think I've ever had a date bring me flowers."

I turn and hand the flowers to Kiersten, who's all but busting at the seams with a giant smile on her face.

"You ready?" Mark asks as he trails his hand down my arm causing my skin to erupt in goosebumps. He takes my hand in his as he leads me out the door.

"Are you finally going to tell me where we are going?" I give a little pout. He chuckles, as he runs his finger down the bridge of my nose. I scrunch up my face. I'm taking that as a no.

"Nope." He opens the door giving my hand a light tug and leads me out towards the passenger seat.

Since he clearly isn't going to tell me where we're going then I'm going to play twenty questions the entire car ride until I either annoy him so much he has to tell me or until we arrive. It's a game I used to play with my brothers when I was little. It has proven to be 95% effective. At this point I don't care which comes first because either way I will know the answer. It would just be so much easier if he told me. It doesn't take too long before I give up on my game. He's finding too much amusement in my need to know. I'm not sure I like how much he likes being in control of the situation.

I try to guess where we are going based on the streets he turns on, but he caught on to me and has made multiple turns to make us go in a circle so that I can't. I harumph in my seat and cross my arm trying to look annoyed, but Mark puts his hand on my knee and gives it a light squeeze and I can't keep a straight face. A smile escapes me, and I start giggling. Which only encourages him further to try and tickle my side. I try to squirm away from his reach, but we're in a car so there isn't anywhere for me to go.

"Watch it, Mister Winters!"

He gives me a devilish grin. "What am I supposed to be watching?"

"The road!" I point ahead. "You're driving."

He dips his head in my direction, giving me a wink, then turns back forward. "Fine. Have it your way."

He pulls my hand from my side and puts it in his, resting our entangled hands on the arm rest between us. As I give it a squeeze, I can't help but revel in all that has happened in the last few days. Never in my wildest dreams did I ever think that I would be sitting in a car with Mark Winters. On a date. Holding hands. And NOT for the first time!

Finally, he pulls into the parking lot, and it takes me a minute to get my bearings on where we are. "The farmer's market?"

"Is that okay?"

I smile up at him, "It's perfect. And it's Tuesday!"

His eyebrow quirks up.

"A lot of local artists and craftsmen come on Tuesdays," I explain. "It's sort of like a mini flea market within the farmer's market." I tug him forward. "Well, are we going in or are we just going to stand here all night?"

Mark follows my lead, then suddenly he steps away, my hand still in his and I'm spinning in towards him. I land right by his side with his arm around me, having never let go of his hand.

I nod my head at him. "Not a bad move."

I use my free arm to reach around him and pinch his side making him squirm like he made me in the car. "But mine's better," I whisper in his ear, making his Adam's apple bob as he gulps.

And that is how you take back control.

Composing himself, he says, "I figured we could walk around for a bit and then get some dinner at the food trucks?"

"Sounds good to me!"

Tonight is, in a word, perfect. I couldn't have planned a better night if I tried. All the years I spent dreaming what it would be like to go on a date with Mark, I never thought of something this magical.

We walk. We talk. The food is amazing. Twinkle lights begin to turn on overhead and light the walkways. There is a band starting to play over on the stage. It's a picture-perfect moment. I'm sad the night will soon be over. We both have work in the morning. Not to mention how I'm still recovering from the lack of sleep the last few nights.

Mark nudges me. "What's going on in that pretty little head of yours?"

I sigh. "I was just thinking how I'm not ready for tonight to end." I look up into his perfect, chocolatey brown eyes. "It's been the perfect date." I nudge him with my hip. "Thank you."

"How about we grab ice cream and go listen to the band play?"

I nod in agreement.

As we approach the stage area, I find some seats near the back.

"What kind of ice cream do you want?"

"Surprise me."

Mark rolls his eyes. "Not this again."

"What?" I bat my eyelashes at him. "I'm not picky."

He rolls his eyes again but turns towards the ice cream stand.

"Mint Oreo!" I call after him.

I sit and listen to the band play as I wait. I see an older couple a few tables up. They're holding hands, and my heart swells. It might be my overly-romantic heart, but that's the life I want. To still want to be with the person you love, choosing them over and over even after all those years. It's beautiful. I don't even realize I'm crying until I feel a tear drip from my cheek. I wipe my face and laugh at myself.

"One Mint Oreo." I jump when Mark's arm brushes mine as he sits down offering me my ice cream.

"Thank you." I give a slight shiver.

"Are you cold?" Mark asks as he hands me his cone and starts to remove his jacket.

I shake my head. "I'm good."

I link my arm with his and lean my head on his shoulder as we eat our cones. He begins drawing circles on my knee with his finger and thumb. I can't help but sigh with complete and utter contentment.

We throw away our trash and start to leave when the band begins to play an REO Speedwagon song. Mark leads me towards the makeshift dance floor and pulls me into him. He wraps his arms around my waist, and we begin to sway. He twirls me out here and there, but mostly, he just holds me close.

I lay my head against his chest as I start to trace the stitching of his shirt with my finger. "Thank you again for tonight. It really has been perfect."

"Thank you for coming with me." He shifts to meet my gaze. There's a look I've never seen before. It's soft and tender yet intense. It makes my heart flutter and my stomach do backflips. He pulls me in closer to him. "This thing we're starting; I'm all in."

"I'm all in too. Even if it does seem a little crazy."

"Is it really that crazy?"

"No," I shake my head. "To be honest, it's something I've wanted for a long time." I pull away from him enough to fully look at him.

He smiles down at me, "Me too."

I raise an eyebrow. "I mean way longer than three weeks."

Mark laughs, "So do I!"

I pull even further away and eye him questioningly. "Wha—how long?"

"How long what?" Amusement tugs at his lips. He's playing with me again.

"How long have you felt something for me?"

"Ben's wedding."

I freeze. "Ben's wedding? That was three years ago?"

"I'm painfully aware!"

I smirk. "You've been pining for me for three years?"

He gives a sheepish grin. "I wouldn't say pining, and it might have crossed my mind a time or two before then." I gape. I don't know what to say. "There might have been a teensy, tiny bit of jealousy when you brought what's his name home for Christmas."

I don't have words. I don't even know what to do with all of this new information. All this time. All these years that we could have—I can't even wrap my head around it.

"There's more," he confesses. I'm not sure how much more I can take. "It took everything out of me not to kiss you that night." He doesn't have to say which might. I know exactly what he is talking about.

"Why didn't you?" I barely whisper.

He rubs the back of his neck. "You had just broken up with your boyfriend. I didn't want to complicate things for you. Especially when I wasn't sure I even knew how to be a boyfriend. In case you haven't noticed, relationships haven't exactly been my forte."

My head is reeling. So many thoughts. So many emotions.

"I would have let you, you know."

"I know." He pulls me back into him as the song finishes. I can hear his heart thumping loudly in his chest. "How long?"

"Huh?" I don't dare look up at him.

"How long have you had feelings for me?"

I make myself look up. "Umm, welllllll..." He looks at me expectantly. "It's been a bit longer than you," I confess. I feel heat creeping up my neck.

"How long?" I hear the smile in his voice, and I hate him for it. Only I don't hate him at all. The complete opposite. "Come on, I told you."

I take a break and steal my resolve. "Okay. Fine." I look at him making full eye contact. "I have pretty much been in love with you since I was about twelve."

He smirks. "Since you were twelve?"

My embarrassment hits me, and I bury my face in his chest.

"So the theme songs?"

I nod.

"The jerseys?"

"Yes," I say, muffled into his shirt.

He puts his arms tighter around me. "Why?"

I try to extricate myself from him, but he holds me firmly in place.

I shrug. "You saw me."

My eyes start to brim with tears as the full embarrassment starts to hit. "I read *Persuasion* fourteen times the summer you left for college purely because I knew that's the book where your mom got your middle name."

The tears start falling, but I'm laughing now.

"Why are you crying?" He wipes my cheek with his thumb.

I start to turn away. "Because it's embarrassing!"

He cups my face with his hand, and I feel the trail of his other hand as it slides from my waist, and up my back. There is a fire in his eyes, so intent on mine, his head dipping ever so slowly towards my lips. We are magnets pulling towards each other. I lift my head as he lowers his.

"What's going on?"

CHAPTER 20

Mark

MILLIE AND I both freeze. My blood turns to ice. I don't know how long Ben has been standing there or how much he has heard. When it comes to Ben, it's best you approach things as if he were a woodland creature. Slow movements. No loud sounds.

Millie steps away from me and puts a good three feet between us. I stand completely still, unable to move. I knew that this conversation would need to happen someday; I mean she is his sister, but I really wasn't thinking it would be tonight. Not on our first actual date.

"Hey, Ben." My voice seems way too high right now. "What are you doing here?"

His eyes are dark and calculating. "Picking up some ginger root for Belinda, she's been having some rough morning sickness. What are you two doing here? Together?"

Millie thinks faster on her feet than I do. Just as I'm about to come clean about everything, she jumps in.

"Mark asked me to help him fix up his new place. He mentioned he liked some items that you and Belinda have so I brought him here to see if we could find anything." She pauses. When Ben doesn't say anything, she continues, "Since we had to come after work, I suggested we meet up for dinner and then walk around."

I'm stunned. How did she come up with that so quickly? I don't like lying to anyone, especially my best friend, but something of this magnitude will take a gentle hand. It may or may not need a full PowerPoint presentation complete with charts and graphs. Ben looks at me and then back to Millie. He's not buying it. At least not fully.

"You two were looking pretty chummy on the dance floor." Maybe it's my guilty conscience, but I swear his eyes are burning into my soul.

That's it. We're caught. Game over.

Millie's voice breaks through my panic. "Have you ever known anyone to get chummy during an REO Speedwagon song?"

"I guess not," Ben concedes. His whole demeanor shifts. "So did you find anything you like?"

All eyes are on me. "Where?"

"At the market," he says slowly, like it's obvious, because, well, it is. We are literally standing in the middle of the market. "Millie said she was helping you fix up your place."

That all-too-familiar pit is forming in my stomach again.

"We haven't been here too long. Haven't made it that far yet. We had dinner and were just finishing some ice cream while listening to the band play when we ran into you." At least that part wasn't a lie.

"Cool. Well, I need to get back home with this ginger." He's about to go when he turns back to face us. "There are lots of cool things here. I think we came and looked at least four or five times before we decided on any specific pieces. Let me know what pieces we have that you liked, and I can give you their information."

"That would be great," Millie says. "I'm sorry Belinda isn't feeling well. Let me know if she needs anything."

He nods.

"I'll call you this weekend sometime," I call as he turns and starts to walk back towards the parking lot. I hold my breath until I see him exit towards a row of cars.

I turn towards Millie. "Did I ask you to help me fix up my place?"

She shrugs. "I panicked. It was the first thing I could come up with."

"No, I'm the one who panicked."

"You do realize that I'm going to have to fix up your place now right? Because Ben will notice."

I give her a sly grin. "Ben hasn't been over yet."

She matches my grin. "But he will notice if it looks like a full-on bachelor pad."

I grab her hand. "Good thing I was already planning on asking you to help me then."

She pulls my arm over and around her shoulder. "Oh, were you now?"

I purse my lips like I'm thinking about it. "Hmm-hmm."

Millie's eyes dance. "Sounds like a win-win to me. I get to spend time with you, and I get to spruce up your place all at once."

"You've never been inside my place; how do you know it needs any sprucing up?"

"You're a single, straight man who lives alone. Unless you hired someone to help you, or your mom and Rosie helped, it needs to be fixed."

"Fine. But did you really have to tell him I liked pieces from his house? Now I'm going to end up with some crystal-encrusted monstrosity in my house."

Millie doesn't even try to hide her smile. Her laugh comes bursting out like some sort of cackle. Then she snorts which makes her laugh even harder. I love how much she doesn't hold back what she's thinking or feeling. It's just so. . . Millie.

"I promise you won't have to have anything with crystals in it." She nudges me in the side with her elbow. "Unless you decide you just can't live without it."

I puff out a laugh. "Fat chance. For the record, this is not the date I had planned."

Millie curls into me. "It's been the perfect night." She looks up at me. "Maybe leave Ben out next time."

I lean my forehead against hers. "Deal."

Nothing about coming home has gone as I expected, but the most unexpected has definitely been Millie. All of this is more than I could have ever imagined. I'm not falling for her. I've already fallen.

AFTER I DROP Millie off back at her place I can't help but marvel at what an amazing night it's been. How amazing she is. It's the most honest and vulnerable I have ever been with anyone. You'd think I would be terrified right now, that

I would be over-thinking every last detail, but I'm not. I'm completely cool, calm, and collected.

I'm so distracted in fact that when my phone rings I don't even look at the caller ID before answering.

"Mark." My father's voice hits me like a bucket of ice.

"Dad."

"You quit your job, moved out of your apartment, and you aren't answering your phone. What on earth is going on with you?"

I take a deep breath. My father is really the last person I want to talk to, any day, but especially tonight.

"Nothing is going on with me." An understatement, but it's not like he's asking because he actually cares.

"If nothing is going on then why did you quit your job? We worked too long and too hard for you to get where you were for you to just throw it all away."

"That's just it, Dad!" I snap feeling bold from a distance. "I told you from the beginning that I didn't want help. Not with school, but you interfered. I didn't want help getting a job, but you went behind my back and called in a favor to your old college buddy. Then I find out that you yet again went behind my back and were working behind my back to get me the promotion. A promotion I wasn't sure I wanted."

"Don't be ridiculous, Mark, of course you wanted the promotion. The youngest partner in firm history? Even I didn't do that when I was starting out, and I was very good."

I roll my eyes. Even when we are talking about me, it's about him. How did I ever let myself fall under his spell?

"Well, I didn't want it, so I left."

"This doesn't have anything to do with Natasha, does it?"

"No. It has nothing to do with her."

"She was never good enough for you."

I scoff. Dad could do nothing but sing her praises the entire time Natasha and I were together. After we broke up, he tried for months for me to get back together with her, claiming, "You have the same values and goals."

"Why don't you come by for dinner tomorrow night and we can figure this whole mess out. Unless there's something else you aren't telling me?"

He's fishing. He already knows I moved out of my apartment which means he already knows I've moved, but he doesn't know where. At least he's not certain.

"I'm busy tomorrow night." I have plans with my mom so it's not even a lie.

"I'm sure your mother is gleeful that you came crawling back to Ridgeview." And there it is. The fatal blow.

"How long have you known?" I ask, completely defeated. Of course he found me. I was a fool to think I could just move and get away from him and his tyranny.

"Did you honestly think I wouldn't figure it out? I mean, Ridgeview? Seriously, Mark? That town is nothing but a dead end."

I don't have the energy to defend myself right now, not that it would work.

"It's been a long day, so if you're done with the inquest then I'm going to hang up." Before he can respond, I hit the end button.

I try to go back to that feeling I had tonight when I was with Millie, but the looming presence of my father overshadows any and all happy feelings.

CHAPTER 21

Millie

TONIGHT WAS PERFECT. Well, if you omit the part where my brother showed up, then it was perfect. I know I should have just been honest about our date when Ben showed up, but I really didn't want to deal with his dramatics. Not tonight.

No one was home when Mark dropped me off, so after changing into my pajamas and failing to find anything to watch, I decided to pull out my laptop to start looking at Pinterest for ideas on how to fix up Mark's place. Nearly two hours in and I may or may not have also looked up city plans to get an idea of the floor plan since I still have only been on the front porch. According to Google, the townhomes in that neighborhood are 2-3 bedrooms, depending on if it was a single or double story, 1-2 bathrooms, and then a living and dining area off of a kitchen.

> **MILLIE:** Single or double story?

> **MARK:** What?

MILLIE: I'm looking up ideas for your place.

MILLIE: Single or double?

MARK: Double

MILLIE: Bathrooms?

MARK: Yes.

MILLIE: How many?

MARK: 2

MILLIE: Bedroom?

MARK: Amelia Jacobson, are you thinking about my bedroom? Or just trying to picture it?

My face heats.

MILLIE: NO!

MILLIE: I MEANT to put an s on that!

MARK: Millie, calm down. I knew what you meant. I'm just messing with you.

MILLIE: You're such a jerk!

> **MARK:** Yeah, but you like me.

> **MILLIE:** Do I?

> **MARK:** Yeah. You do.

I'm grinning like a fool. Ear to ear.

> **MILLIE:** Yeah. I do.

I stretch and look at the clock. I really need to get some sleep. I close my laptop. I climb into bed and try to get comfortable. That's when my brain decides it's time to start racing. Everything is swirling together, but one thing is clear. I need to talk to Jonathan. I send a message before I can chicken out.

> **MILLIE:** Are you free for lunch tomorrow? I know you're busy.

> **JONATHAN:** I always have time for you. Do you mind coming to the high school?

> **MILLIE:** Not at all! What time is rehearsal? I can come around then.

> **JONATHAN:** That would be amazing! I need to pick your brain about one of the numbers, it's just not working right and I can't figure it out.

> **JONATHAN:** 2:30 in the auditorium.

> **MILLIE:** It's a date

I ARRIVED AT the office early this morning, because as much as I want to spend all my time with Mark, I also know that if I see him at all it would distract me. I needed to get in, get stuff done, and then leave by 2:00 in order to make it to Jonathan by 2:30.

I have so much I need to catch up on since I missed work Monday. There is a pile a mile high sitting on my desk taunting me. I slam my head on my desk with a groan.

Trina plops down next to me. "What's up with you?"

I sit up. "What do you mean?"

"You just seem distracted. Even more than before."

I quirk my face.

"You're dating someone!" Trina screams.

"Shh!" I hiss. "Not so loud. And how did you figure that out?"

"Distracted. Smiling all the time. All the signs were there. Don't know why I didn't make the connection earlier."

"I mean, it's not official or anything. It's only been three days. We've only technically been on one date."

"But you like him."

I nod and I can't help but smile. "Yeah. I really like him."

"Uh, you're so..." she motions all around me, twitterpated. I've never seen you like this."

"I've never felt like this before."

"So, tell me all about him. Name? Job? What kind of car does he drive?"

I raise my eyebrow.

"I'm not going to stalk him!"

"I know." I think. I honestly don't know if Trina would stalk someone or not. She might.

"So, tell me about him."

"Okay. Well, his name is Mark."

Trina's eyes go wide, and she starts flailing her arms. "Wait! Mark? Mark as in the new guy at Lexington?"

I nod.

"You saucy minx!"

"I'm far from a minx," I deadpan.

"Umm, says the woman dating the new hot guy of the building."

"It's not like that. He's just Mark. He's always been—"

"Wait." Trina picks up my picture from the hike. "Isn't this guy named Mark?"

"Umm-hmm." I nod.

"So Hike Mark and Lexington Mark are…"

I keep nodding. "The same person."

Trina starts hitting me. I wave my hands in surrender. "Stop hitting me!"

"Sorry. I'm just so excited for you!" She leans, in closer and whispers, "He's so hot!"

I roll my eyes.

"Yes, he is attractive, but he's so much more than that," I gush. I can't help it.

Trina sits back down in her chair. "Well, I'm happy for you."

"Thanks. It's still new, but I feel really good about this."

"And apparently he can't stop thinking about you either." Trina waggles her eyebrows as she hands me my phone.

MARK: Hey, beautiful. Missed seeing you this morning.

MILLIE: I came in early to try and catch up on some work.

MILLIE: I missed you, too.

MARK: Are you available for lunch today?

MILLIE: I have lunch plans already, but I'm available for dinner.

MARK: Work lunch?

MILLIE: No.

MARK: Have a hot date or something?

MILLIE: Or something.

MARK: Oh…

MILLIE: Mark, relax. I meant what I said last night. I'm all in.

MILLIE: I'm meeting Jonathan for lunch.

MARK: Jealousy is not a good look on me.

MILLIE: Green's a good color on you.

MILLIE: Brings out your eyes.

MARK: You're going to be using that against me, aren't you?

MILLIE: Most definitely

MILLIE: Dinner?

MARK: Can't. Have plans with my mom tonight.

The fact that Mark has plans with Helen shouldn't give me heart palpitations, but just knowing how much she will love the one-on-one time makes me smile. I don't think Mark could do anything that wouldn't make me smile. As much as I thought I liked him when I was younger, it has nothing on how I'm feeling about him now. Sometimes real life can be better than the movies.

I PULL INTO the high school parking lot a little later than planned, but I figure Jonathan will forgive my tardiness when he sees what I brought for lunch. I gather up all the bags and make my way towards the auditorium. I admit, I might have gone overboard with getting some of his favorite things. With any luck, he will be so distracted with the musical that he won't think too much about it.

It still feels strange to be visiting Jonathan on our campus even though he has worked there for two years. It's hard not to feel at least a little reminiscent each time I step foot past the front gates. There are memories at every turn. Muscle memory takes over, and I take an old shortcut through the English building. The bags of food in my hands are getting heavy so I pick up my pace. I can comb through the memories later.

Pushing through the double doors of the auditorium, that familiar scent hits me mixed with a slight pang of loss. Sometimes I miss music and theater so much it hurts. I'm happy with my life and where I am, but sometimes I wonder what would have happened if I would have been brave enough to have kept it up in college.

"Hey, stranger!" Jonathan runs up, wrapping me in a big hug.

"Hey! I have lunch!" I hold up all the bags.

"I can see that." He eyes the bags. "How many people are you planning on feeding?"

"I know you've been having lots of extra rehearsals, and I figured you haven't been eating dinner, so I brought enough for you to have the leftovers."

"Always looking out for me." He takes the bags and leads the way to his table in the middle of the hall.

As I walk behind him, I am struck by the similarities and differences between the two brothers. If you didn't know they were brothers, you'd hardly guess that they were even related. Jonathan is shorter than Mark by three or four inches. Mark is broad shouldered with a muscular athletic build, while Jonathan is slender and narrow. Jonathan is blond and blue-eyed. Mark is the epitome of tall, dark, and handsome with his dark hair and dark brown eyes.

Jonathan calls his students to attention and introduces me. "This is Amelia Jacobson. She is here to watch some of our numbers and give us some feedback. I want all of you to be respectful and know that I asked her to be here as a personal favor. She knows what she is talking about. When we were in school, she was lead in most of our productions junior and senior year. Including the one that we are doing this year. Listen to her. Ms. Jacobson is here to help." He looks over and winks at me. "Besides, she will be much nicer about it than I ever am."

The whole class laughs.

Even though I've only visited him a few times, I have seen how much these students love him. He's strict and pushes them, but it is with nothing but love. He wants this program to be for them what it was for us. A safe place. A place where they feel comfortable to be their true selves and a place that they feel validated and valued.

"Amelia?" I eye him.

He shrugs. "It's your name."

"Yeah, that no one other than my grandmother calls me." And Troy, but that's a different situation entirely.

"Do you want me to call them back and correct them?"

I roll my eyes. "No."

Jonathan laughs. "Because I will."

"Yes."

"Thanks again for coming. You know this show like the back of your hand for how many times we've been in it over the years. And there's just something that isn't working right. I need a second opinion."

"Which show are you doing?" By the look on his face, I'm guessing I'm already supposed to know that. Did he tell me, and I forgot? I don't remember him telling me. I don't even remember the last time I've really talked with Jonathan. I've been so distracted with Mark. I clear my throat and look back at Jonathan who is watching me carefully.

"I must not have told you; we're doing Guys and Dolls." He shifts in his chair. "It's been a while since we've talked. I don't think I've seen you since you were sleeping with my brother."

"I didn't sleep with Mark, and you know it."

"No. I don't know that."

"We fell asleep watching a movie. You know, like you and I have done a thousand times."

"I just find it funny."

"Find what funny?" My defenses are up. Armor in place.

"That you were spending time with Mark in the first place."

This is the perfect opportunity to be open and honest. Just tell Jonathan about dating Mark. Sure, he will be mad, but he will get over it.

"You're right, it has been a while, but I'm here now. Anyway, I'm sure you told me, things have been pretty busy with work. I have two different launches happening within the next few weeks," I explain.

"That's exciting."

"It really is. One of them is for Franklin Davis."

"Is he still being all crazy about contracts?" Jonathan laughs.

"You have no idea! Mark finally got the wording right on this last one. It's the seventh copy, and he finally signed it yesterday!" I stop in my tracks and know right away my faux pas. I try to swallow down my guilt. "I guess it's been so long since we've talked, I haven't had the chance to mention that Mark works in the law office in my building."

Jonathan's eyes narrow. "No. You haven't."

"Small world, huh?" I say weakly.

"It would appear so."

I push the bags towards him. "You should eat. Don't want it to get cold."

Jonathan looks into the bags. "It's salad."

"Don't want it to get warm then." I unload the bags of food onto the table. "You said there was a number you wanted me to see?"

I am trying to sound more upbeat. Things just got pretty heavy. I came here to spend time with Jonathan and to help him with his show. And that's what I'm going to do.

The rest of rehearsal goes pretty smoothly, despite the awkward tension we started out with. Jonathan has a really talented group. They are amazing. They have put in a lot of work, and it shows. I can't wait to see the final product. It was also nice spending time with Jonathan; it's been way too long since we have spent time together, and I know a lot of that is my fault. I've been so afraid of what he will think about me dating Mark that I have completely neglected our friendship, which is totally unfair. Jonathan has been there for me through thick and thin over the years and deserves better.

CHAPTER 22

Mark

Birthday ✤ 3 Years Ago

"**I** JUST WANT TO thank everyone for coming tonight and celebrating my Marky. Happy birthday, Baby!" Natasha raises her glass in a toast.

"To Mark!" Everyone shouts in unison.

I look around the room and I hardly know a single name of anyone toasting in my honor. That seems to be the most consistent birthday tradition. Happy birthday to me from a room full of strangers. Well, they aren't exactly strangers, I do work with them, or at least most of them. I think.

A well manicured finger glides up my arm. "Penny for your thoughts." Natasha coos into my ear as she leans up to kiss my cheek. I can tell she's had a few drinks by the way she's swaying.

I smile down at her, "Just thinking about how lucky I am." I pull her into me and I'm about to kiss her when she straightens.

"It's Mr. Watson and Mr. Bancroft," She whispers, "I can't believe they came! I'm telling you, you are a shew in for that promotion." She straightens my tie. "They wouldn't come to just anyone's birthday celebration." She moves her body to stand next to me like we are some kind of power couple.

"Good evening Mr. Watson." Nat sounds way too eager, "Mr. Bancroft."

"Ms. Reszke." Mr. Watson says, then turns his attention towards me, "Happy birthday, Mark." He shakes my hand.

"Thank you, Sir." I nod to Mr. Bancroft, "Mr. Bancroft."

"Yes, well anyway," Mr Bancroft says as he waves his hand in the air, "This isn't exactly my kind of gathering, but Watson and I wanted to tell you that we are very impressed with the work that you have been doing and that it has been noticed. Keep it up, son, and you'll be on the fast track to partner in no time."

I can feel the excitement radiating through Nat as she squeezes my waist pulling herself in closer to me.

"Thank you, Sir, it's challenging work, but I'm always up for a challenge."

"That's what your father said when we first talked about your first interview."

Wait, what? Bewildered, "My father, Sir?"

"Oh, Jack and I go way back." I stare at Mr. Bancroft in disbelief, "I'm sure he's told you all about our rivalry throughout our Yale days. He always kept me on my toes." Mr. Bancroft continues with his story, but I don't hear any of it. I'm still in utter shock and the feeling of betrayal is building. All I had wanted was to make my own way. I didn't want any handouts. That's why I didn't want my dad's help finding a job. That's why I hadn't asked him to write I letter. I had always assumed that he had, but I never imagined that he had gone behind my back and not only talked with his old school frenemy, but that they had gotten together and discussed my interview?

This is all too much to handle. The room starts spinning. I need to sit down.

Mr. Watson and Mr. Bancroft leave, and Natasha is gushing. "Oh, Marky! How wonderful! I told you you were at the top of the list for that promotion! Can you just imagine? The youngest junior partner in Watson and Bancroft history!"

I look at her blankly. "Uh huh."

"What's wrong? You look overwhelmed." She leans up and kisses my cheek. "Of course you are overwhelmed, what am I even saying. Our bosses not only showed up to your birthday party, but they showered you with compliments. I would be enthralled with emotions too!" Natasha giggles. "Oh, Marky, can you just imagine? Oh, the life we are going to have!"

"I think I need to sit down." I head to the nearest table.

"Are you sick? You don't look to good." Natasha says concerned.

I make it to the chair and look up into her big brown eyes, "Do you want to get out of here?"

"Get out of here? We can't leave, Marky, it's your birthday party!"

I look around the room again, "I honestly don't think they will even notice. I hardly know anyone here."

Nat's face drops. "You don't like it? I spent weeks putting this together and you don't like it."

I know I've messed up and need to make this better. I take her hands in mine, "No, I do like it." She gives a glimmer of a smile, "I love it, really. We don't have to leave. It was just a thought."

"Oh good! I'm so glad you like it! I was so worried." Nat continues to go on about the planning process and I try to act like I am interested, but truth is I'm not. I hate birthdays and I always have. They are never what you hope they will be and after years of disappointment you start to kind of hate them.

It's still too crowded in here and I need to get away, but I need to find a way that won't insult Nat. "Why don't you make the rounds, you are the hostess after all, I think I see James over by the bar." Natasha agrees and as I make my way towards the other side of the room I hear her squeal with glee, she is loving all the attention. She can have it. Once I make it to the bar I wave to my co-worker, he waves back. I continue my way to the back door that leads to the restaurant's back patio. Natasha rented out the entire place tonight so it's quiet. Just what I was hoping for.

I close my eyes and try to center myself. I count up and down to ten. Inhale. Hold. Exhale. Hold. Another breath slowly in then slowly back out. I open my eyes and look out on the view. The city lights are beautiful, but I'm more taken with the stars. It still amazes me how many stars there are. It's calming.

My phone dings with another birthday message in the birthday group chat Mom started earlier. I'd like to personally thank Rosie for this nonsense since she's the one who taught her how to even create a group chat. It's been nonstop messages all day from my family and the Jacobsons. I'll read them later. I know everyone means well. I just don't have it in me right now to respond.

When I finally make it home I am completely spent. My social battery has nothing left; I am all peopled out for the next month at least.

Todd walks into the kitchen, having clearly just got home himself. "How was your party?"

"How was work?" I ask dryly.

He grins, "That good huh?"

I groan, "It was the worst. I hardly knew anyone there."

"What were you expecting? Natasha probably just invited the entire office and few choice clients."

I sulk onto the counter, "I swear most of them didn't even know it was my birthday. They just thought it was some office party until the speeches started."

Todd's eyes go wide, "Speeches? As in more than one?"

I lift my head from the counter, "Yep."

"Ah, man, I'm sorry. That's rough."

"Not even the worst part."

"What, was Jack there or something?" After living together for almost nine years I don't have to explain why my dad showing up in anyway makes things complicated. He's seen it firsthand and thankfully doesn't ask too many questions just lets me say what I want to say and then moves on.

"Not physically, but I did find out that he not only went to Yale with one of my bosses, but they got together and discussed my interview."

"No!"

"Yep."

"Man, just when I think he's done everything he does something else."

"Same." And just like that Todd knows that I'm done talking about it and changes the subject.

He pushes a box towards my head which is back on the counter, "This came for you earlier."

"What is it?" I ask.

"How should I know? I didn't send it."

"Who's it from?"

"Do I look like a shipping label to you? How should I know, the box was at the door when I got home so I brought it in."

I inspect the box, but I don't recognize the address and it doesn't have a sender's name. I decide not to open it, like everything else I'll get to it later. Right now I just want to be done with today. I take it with me and head to my room.

As I lay on my bed I can't stop thinking about that stupid box. Who sent it? What's in it? I finally give in to my curiosity and go and get a knife from the kitchen to cut through all the tape.

Inside is another box covered in zip ties. What the heck? After finally cutting though what had to be fifty zip ties, *who just has a bunch of zip ties laying around?* Underneath all those zip ties is more tape. I finally get through all of that tape to open the box to find another box. What is going on? I'm done. I don't even care anymore. *But I do! Dang it!* Whoever sent this is evil. After three more boxes within a box and what had to be a full role of tape, I finally see what's inside. It's a card. All *THAT* for a card.

Happiest of birthdays Mark! I know you hate them, so I had to make it exciting somehow. Hope you enjoyed your day in spite of yourself.

Love, Millie

P.S. I was going to send muffins, but I didn't want to risk you not opening this and them getting all gross because that would be a serious waste of perfectly good muffins. So here is a picture of muffins you could have had if you weren't such a kill joy.

I can't help but smile. All the stresses of the day melt away.

MARK: How much tape did you end up using?

MILLIE: You opened it?!

MARK: Yes, I opened it. Wouldn't want to miss out of a prime food picture.

MILLIE: That's what you get for being a Birthday Grinch.

MARK: Thank you for the box.

MILLIE: You're welcome.

MILLIE: HAPPY BIRTHDAY!

I laugh in spite of myself. I feel lighter than I have all night. I end up fall asleep with a smile on my face.

CHAPTER 23

Mark

I KNOW IT SHOULDN'T bother me that Millie is having lunch with Jonathan today, but the idea of her hanging out with anyone other than me when all I want to do is to be with her is just driving me nuts. It's only been eighteen hours since I saw her, but I miss her. Our lunches make my days so much easier.

I also want a distraction from all that is my father. He's sent me multiple text messages today about how I hung up on him, about how I'm throwing my life away, how I can't just run away from my responsibilities, how I'll waste away in Ridgeview. And there's my personal favorite: Don't let your mother brainwash you.

I haven't responded to any of them. I did send a text to Todd just checking in on how intrusive my father has been in his life. Todd claims that he hasn't bothered him too much, but I don't really believe him. I know my father, and if he wants information it's only a matter of time before he finds a way to get it. I'm still not sure how he found out I was back in Ridgeview. The thought of it gives me chills.

At least I still have a safe haven in Lexington. I don't have to shadow Troy anymore, thank goodness, but I still don't have too many of my own projects. I help here and there where I can, but there's nothing that is fully mine. Miles has told me time and time again that Lexington shares all of its clients, and I get that, but I'd still like to show more of what I am capable of doing. I have been getting a lot more of the Quimby contracts. Partly thanks to Millie and partly thanks to that contract that I did for Franklin Davis. That guy is something else. It took seven contracts before he was willing to sign. Seven! Back in Charleston the most back and forth I ever had to do was three, and that was for something way bigger than a book tour.

"Knock, knock," Nancy says as she opens my door.

"Hey, Nancy. What's up?"

"Nothing. Just noticed that you hadn't left for lunch yet. You've usually left and come back by now."

I look at my watch; it's 3:30. When's the last time I ate? Maybe that's why I'm so moody. "Decided to work through lunch today."

"Ah." She watches me a little too closely for comfort. "Is everything okay, honey?"

"Yeah!" I say way too excitedly. "Why do you ask?"

"Because you're acting…" She trails off.

"Strange?" I offer.

"That's one way to put it."

I groan. "It's Millie."

Nancy comes the rest of the way into my office and closes the door. I motion towards the open chair.

"Tell me all about it. I thought things were going well. Last I saw you two, things seemed to be going very well."

I chuckle. "They're going better than I ever imagined."

"Then what's the problem?"

I sigh. "That's the thing, I don't know! Millie is amazing. She's warm. She's funny. She's freaking adorable. She's perfect." I throw up my hands, "It's just... things with our brothers have made things complicated."

Nancy waits for me to continue.

There is something about Nancy that just makes me able to open up and tell her things. So I do. I tell her everything that has happened since Saturday. From the bad blind date to going to breakfast at the crack of dawn. I tell her about the fight with Jonathan and how I tried to stay away from Millie to save their friendship even though it made me miserable. But when Millie showed up on my doorstep rambling on and on about cookies, I knew I couldn't let her go.

"Now she's at lunch with my brother, and I'm the green-eyed monster because he gets to spend time with her, and I don't." Nancy is far too amused with my current angst. "What's that smile for? It's not funny! I'm jealous of my brother for having lunch with his best friend. Someone who only a month ago I had never spent more than a few hours at a time alone with."

"You love her." Nancy is so matter of fact that it takes me back.

"What?"

"You. Love. Her." She emphasizes each syllable of each word.

"We've gone on one date. I don't love her." Her gaze is trained on me. "I haven't even kissed her yet."

"Then kiss her already! For heaven's sake, honey, you've been alone with her enough."

"We keep getting interrupted!" I rake my hand through my hair in frustration. Trust me, I want to kiss her. I've tried to kiss her. Multiple times I've tried to kiss her. Something always happens right before contact is made. It would be comical if it wasn't so frustrating!

"When will you see her next?"

"No set plans. I was hoping I'd see her today, but she had a busy day with work and then lunch with my brother."

"Well, then, I say plan something that will give you optimal opportunities. And limited obstacles."

Nancy leaves, and I stare at the few papers on my desk. Nothing is due in the next couple of days, and I have zero desire to work on any of it. I look at my watch. It's early enough that there is time to go to the gym to blow off some steam and still go home and shower before I need to head to my mom's for dinner.

When I turn into the gym parking lot, there are hardly any available spots left. That means it's crowded, not really what I was hoping for. I've never understood how people who claim to be workaholics can also be gym rats. After how I have felt all day, I may have new insight into that. As I start to get out of the car, I decide that as much as I need to blow off some steam, lifting weights or running on a treadmill isn't going to cut it. I need to physically hit something. Without giving myself the chance to second guess, I get back in the car and head towards the one place I always went to clear my head as a kid: the batting cages.

I've rented the batting cage for the next half hour. I set the ball machine on easy at first, but it soon becomes too slow, so I increase the difficulty. One hit. Two hits. Three hits. Four. Hit after hit, my head gets clearer. I take a deep breath, place my feet, grip my bat, five. I stop keeping count as I get into the rhythm of each ball release. Man, it feels good to be back at it. After my knee injury in college, it was too hard to even watch a game knowing I'd never get to play again.

When I'd come home to visit Ben, Danny, and Matt, they would invite me to come to the batting cages like we used to when we were growing up, but I couldn't do it. They didn't get how much it sucked that I couldn't play anymore. Danny stopped playing when he went to college, choosing to focus on his studies. Ben quit playing shortly after he and Belinda started dating. Matt stopped playing when he became a single parent and had a child to support. I on the other hand didn't make the decision; it was made for me. One minute I was playing as a draft hopeful, and the next I was just another washed-up could-have-been.

I wasn't able to go back to a batting cage until a couple of years ago when the firm decided they were going to participate in a baseball league. The one (and only) positive to my father being in cahoots with my bosses was that he mentioned to them how I used to play; they quickly recruited me to play on the firm's team. The firm didn't do well in the league, but I started going to the batting cages every week up until I moved. So I guess you could say in that one instance my father actually did something good for me, even if it wasn't the outcome that he was wanting.

After two reps, I take a break. When I turn around, I see Nick Klinefeld walking towards me with a grin on his face.

"You still make it look easy, Winters." He stops on the other side of the fence. I haven't talked to him since I watched his team play.

"Hey, Nick."

"I just wanted to say thanks again for coming and watching the boys play the other day. It's always good to get a different perspective. I've coached a lot of these kids since they were in little league, and I can get a little tunnel vision."

"No problem. It was nice to be that close to a field again. I haven't had time to go to a game in a very long time."

Nick rubs the back of his neck, which used to be his tell when he had something on his mind. I guess that hasn't changed. "I know you're busy with work, but there is a spot open for an assistant coach."

I'm not even sure what to do with this information. "Assistant coach?"

"We've been down a couple coaches for a while now, and to be honest, it's exhausting. If you were interested, I was thinking I could talk to the school board about it?"

"You want me to be an assistant coach?"

"You'd be great! You've always been a great player, and you have more experience outside of high school than any of the rest of us. You've played multiple positions. And played them well. You could give a better insight to what it would take for them to play college ball. We have a couple that could go all the way, they just need someone to help guide them in the right direction." Nick senses my hesitation. "We could try it out for a couple games—you know, join us for a few practices then come to the games and see what you think. It can be as preliminary as you want it to be. Just think about it."

I was still baffled he would even think of me.

"I'll think about it," I promise.

He turns and walks away, and I start another rep of pitches. The idea of coaching is intriguing, definitely something I have never done before. It would be nice to be on the field again—I've missed it. Am I really considering this offer? I think I am.

"YOU SHOULD DO it!" Millie cheers from her curled position on my couch. She's been making me a pro/con list since I told her about Nick's offer ten minutes ago. It's all I've been able to think about since he asked me yesterday. Well, that's not true. I couldn't stop thinking about a certain redhead who has taken full residence in my mind and heart. I thought about the coaching position when I forced myself to not think about Millie.

"But coaching? I've never coached before."

"No, but you have played since you were three, and I'm pretty sure you were team captain on almost all of those teams." She gives me that dimpled smile that makes her eyes sparkle. I plop next to her and run my hand up and down her legs, and she uncurls and drapes them over my lap. "Don't let the fact that you're scared stop you from doing something you want to do. You were scared when you switched to pitcher, but you still did it. And look where it got you. You got a college scholarship. Not many people can say that."

"You really were paying attention all that time weren't you?"

She smacks my arm. "Quit deflecting. You want to do this. Call Nick and tell him."

"I guess I could at least try it out. Worst-case scenario, it isn't a good fit, and I walk away."

"See, you've already made your decision. You just wanted someone to agree with you."

"I missed you."

"I didn't see you for one day." She blushes. "I missed you too."

The timer dings.

"Dinner's ready." I ever-so slowly move Millie's legs from my lap, gliding my hands over the smooth skin as I do.

"I still can't believe you wouldn't let me help," she protests.

"It's a frozen lasagna. Even I can handle that."

"I recall you once ruining Top Ramen."

"That was fifteen years ago! And way more steps!"

She rolls her eyes. "Fill pot with water. Boil water. Put in styrofoam. Cook. Add provided salt packet."

"See. More steps." I pull the lasagna out of the oven. Parts of the cheese on top are burnt, and the center is still ice cold. I don't know what else to do. I push it back into the oven.

Millie snorts out a laugh. I narrow my eyes at her.

"Don't you dare." I head towards her.

"No!" Millie tries to run, but my island blocks her only escape route. I grab her, throwing her over my shoulder. She shrieks as I tackle her to the couch and start tickling her.

"Stop!" She gasps between bouts of laughter. "I concede!"

We sit there just staring at each other for a long moment. My eyes fall down to her full pink lips and back to her eyes. As I start to lean in closer, I pause. Is there anything that could possibly stop this from happening this time?

No sprinklers. Check.

No brothers. Double check.

We are completely alone.

I gulp as I lean my head closer to her's. Before I can close the gap, Millie's hand is clutching my shirt while her other one grabs my neck pulling me into her. Our mouths crash together. Slow and timid at first. Then, with a surge of urgency, I can't help but deepen the kiss. Millie's hand is in my hair pulling me closer and closer, yet nothing feels close enough. My hands roam down her back to her hips. This moment is everything we have been building towards. It's years of waiting and longing for the right time.

I'm completely lost in this kiss when the fire alarm starts going off. I groan as I pull myself away. Ending the kiss. "Seriously!"

Millie takes a couple shallow breaths then starts laughing uncontrollably. I go into the kitchen and pull a now completely charred lasagna out of the oven. I sigh as I plop it straight into the sink. Why is cooking so hard?

Millie comes behind me and wraps her arms around my waist. "What do you want on your pizza?"

I turn to face her, putting my arms around her. I lean down and give her a light peck on the cheek before resting my chin on her head. She starts laughing again, and before I know it, I'm laughing harder than I have ever laughed in my entire life. My whole body is convulsing with deep, guttural laughs. I wipe my eyes. As I shift our bodies so that we are standing side by side, I put my arm around her and pull out my phone.

"I don't care. You choose. Anything. As long as—"

"It doesn't have olives or mushrooms," Millie finishes. "I know. I was watching, remember? I'm watching you, Wazowski, always watching."

I look at her in confusion.

"Monsters, Inc."

I shrug.

"You've never seen Monsters, Inc.?"

"No," I say, still not sure what is happening.

She shoves my phone back at me. "You order the pizza. We're fixing this. I can't believe you've never seen Monsters, Inc.!"

CHAPTER 24

Millie

I PARK MY CAR in my usual spot in the parking garage. Mark is waiting for me, leaning against his car. He walks over and opens my door for me, helping me out. His eyes roam over me. I'm suddenly very self-conscious of my form-fitting dress. His Adam's apple bobs up and down, and I have to stop every impulsive thought of grabbing and pulling him towards me. The same fight is evident in his eyes.

"Wow. You look—"

"You don't look too bad yourself."

"I think pink is my new favorite color."

My blush no doubt matches the color of my dress.

Mark pulls me into him, leaning down to give me the lightest kiss. It's barely a peck and yet it sends fire down to my toes.

"We should probably head in there," he whispers in my ear, making it way too hard to concentrate on what he's saying. I'm pretty sure that man carries every ounce of oxygen I need for survival. All I'd need to do is pull his mouth down to mine, you know, for survival purposes. Not because I want to kiss him or anything. This is purely a biological need.

"Mm-hm."

He gives a soft chuckle. "Come on."

The elevator seems to be taking forever today. I hit the button for the tenth time when Mark suggests taking the stairs. I groan. I did not wear the shoes for the stairwell. I look longingly at the elevator one more time before agreeing. He pulls me towards the door as I reluctantly follow. We take our time climbing the flights. Partly so we (Read: me. Mark clearly puts time in at the gym. I, however, do not.) don't show up to work all sweaty and gross. But mostly it's the perfect excuse to spend some more time together this morning.

Finally making it to the third floor, I'm about to open the door to our hallway when Mark gives my hand a tug and pulls me towards the opposite wall. He pulls me into him and covers my mouth with his. My hands trail up his chest and up his neck. He groans as my fingers find the hair at the nape. His hands are at my waist pulling me in closer, and he deepens the kiss. My breath catches as he moves his attention to trailing kisses along my jaw and down my neck.

I freeze when I hear a door somewhere below us open. Mark protests as I push him away.

"Did you hear that?"

His breath is hot on my skin as he catches his breath. "Hear what?"

Someone is climbing up the steps.

I look at Mark. "That."

He groans again as he pulls us back towards the door. I stop him one last time before he can pull the handle and give him a quick kiss. "Meet me for lunch?"

"Of course." He kisses me again. "Especially if there is more of that."

"Maybe." I give him a wink then open the door into the hallway that separates our offices.

> **ASHLEIGH:** The girls have been begging to go to the beach. Want to join in?

> **MILLIE:** Of course! I'll bring the s'mores supplies.

Ashtyn's and Austyn's bright orange and yellow swimsuits make it easy to find Danny and Ashleigh when I arrive at the fire pits. I managed to get here early enough that I have plenty of time to play with the girls before it gets too dark and cool.

"Hey, sis. Glad you could make it." My brother pulls me into a big bear hug.

"Thanks for the invite."

"Aunt Millie!" The twins shout in unison as they run up and tackle me, making the three of us fall into a heap in the sand.

"Girls! Give her a moment!" Ashleigh isn't even trying to hide her laugh. I grin over at her.

"At least this time there was sand." I stand up and dust off as I remove my coverup.

"Cute suit! Is it new?"

I look down at my retro two piece. "I got it for that cruise I went on last year."

"Well, it's adorable."

I bend down to put my things in my beach bag when I see an all too familiar figure walking towards us. Even from this distance I can see his all too sexy dimple on full display as he notices me. I look over at Ashleigh as she watches me. "Mark is coming?"

She gives the most mischievous grin. "Did I not mention that? How forgetful of me."

I roll my eyes. "What are you up to?"

"Nothing."

I try to glower at her, but my smile is too big. "Liar."

"Mark is here!" Ashtyn takes off running. Mark barely catches her as she lunges at him. The sound of their laughter carries, and it makes my whole heart melt at the sight.

Ashleigh nudges me. "I think you might have some competition for Mark. Ashtyn has been talking about him nonstop all week."

I smile at the thought. I love that Mark has spent time with the girls and that they love him so much.

"Aunt Millie, Ashtyn and I want to build a sandcastle! Will you help us?" Austyn asks in the sweetest little voice I could never say no to.

"Of course!"

"Mark too!" Ashtyn hangs on his neck as he carries her and points him towards us. He catches my eye and gives a wink as he puts Ashtyn down. I'm a melted puddle. Ashtyn runs over to Austyn, and they gather all of their sandcastle building supplies.

"I didn't know you'd be here." Heat rises throughout my body as Mark's hot breath rolls over my skin as he leans his now very bare chest to my back.

I swallow. "We didn't exactly talk today."

He leans in closer and burying his nose in my hair. "You smell good."

I shiver but remember where we are and step away. I turn to face him, and it's difficult to breathe when I see all that is usually covered by his shirt. I pull my eyes away and see the pleased smirk on his lips. I narrow my eyes. "Behave."

He puts up his hands in surrender, but his eyes are still blazing as he looks at me. "Always."

I swat at him as he starts to walk past.

We spend the next twenty minutes building sandcastles with the twins. After we finish, the four of us stand back to look at our creation. I don't dare look up at Mark's face, I know if I do I'll be even more of a goner. I've fallen hard for this man, and if I look at him there's no saying what I would do, but I'm fairly certain it wouldn't be appropriate for my three-year-old nieces to witness.

I'm completely unprepared for the sudden sensation of being lifted off of the ground and thrown over Mark's shoulder as he yells, "Last one to the water is a rotten egg!"

"Put me down!" I yell, kicking and flailing.

"Never!" His laugh rumbles throughout his whole body.

Ashtyn and Austyn are shrieking in delight and running after us. I look behind them and see Danny and Ashleigh at the pit, high-fiving each other. I am never going to hear the end of this.

The sand starts to decline as we reach the shore. Mark picks up speed, not stopping until he is waist deep, then tosses me into the ocean. I gasp from the shock of the cold water hitting my skin. I struggle to find my footing as I stand up. I glance up to see a look of pure delight.

"You're going to pay for that!" I leap at him, making us both fall backwards back into the water.

When we break through the surface of the water, Mark's arms are around my waist holding me closely. He gasps as my fingers trail the water beads as they fall down his torso and arms. A glimpse of orange and yellow in my peripheral reminds me of where we are, and I slip out of his arms and swim back towards the shore.

We spend the next hour splashing and playing with the girls until the sun sets and the temperature starts to drop. After drying off and curling up in an oversized sweatshirt next to the fire, I watch everyone cook their hotdogs and s'mores. I lay my head on Danny's shoulder as I have so many times before. He affectionally flicks my nose like he used to when I was little. "You look happy."

I lift my head and face him. "I am."

"Good." He nods. "I'd really hate it if I had to hurt him for hurting you."

A little sliver of guilt plants itself into my subconscious. There are so many ways this could blow up in my face. Up until now it's all seemed so easy, but that's not real life. That's storybook or movie life. That's the main character storyline, and I'm not a main character. Right?

CHAPTER 25

Mark

"WHAT DO WE want to do for dinner? We can go out? Order in? I think I have something in the freezer, but that didn't go so well last time."

"How about we order in?" Millie suggested. I'm liking where this is going. "Then you can give me a tour." I'm really liking where this is going. Millie swats at me. "Get your mind out of the gutter."

"It wasn't." It wasn't in the gutter, but rather—places it still shouldn't be.

"I need to know the full layout if I'm going to help you fix up the place." She gives me a coy smile, "And we never got past the living room last time I was over."

"No, we didn't." I grin back as I think about that kiss. Was that really just two days ago? So much has happened since then. So many kisses. Many, many kisses. The best kisses of my life. "You really don't need to fix anything up. My place is fine."

Millie scrunches her face like she smells something bad, pointing all around her she says, "This is not fine. You've lived here for over a month, and you still haven't unpacked everything."

I know I'm beaten. Not that I'm fighting her too hard. I'd find a way to give her the moon if she asked for it.

"Fine. But we don't need to work on the whole place. I'd feel guilty having my girlfriend doing all that work."

As soon as it came out, I knew what I had said. Her eyes are as big as I have ever seen them. Her jaw drops open. She's never been silent for this long before. I don't know what to do. Was it too soon? It doesn't feel too soon. In fact, it feels very, very right. I really need her to say something.

"Did you just say girlfriend?"

I lean in towards her, backing her against the kitchen counter. My hands are on her hips, and I dip my head to whisper in her ear. My voice is low and husky as I say, "Yeah. I did."

Millie shivers in my embrace. Her lips part as she places her arms around my neck and starts to twist her fingers in my hair along the back of my neck. I've grown very addicted to this feeling. I can't take my eyes off of her. I start to lean my head down as she lifts her head to meet mine, our breaths have intertwined. Our lips are just about to brush when there is a knock at the door. I groan. Whoever it is, it better be an emergency.

"It's probably the food." Millie slides her hands down to my chest and stays there for a moment before giving me a slight shove.

"We haven't ordered anything," I whisper. Not ready to back away from her just yet.

"You're right." She quirks her eyebrow. "Who do you think it is?"

I have a couple of guesses, but I don't like any of them. Another knock.

"Guess I better answer." I look through the peephole, and it's my neighbor, Krystal.

"Just my neighbor, she'll go away."

"Just answer it." Millie all but shoves me towards the door. I give her a skeptical look. "What?" She shrugs. "You're already standing there. She can probably hear us through the door talking. Just answer it."

I really don't want to. Ever since I moved in, Krystal has been coming by for help with random things. Sometimes I help her, but I usually try to stay clear. I definitely never go into her house, and she never comes into mine. I want all the witnesses I can when she is around. She's the type of woman I assume would be the perfect match for Troy. Then again, that's an insult to any woman.

"Are you sure?" I give her one last chance to change her mind before I reluctantly open the door. Mentally bracing myself for whatever is about to happen.

"Hey, Mark," Krystal coos. She's dressed in a sports bra and something that can barely be called shorts with how little fabric there is. Let's just say there is little left to the imagination. Even if Millie wasn't standing three feet away, I would be feeling uncomfortable. "I was just getting back from my workout, but I seem to have locked myself out of my place." Sure, she did.

"That's too bad." Thanks to the last unwanted conversation with this woman, I know she lives in the section of condos that are rentals. "Have you called your super? I'm sure he has some extra keys."

"He didn't answer. And it's getting cold. And dark." She tries to enter the doorway. I fill the doorway and block her from entering. "Can I just come in for a minute? Then I can call him again."

I continue to block her. Her eyes gleam up at me, making me even more uncomfortable. She's a snake stalking her prey. And I'm her prey. She pouts and runs her hand along the top of her bare chest. At least that's what I assume she's doing. I've firmly planted my eyes on the spot between her eyebrows. For a brief moment I wonder how offended she'd be if I told her her eyebrows aren't even, then I think better of it. She might make me uncomfortable, and her visit is entirely unwanted, but I'm not a jerk.

Krystal starts to make another advance towards the door when Millie shows up next to me holding a blanket out toward Krystal.

"Actually, my boyfriend and I were just getting ready to leave. I'm so sorry about your keys. It must be hard not having a place to hold a house key." Millie's eyes darken as she gives Krystal an up and down glance. It's kind of frightening. "You're more than welcome to use this blanket so you don't freeze while you wait for the super." She leans in closer and whispers, "I hear ruptured implants can be pretty painful."

I'm not sure who's more shocked by Millie's words, me or my red-faced neighbor. It takes all of my self-control not to laugh as Krystal turns and stalks off.

"I guess that's a no on the blanket then?" Millie calls after her.

I turn to face Millie, gaping.

"Why are you looking at me like that?" Millie smirks.

"I've just…I…I have no words."

"That's your neighbor?"

"I told you I didn't want to answer it."

"Does she do this kind of thing often?" Millie is trying to sound casual, but the jealousy in her voice is palpable.

"You were jealous."

"I was not!" She defends.

"Yes, you were." I use air quotes and repeat, "My boyfriend and I were just leaving." I mock her voice, maybe adding a little more sass to the tone for dramatic effect.

She shoves me. "Shut up."

Her lips twitch. I pull her into my arms and hold her tight against me kissing the top of her head. "So now that we have become official in the most unconventional way possible, what, pray tell, would you like to do for dinner, girlfriend?"

Millie half-heartedly pushes away from me. "Well, boyfriend, a burger, fries and then some Home Depot sounds like the perfect night to me."

I groan. "You're not letting go of this any time soon, are you?"

She removes herself from my grasp and grabs her purse and jacket then pulls me back to the door. "Nope." She stops mid stride. "Oh, and grab your keys. I hear the super isn't answering his phone tonight."

I barely contain my laugh.

"ABSOLUTELY NOT," I protest. We're standing in the middle of Home Depot looking at paint colors. Rows and rows of colors to choose from, not that my place needs paint. The previous owners painted right before I bought the place. Sure, it's that early 2000s taupe that everyone and their brother used, but it's practically brand-new paint. Millie has completely lost her mind if she thinks I'm going to let her paint any of my walls black.

"Just an accent wall!" Millie argues.

"You're not painting my walls black." I put my hand up to stop her argument. "Not even if it's just one wall."

Millie pouts, and it's adorable that she thinks that's going to make me cave. I might give in on a lot of things, but this is one hill I'm willing to die on. She pouts her lips more and gives me the biggest sad eyes she can muster. I groan. I can't take the doe eyes. I'm about to give up my resolve when a store employee comes up to us.

"Anything I can help you with?" Bright, according to the name written on his apron, asks.

I say, "We're just looking," at the same time that Millie says, "Yes!"

For the next twenty minutes, I stand back as Millie and Bright go back and forth about different color schemes. When Millie and I finally leave the store, we have a cart full of sample paint colors. I technically lost this round, but since none of the paint colors are black, I'm counting it as a win.

I also realize that I finally understand what Ben meant when he said once I found the right person, I'd be willing to do anything to make her happy. And I would. I would do anything to make Millie happy.

Even paint my walls black.

CHAPTER 26

Millie

$\mathcal{I}$'VE BEEN STARING at the same page for the last twenty minutes. I should just give up for the day, but Sheila wants notes by the end of the day tomorrow and I'm only halfway through.

"Are you okay?" I nearly jump out of my skin when I hear Trina's voice. I hadn't even heard her come back into the office.

"I'm fine," I squeak out. Maybe if I don't draw attention to it, she won't notice.

"Clearly," Trina laughs. "Are you going to turn the page any time soon or are you just going to memorize that particular passage?"

I glare and make a point to turn the page. I have no idea what's going on anyway so what's one more page?

"So, is this a good distracted or a bad distracted?"

"I'm not distracted." I turn another page.

"Sure you're not." Trina gives my shoulder a little shove. "Now spill." She swivels my chair so that we are face to face. "How are things with Mr. Hottie?"

"Amazing. Wonderful. Basically perfect." I sink into my chair.

"But…?"

"But nothing. Things are great. Mark is great."

"So you've said, but Millie, for someone who's dating her dream guy, you don't seem like everything is so amazing and great."

"It has nothing to do with Mark. Mark really is great and wonderful. He's an even better boyfriend than I ever imagined existed. It's just…I don't know."

Trina sits back in her chair with a thoughtful look on her face. "Have you told your families about the two of you yet?"

"Danny and Ashleigh know. And I'm pretty sure Mark's little sister knows."

"But not Jonathan?" And there goes the all too familiar pit in my stomach. "Look, I know I've only met Jonathan a couple of times, but he's your best friend. He wants you to be happy."

I nod. I know she's right. I need to tell him. I know I need to tell him. I just don't know how. He's always been so standoffish when it comes to his brother. Jonathan has always kept our friendship as separate from our families as possible considering the circumstances, and here I am making the two collide.

Trina places a hand on my shoulder. "Just don't avoid him. I know you don't like difficult conversations, but avoiding him is just going to make it worse."

I groan into my hands. I know Trina is right. I need to tell Jonathan. Not telling him about me and Mark isn't fair to either of them. And as hard as it is for me to say, it's not fair to me.

I sit up straight and start coming up with a plan. Because everything needs a well-thought plan. And every plan starts with a pro/con list.

"HEY, BEAUTIFUL." MARK'S deep baritone rings through the office, and I can't help but smile. All my worries of earlier wash away.

"Hey. I wasn't expecting to see you today. I thought you had a meeting with a client?"

Mark wraps me into his arms and kisses me on the top of my head. "It went really well. So well, in fact, that we finished earlier than planned. Did you already have lunch? I was thinking of getting out of the office for a bit."

"She's available!" Trina bounds into the room to stand next to me, sticking her hand out towards Mark. "I'm Trina. It's sooo nice to finally meet you!"

Mark chuckles. "It's nice to meet you, Trina. I've heard a lot about you."

He gives her a little wink, and Trina giggles. I roll my eyes. This man is too charismatic for his own good, and he knows it.

"I'll let you and Millie get going, but I just have to say you are even better looking in real life than you are in your picture." My eyes go wide, and my face is instantly flushed.

"Trina," I grit out through my teeth.

"What?" She shrugs.

"I feel like I'm missing something. What picture?" Mark looks back and forth between us.

"It's nothing. What did you want for lunch?" I try to shove Mark out the door, but it's pointless. The man is solid.

Mark grabs my hand and twirls me into him. He looks down at me. "I do believe the lady said something about a picture?"

"It's over on her desk!" Trina says unhelpfully. I glare at her as Mark pulls me with him towards my desk. She grins at me as we pass. "It's in the frame. The one by the cup of pens."

Mark drops my hand and picks up the frame. "I remember this hike." He looks over at me. "I can't believe you've kept this picture all these years."

"It's one of my favorites."

"Mine too. Could I get a copy of this?"

I nod. There's a sentimentality that I haven't seen in him before. I just sit and watch the rare moment.

"A DOUBLE DATE?" Mark groans. "With who? You know I'm not the most comfortable around strangers."

"My roommate and her boyfriend. You met them briefly when you came over? Amara and Duncan?"

"I guess that wouldn't be too bad."

"You can be pretty charming when you want to be."

He sighs as he sits on the desk. "This is really important to you, isn't it?"

I step closer and wrap my arms around his neck. "It really is."

Grabbing my waist and pulling me in even closer, Mark rests our foreheads together. "Then let's go."

Honestly, I thought it was going to take a whole lot more persuading to get him to go along with the double date idea that Amara and I came up with last night after I got home. Up until I started spending time with Mark, she was the only roommate in a relationship, and Duncan's best friend is never seen with the same girl twice.

I squeal, "Really?"

He gives me a partial grin. "Yes." He buries his head in my neck. "As much as I'd like to keep you to myself."

I giggle as he starts trailing kisses along my neck and throat.

"Stop it." I give a halfhearted shove. "We're going to get caught."

He presses his lips to my ear. "I don't care."

Giving my lobe a little nibble, he starts kissing my neck again. If he wasn't already holding my waist, my knees would completely buckle out from underneath me.

"Knock, knock." The door opens and I can't bounce back fast enough. I turn to face a thoroughly surprised Nancy. "Oh! I didn't know you two were—"

I feel my blush down in the depth of my soul.

"Hi, Nancy," Mark says in a voice that is completely unbothered by the fact that we were just caught making out in his office.

Nancy's face breaks out into the biggest smile I have ever seen. "Hello. I have that file for you." She hands Mark a folder then looks over to me. "Always nice to see you, Millie."

Then she turns and leaves, closing the door behind her.

"You alright over there?" Mark asks, clearly fighting back a smile. I can't look at him. I'm still so embarrassed about being caught by Nancy. "Mills?"

A twinge of worry laces his voice. I rub my hip after running into the corner of the desk. I plop into the chair.

"I'm fine." I sheepishly peer up at him.

His face softens as he gets up and comes over to kneel in front of me. "You sure?"

I put my hands on his broad shoulders. "Yes, I'm sure." I lean down and kiss his cheek. "Maybe no more making out in your office though."

We sit with our foreheads together. As soon as our eyes meet, Mark's mouth tugs at the corners as he tries to hold in a smile. A snort escapes him which causes us both to erupt into laughter. I wipe at my eyes and try to fix my makeup the best I can before heading back across the hall to my desk.

I wave awkwardly as I pass by Nancy's desk on my way out the door.

"Good seeing you, sweetheart."

"Bye, Nancy."

She winks pointing towards Mark's closed door. "That's a good one in there."

I smile. "Yes, he is."

"You two should come to dinner sometime next week."

A weight is lifted, and I relax. "Give Mark some dates, and we will make it happen."

"Sure thing, sweetheart. You have a great rest of your day."

MINI-GOLF MIGHT NOT have been the best idea for a double date. At least Duncan and Amara have been good sports dealing with the ultra-competitiveness that is me and Mark.

"We don't need to keep score," I say, trying to make it sound like it isn't a big deal. I'll just keep score in my head. No one will be the wiser.

Mark nods in agreement. "Yeah, what's important is that we're having fun. Not who's winning."

"Says the person winning," Duncan mutters.

Amara elbows him. She plasters on a smile. "The whole point of tonight is for us to all get to know each other better."

"Exactly!" I respond.

Amara and I eye each other. This isn't going as smoothly as we had hoped. We probably should have done that pottery class Amara had mentioned. Maybe if we only play one round of golf tonight? At this rate it's going to take all night anyway. I knew my family was intense when it came to any sort of sport or game, but this complete and utter lack of competitive spirit is ridiculous. Even with all of us playing, we would have been almost done, and that's if the kids and wives were here. Just the nine of us Jacobsons? We'd be on round two, forming new alliances and strategizing how to make the winner of the last round lose.

After a rather (agonizingly) long round of mini-golf, we had decided to head to Pete's Pie Palace for pie shakes. Food is always safe. And who doesn't love pie? Or at least ice cream?

When we get to Pete's, the line is pretty long so Mark and Duncan go put in our orders while Amara and I get a table. I keep watching them in line, but they aren't talking much. I don't know if that's because they don't know each other or if they're both miserable.

"How do you think it's going over there?" Amara asks.

"I don't know. They aren't talking much."

"Mark's pretty reserved, right?"

"I mean, yeah, but to not talk at all? And it's not like Duncan is shy. He usually never stops talking." I turn back around and face Amara. "Sorry. I didn't mean that. It's just—"

She puts her hand up to stop me. "No. You're right. Duncan usually does talk a lot but not in new situations. At least not if he doesn't have to."

"What are you talking about? I've never seen Duncan have a hard time talking to anyone."

"Yeah, but he was probably with people he's comfortable being around or he was working a gig. He's pretty quiet until you get to know him." She cranes her neck to look over at the guys. "But once he's comfortable, he's the best guy around."

I smile watching Amara. I love seeing her light up when she talks about Duncan.

Amara turns back towards me. "What?"

"Nothing." I grin. "I just like seeing you so happy."

A blush lightly colors her cheeks. "Thanks. And for the record I like seeing you so happy too. It's been a long time since you've been this happy." She pauses, but doesn't continue.

"What?" I eye her. "You look like you want to say something."

"I don't want to overstep."

"Overstep?" I ask, confused. What could she possibly want to say that would seem like overstepping? "Amara, you know you can talk to me about anything. What is it?"

"It's just—it's just I don't think I've ever seen you this happy. And it's just nice to see you actually putting yourself first for once."

I'm taken aback a little by her words. I mean, I know I don't always prioritize my wants, but I wouldn't say I never do.

Amara continues, "You know I love Tori and Jonathan, they're some of my best friends, but they both have just strong personalities that sometimes I think you get lost. You love them so much, and you want them to be happy so you just give in and follow their lead."

I'm stunned by her words, not because I'm upset, but because I know deep down she's right. I do bend over backwards to make them happy. I will always give up my idea for plans if they have something else they want to do. Even if I hate it. I go running on Saturday mornings, for goodness sake! Poorly, and I slow them down considerably, but I still go. Is that really why I'm scared to tell Jonathan about me and Mark? Am I worried he'll talk me out of it? Tell me that this isn't a good idea, even if this is the best and healthiest relationship I have ever been in?

"I shouldn't have said anything."

I grab Amara's hand. "No, I'm glad you did. I just—"

"Who's ready for pie?" Duncan sing-songs as he and Mark set the shakes on the table and sit down.

Amara raises her hand. "Me!"

We pass spoons and napkins around the table and start to dig into our food.

"What is that?" Duncan stares at Mark's shake with skepticism.

"A blueberry pie shake." Mark says while taking a big bite.

"Why is it purpley brown?" Amara wrinkles up her nose.
I snort a laugh.

"What's so funny?" Duncan asks.

Mark smirks and points his spoon at me. "Want to explain or do you want me to?"

I laugh. "I will." I turn to Duncan and Amara. "One night when we were growing up, our parents left all of us kids alone, and we got bored so we started mixing up random concoctions and daring each other to eat them."

Amara rolls her eyes. "Your family is so weird."

Mark snorts. I elbow him. "Anyway. One of the concoctions was blueberry pie filling and chocolate ice cream."

"Ben bet me I wouldn't eat it," Mark says, taking over the story.

"He not only finished it, but he's been eating it ever since," I add.

Mark shrugs. "It's good!"

"Eww!" Amara laughs. "That's so gross."

I start laughing and take a bite of his shake with my spoon. "It's really not that bad."

Mark puts his arm around me and pulls me in kissing the side of my head.

"You two really were made for each other," Amara gushes.

CHAPTER 27

Mark

THE PAST MONTH has held some of the best days of my entire life. I still can't believe that this is real life. I've found a balance between work and a personal life. Millie and I spend almost every waking hour together, whether it be at work or at home. We've gone on another double date with Duncan and Amara, and they are growing on me. Honestly, Amara has grown on me much more than Duncan. I know I can't fault the guy for not having my level of competition or work ethic, but it's there in the back of my head when we hang out together as couples.

Couples. I'm part of a couple. I'm in a couple with Millie Jacobson, and not just a couple of people. It blows my mind.

I jokingly told Nancy that I wish she and her husband, Marty, would adopt me and be my parents after she invited Millie and I to come over for dinner. As amazing as Nancy is at the office, she's so much more when she's in her element. Marty brings out a whole new side of her. It's nice to see a healthy relationship that isn't Dan and Norah Jacobson. It amazes me that they aren't as rare of a relationship as

I grew up thinking. Nancy and Marty have been together since they were twenty and raised their children in seven different states. I could never imagine my parents doing that. They weren't able to even live in the same city their entire marriage.

Last Wednesday Marty asked if I like fishing. When I told him I'd never been fishing, he told me that he would teach me. We're going on Saturday before the sun comes up, which means we will make it back in time for my first official game as assistant coach to the Ridgeview Hawks baseball team.

With everything going so great in my life right now, it's hard to understand this lump that seems to be lodged in my throat as I sit in my car avoiding going into my mom's house. I know I have about 3.5 seconds before she notices my car sitting here and she or my little sister come charging out to retrieve me. Rosie is home for a long weekend, and Mom insisted on a family dinner. Just the four of us. I tried to convince Millie to come with me, but she told me that this is family time. It might also be because we still haven't told our families about us. Sure, Danny and Ashleigh know, and I'm pretty sure Maeley and Rosie know. They at least suspect.

Millie and I had both agreed that telling our families officially needs to happen after we talk with Ben and Jon, but we're both cowards when it comes to telling them, so here we are still keeping a giant secret. Coward might be too strong of a word, at least when it comes to Millie. I'll fully claim my cowardice.

Over the years, Ben has berated Millie for some of the most ridiculous things. When we were kids, Jon and Millie were in a play and weren't old enough for our parents to let them walk home alone so Ben and I were asked to stop by the elementary school and walk with them. It wasn't a big deal, but Ben made it seem like Millie had gone out of her way to make his life harder. I never understood why he was so hard on her. Even at Jacobson family dinners I've been to since I moved back to town, it doesn't make sense why he is so combative with her.

I don't blame her for being gun-shy when it comes to telling him we are dating. If I was her, I would be timid to share things with him too. I know he'll be mad at me, but he'll get over it. He always does. It was one of those things he put into our "Best Friend Code" when we were in middle school. "Always forgive the other person." At the time I figured it was because we had been in an argument about something happening on our baseball team. I will give him credit for holding his end of that contract nearly twenty years later. As unfair as it is, I'm not so sure he'll forgive Millie as easily even if she is his sister.

Ben's relationship with his siblings is hard to explain, mostly because I don't understand it. Things are even harder to understand since I've been away for so long and he married Belinda. She's definitely a sore subject when you talk with the family as a whole. She doesn't like them and looks for any excuse to avoid family events, which doesn't sit well with a family that does literally everything together.

Add in my family relationship dynamics, and it's a wonder Millie and I are doing as well as we are. I know she's stressed, and I wish I could take that away from her. I wish I could promise her that everything was going to work out and that everyone was going to be as happy as we are about us. That's the biggest thing holding me back: I'm happy. For the first time in my life, I have hope that I could actually not only be in a relationship but build a life with someone, have a family of my own. If you would have told me six months ago that moving back to Ridgeview would be the best decision of my life, I would have told you you were crazy. Now I wonder why I didn't move back sooner. Or even why I ever left.

Headlights beam behind me as Jon pulls his car up the drive and parks behind me. It's time to face the music, or I guess in this case, the performing arts teacher.

"What are you doing sitting in the driveway?" Jon looks at me inquisitively. A look that reminds me so much of our father that I almost want to smack him right here and there.

I relax my fist; it's not his fault we share DNA with the man. Nor is it his fault that I have the relationship with our father that we have. Jon never sought Dad's approval like I did. He's always had a confidence that I have equally admired and resented. It's probably why it was so easy to push away from him when I left. Can't envy something you don't realize you're missing.

"Just pulled in right before you." Jon's eyebrows quirk, and I know my excuse is flimsy. I can see the water under my car from my air conditioner just as much as he can, but he doesn't push any further.

"Help me carry in dinner?" he asks while opening his back door.

"I thought Mom was cooking?"

"She was going to. That's why I volunteered to pick something up." There's a hint of amusement in his voice.

"Good call." I grab a couple of the bags. "I could have bought dinner."

Jon's annoyance is evident. "It's not a big deal. I can buy dinner."

"I never said you couldn't."

"No, you just implied it," Jon says bitterly. "You always do this."

"Always do what?" I ask, confused.

"Assume you're the only one who can take care of this family. It wasn't your job when we were kids, and it isn't your job now." His words cut right through me.

"I didn't mean to offend!" I didn't, but I can see how it might have come across like that. "I just meant—thank you." It's not much, but it's something.

"Thank you?"

"Yeah. Thank you for picking up dinner. You probably saved all of us from food poisoning." The air is stagnant with an unspoken tension that is always present when my brother and I are alone. We stand there at a standstill just looking at each other holding bags of food. Now would be the perfect time to open up to my brother about how much I would change if I could go back and how I wish our relationship was different, but I can't seem to make myself be that open. Not sitting in our mother's driveway.

"There you two are!" Mom calls from the front door. "Get in here so we can eat and catch up!"

We both turn towards the walkway, and I take a step back, letting Jon go first. I take a big breath and let it out slowly. This would be so much easier if Millie were here. She calms me better than any breathing technique ever could.

"Where do you want these?" I motion to the bags in my hand as I enter the dining room.

"Oh, anywhere." Mom waves her arms. "I just can't believe I finally get all three of you under one roof at the same time!" Her voice cracks, and her eyes are misty.

Rosie rolls her eyes. "You act as if you don't see us all the time."

"I know I see all of you, but it's hardly ever at the same time. And it's never just the four of us. There are always other people around. As much as I love the Jacobsons, it's nice to have a night alone with my kids." She squeezes each of our arms. More guilt oozes in my gut.

I know I've been avoiding her. I've just been so happy with Millie that I didn't want anything to mess it up. Especially my mother. She could take this relationship one of two ways. She could take the usual road where she tells me about how you can never trust anyone and that relationships always fail (I wonder where my issues stem from.) Or else she'll think that it is the best thing ever and put all of her hopes and dreams into my relationship and therefore add a bunch of pressure.

I've made huge strides in my overthinking and have talked about all of this with Millie (due to lots and lots of coaxing on her part). Thankfully she's very understanding of the situation and my inability to process my emotions easily. One of the many reasons why I'm madly in love with her.

Yes, I'm in love with her. I haven't told her yet, but it's going to happen. As soon as we figure out a way to tell our brothers and then our families. That has to happen first. I could so easily tell my family right here and now. Especially when Mom starts asking for life updates like she used to when we were kids.

"Tell me everything! What's new? What's exciting? What's—"

"Mom! We get it!" Rosie interrupts.

"I'm sorry," Mom apologizes.

I pat her arm with my hand. "No need to apologize. It's been a long time, like you said."

Mom wipes at her cheeks. "I'm just so happy you're all here."

Jon wraps her up in a hug. "We're happy to be here, too."

He and I make eye contact, forming an unspoken agreement. Whatever it is that we have going on between us, it doesn't matter. What matters is that we are here for Mom and Rosie. We owe them both that.

Rosie stands up from her seat. "How about I go cut up that cake, and we can delve into our lives over devil's food and ice cream?"

"We haven't even had dinner yet, and you want dessert?" Jonathan follows after her.

Mom smiles as she hears them bickering in the kitchen. Then her eyes land on me. "So, when are you going to tell your brother?"

I gulp. What does she know?

"Tell him what?"

Her eyes narrow. "About you and Millie."

My mouth gapes open. "How?"

"I saw the two of you at the movies last week. I was about to go say hi, when…"

She leaves the sentence hanging in the air, but I don't need her to fill in the blanks. I know exactly what she would have seen: Millie and I being very couple-y.

"How long have you two been seeing each other?"

"A few weeks." I try to stop the hyperventilation that I feel coming on. "We've been spending time together pretty much since I got back." I can't read her expression. Is it hurt? Worry? This isn't how I wanted her to find out. I take another staggering breath. "I didn't mean to hide it from you. We were going to tell you, I swear."

My eyes are pleading. There might be a lot of things that I don't talk to my mom about, but this isn't—wasn't going to be one of them. Mom nods. She's about to say something else when Rosie and Jon come back in the room, the latter grumbling about how cake shouldn't come before dinner.

"What's going on in here?" Jon raises an accusatory eyebrow at me.

I clear my throat. "I was just telling Mom about how I have accepted a position as the new assistant baseball coach at Ridgeview."

Jon's eyes go wide. Rosie throws the plates she was holding down on the table and rushes over to give me a hug. "This is huge!"

Mom's eyes are misty again. "You're going back to baseball? You said you would never—"

I interrupt her. "It was hard wrapping my head around ever being able to be on the field again, especially after all that happened." I shrug. "I don't know. I missed it. I'm still pretty rusty. And I'm definitely not 19 anymore, but I'm really liking being back. And I love the challenge. The team is pretty great. It's a good group of kids."

Just thinking about it makes my insides surge with excitement. I might not have been able to go all the way, but who's to say I can't help the next Mickey Mantle get on his way.

I look over at Jon who is still holding two plates of cake in his hands, just staring at me.

"I meant to tell you," I say apologetically. "I know the high school is your turf."

"My turf? What is this, West Side Story?" He sets down the plates. "I forgot forks."

I look at Mom and Rosie as I stand up to follow him into the kitchen. The drawer slams shut as I enter.

"Hey. I really was going to tell you."

Jon whips around. "It's fine. You don't owe me any explanation." I can hear his teeth grind from here. "Congratulations, by the way. I know Nick has been looking for the right fit for the team for a while. You'll do great. You were one of the best players Ridgeview has ever had."

I'm touched by the compliment, but it doesn't mask the hurt and anger I see in his face. But Jon is an excellent actor, and he soon replaces his expression with a content mask.

"Thanks. First game is Saturday. You should come." I'm as shocked by the invite as he is, but I'm not taking it back. I want him to come. "Unless you have rehearsals or something. Then obviously you can't be in two places at once."

"I'll have to look at the schedule."

It's not much, but it's the best we've done in years.

WHEN I LEAVE my mom's house, it's with a full belly and a full heart. It's been way too long since the four of us have sat around and talked like that. Even longer since we've laughed like that. Have we ever laughed like that? This is the happiest I think I've ever seen my mom, which is good. It's rough when she's sad. That trip she took with her bunco group really seemed to put a pep in her step.

I send a quick text to Millie.

> **MARK:** Just leaving my mom's.

> **MILLIE:** How did it go?

> **MARK:** My mom knows. She saw us.

> **MILLIE:** Oh.

> **MARK:** I'm coming over. Be there in 10.

"I still can't believe she saw us." Millie is baffled.

I nod. I found out three hours ago, and I'm still dumbfounded.

"If she knows, then there is no way my parents don't know."

I nod again. "Probably."

"But no one has said anything to us?"

"I don't get it either."

She stands up from the couch and starts pacing the living room.

"Unless. Unless they said something to Danny or Ashleigh," Millie keeps mumbling to herself as she paces.

I grab her hand and steady her. "You're going to wear a hole in the ground if you keep pacing like that."

She stops and sits on my lap. She leans in and lays her head on my shoulder. I stroke her arm up and down.

"We need to talk to them."

"Your parents? I agree."

She puts her hand on my mouth stopping me. I give her fingers a little peck.

"No. I mean, yes, but I was talking about Ben and Jonathan. We need to talk to them. If our parents know, then let's face it, most of my siblings know by now." She looks into my eyes and I know exactly what she is thinking.

"If they all know then it's only a matter of time. And the longer we go without saying anything the more it looks like we are hiding it."

She wraps her hands around my neck and pulls me in closer to her. "And I'm not hiding."

"I'm not hiding either." My voice is husky and gravelly. Our lips barely brush when the front door opens. In walks Kiersten, Torrance, and of course, Jon.

CHAPTER 28

Millie

"JONATHAN!" I BOUNCE off Mark's lap and beeline it for the front door.

Jonathan's eyes narrowed in on us, and then he turned and stormed out.

"Jonathan! Will you wait up?"

He stops, his shoulders heaving. He's breathing hard.

"Geez, your legs are long," I try to joke, but as soon as he turns and fixes his eyes on me, all jokes end. His eyes are a stormy gray that I have never seen before. I take a step back.

"Tell me again how nothing is going on between you and Mark."

"I'm sorry." My voice is barely a whisper. "I wanted to tell you so many times."

"But you didn't." There is fury mixed with hurt in his tone.

"I didn't know—"

"You didn't know what?" He spits out. His tone makes something inside me snap, and now I'm angry too.

"I didn't know how to tell you. I didn't want you to ruin it!"

"Ruin it? Ruin what, Millie?" His eyes darken even more. "How long?"

"Why can't you be happy for me?!" Tears are streaming down my face, but that doesn't stop me from screaming at Jonathan.

"How long?" He says through gritted teeth.

"A month." I try to calm my voice, but it still crackles with emotion.

"How can I be happy for something I know will hurt you?" His words cut deep. "I thought we had gotten past all of this years ago. You didn't like him anymore."

My heart stops. He knew?

"Didn't you learn a long time ago that Mark doesn't do relationships?"

"Hey!" Mark yells from behind me. "Who are you to decide whether or not I do relationships?"

"Just an active observer," Jonathan spits out. "You've never taken any relationship seriously. What makes this time different? You're going to ruin Millie just like Dad ruined Mom."

Mark squares his shoulders as he stands toe to toe with Jonathan, glaring. "I'm nothing like Jack!" He spits out the disdain in his voice palpable. "And Millie is the furthest thing from Mom."

"At least until you're done with her," Jonathan seethes.

What happens next is a blur. Suddenly both men are wrestling on the ground. There are grunts and sounds of flesh hitting flesh. No amount of screaming is stopping them. I'm too weak to pull them apart.

A car pulls up to the curb and out jumps Ben.

Ben races over and pulls Mark off of Jonathan. I'm yelling for it all to stop through thick tears. I can hardly see.

He looks between them. "What on earth is going on?"

Both Jonathan and Mark breathe heavily. Neither one of them speak.

Ben looks over at me. "Mills, what's going on?"

I open my mouth, but no words come out.

Jonathan is the one to break the silence. "It's nothing." He glares at me and then turns back to Ben. "Just finding out that our siblings and so-called best friends have been hiding a relationship for the last month."

Ben stops in his tracks. His eyes trail back between me and Mark. Then back to me again.

"By the look on your face, I'm guessing I'm not the only one they've been lying to."

Ben shakes his head.

"No." His voice is hoarse. "No. You're not the only one." Ben doesn't say anything else; he drops his head and heads back to his car. He gets something from inside and walks back over to hand me an envelope. "Invite to Belinda's shower. She wanted me to make sure you knew you were invited."

I take the envelope from his tightened fist. He doesn't let go right away, and when he does, part of my heart breaks. I've never seen him like this. So hurt. So dejected. So vulnerable. A new round of tears spring to my eyes. Kiersten's and Tori's arms wrap around me as I hear car door slams in the background.

My roommates' arms are replaced by Mark's. He's holding me close. I cling to him for dear life. Everything I feared and more happened tonight. All the weeks of happiness are wiped away in one night. Mark lifts my chin, making me look into his eyes.

"Hey," he whispers softly, "it's going to be okay."

"How?" I don't even know if my words are audible. "Everything is such a mess."

"Because we're in this together." His voice is solid and sure. It's laced with hope and a promise that I have to cling to.

"I love you." I didn't mean to say it. Not out loud. Certainly not at a time like this. But I do. I love him.

He chuckles softly as he nuzzles his nose into my hair and whispers in my ear. "I am so in love with you."

And that's all that matters. All the rest—all the best friends and all the brothers—it will all work out. Mark Winters loves me, and I love him.

CHAPTER 29

Millie

Christmas ❦ 5 years ago.

THE KITCHEN AND dining room are brimming with people. Loud laughter and conversations fill the air. Everyone is here for our traditional holiday brunch with our friends and neighbors. Everyone is enjoying themselves and the holiday spirit. Everyone except Denham. I haven't seen him since our ridiculous fight last night where he accused me of flirting with Mark. Which, for the record, didn't happen. For one, I'm with Denham and would never do that. And second, even if I wasn't here with Denham, Mark would never flirt with me. I gave up that dream a long time ago. I am and will always be like a little sister to him. I haven't seen Denham leave his room yet today. I want to respect his space, but I also can't just leave things like this. This isn't how Christmas with my family was supposed to go.

Before I can make my decision of what to do, Tori comes bounding behind me, grabbing me in a tight hug, which is impressive considering her hands are full of food from the buffet. Mom's really outdone herself this year.

"What's up, babe?" she asks with her mouth full of muffin, then she suddenly gets serious. "Okay, now really, what's going on? You have your Worry Face on."

"I'm not worried!" I snap, but I don't mean to. I'm not mad at Tori. I'm mad at Denham. And myself. "Sorry. I'm just tired."

She pulls me towards the loveseat at the far end of the room giving us as much privacy as could be expected in such a crowded space. "Millie, what is it? And I'm not buying the tired excuse. You have multiple levels of tired and none of them include catty."

"I'm not being—" I don't even have the mental fortitude to even try and defend myself. "It's Denham."

Tori rolls her eyes. "Of course it is."

"Of course, what is?" Jonathan comes over and squeezes himself onto the sofa making me smooshed between the two of them. We definitely don't fit on this like we used to.

"That Millie has Worry Face and it's all Denham's fault." Tori explains.

"Ah."

I twist to face him, "Ah? What is with the ah? There is no ah."

Jonathan ignores me and talks over my head to Tori. "I see it."

"See what?" I demand.

"Worry Face," he says but still keeps his focus on Tori. "We haven't seen Worry Face in what, five years?"

"At least."

"What's up with this guy? What does she even see in him?"

"You guys know I'm right here, right? I can hear you."

They look at me, then go back to their conversation.

"I have no idea, he's the literal worst."

"Obviously. So what are we going to do about it?"

"I've been trying to come up with something for months, but nothing. I finally figured that he would ruin it all on his own."

"Which he clearly has."

"Hello!" I wave my hands between them, "Remember me?"

"Hi, honey," Tori takes my hand and holds it in hers. "We see you, but do you mind keeping it down? We're having a conversation."

I growl in frustration. "I already have parents. I don't need you two to parent me."

Jonathan takes me by the shoulders and turns me to face him. "Let me say this one thing and then we will stop."

"Fine," I concede.

"I'm guessing that you and Denham had a fight, I'll figure what that's all about later, and then when he didn't talk to you, you were up pacing all night in your room." He looks at Tori. "Which explains the tired comment." He looks back at me. "Then you decided this morning that you would talk to Norah because she's your mom and because she has a special way of putting things into perspective." He takes a breath before continuing. "And then after everyone showed up and Denham still didn't come out of his room, this new perspective has given you Worry Face."

I'm speechless. How did he just do that?

Tori lays her head on my shoulder while she hugs me. "We know you, Mills. This isn't you."

My eyes are brimming with tears, but they don't fall just yet. I haven't taken my eyes off of Jonathan. "I thought you liked him."

Jonathan gives a short laugh. "I hate him."

Tori holds back a laugh, resulting in a snort.

Jonathan continues, "I kind of figured things would fizzle out, and we would all move on and pretend he had never existed."

"One cannot ignore the existence of Denham Narcissus Muller VI."

I roll my eyes at Tori. "That isn't his name and you know it."

Tori shrugs. "But it sounds so much better that way."

She's ridiculous, but it does the job and I'm laughing.

"There's our girl," Jonathan says and pulls me into a hug.

Tori joins in. "Yep. Just needed my partner in crime to finally get through to her." I hear them high-five above my head.

"You guys are the worst." They tighten the hug.

CHAPTER 30

Millie

*J*HAVEN'T STOPPED CRYING since last night. Mark stayed until around midnight before he went home to get some sleep. At least one of us will be rested, because I certainly didn't get any sleep. Around two, I told my roommates I was going to head to bed. I knew it was pointless, but they were all falling asleep, and I knew they wouldn't go to bed until I did.

There's a soft knock on my door before Tori pokes her head in. "Hey, how are you holding up?"

I wipe my cheek and shrug. Tori closes the door behind her and climbs into the bed next to me. "Talk to me. What's going on in that head of yours?"

"I was just remembering that Christmas when Denham came."

"Eww. Why are you thinking of that jerkwad?"

I give a halfhearted chuckle. "I wasn't really thinking about him. More... Do you remember brunch? How you and Jonathan knew what I needed to hear?"

"I mean, I remember talking to you, but I don't remember anything specific."

"Do you think I've become too complacent?"

"What do you mean?"

"That somewhere along the way, I started letting you and Jonathan make all the decisions?"

"You make decisions."

"Yeah, but I always give in if there's something either of you want more."

Tori sits up. "Example?"

"Our Saturday morning runs." I sit up and face Tori. "Tor, I hate running. Despise it. It's the worst. It's not exercise, it's torture."

Tori laughs and pulls me into a hug. "You don't have to run anymore." She gives my shoulders a squeeze then her face grows serious. "And I'm sorry you ever felt like your opinion didn't matter. That's the furthest from the truth."

I slump back down onto my pillow. "It's not your fault I let it happen. I don't know how or when, but I let it happen. Somehow, I lost all confidence and stopped fighting to be heard."

"Well, I'm listening now." Tori sinks back down next to me. "So how are we going to get Jonathan to listen to you too? Because I know I haven't sounded the most supportive, but I really do think you and Mark are good together."

'Really?"

"Mills, I know I can be a bit harsh at times, but even I can admit you've been more yourself since you've been spending more time with Mark. He brings out the best in you. And, it was pretty cool of him for sticking by you last night."

I sink further into my bed, then turn to face Tori. "Thanks, Tor."

IT'S FRIDAY AFTERNOON, and there's only one place Jonathan will be. I head over to the high school and wait in the hallway until the bell rings. I recognize a few of the students as they filter out of the choir room. A few wave and say hi. The line of students thins, and I take a breath and steel myself with as much courage as I can before walking into the door.

Jonathan is standing by the piano looking over the sheet music with the class accompanist. He's all smiles and completely relaxed until he looks up and sees me. He looks away and says a final note to the accompanist then walks over towards his chair and gathers his things. I guess it's going to be completely up to me.

Tori and I practiced and roll-played multiple scenarios, but this is real life and no amount of practice has me ready to actually say everything I need to say.

"The choir is sounding really good." Jonathan doesn't look up. There's a slight pause and then he goes right back to putting his things in his bag. "I listened through the door while I was waiting."

"They've been working hard."

A slight twinge of relief. He still isn't looking at me, but at least he's talking to me now. "It shows."

"Millie, what's this about?" He pulls the strap of his bag over his head as he stands to his full height finally turning to face me. "I know you didn't come down here to talk about how the choir sounds. What do you want?"

"I just wanted to apologize for not being honest. You didn't deserve that."

"No, I didn't." He shifts. "I'm assuming you're not here to tell me you're not dating my brother."

Irritation bubbles in my gut. I keep my tone as even as possible. "I'm still dating Mark. And before you can say anything else, I'm going to keep dating him. He's a good man, Jonathan. He's the best guy I've ever dated."

Jonathan snorts. "Not like that's a hard title to achieve."

"Stop. Just stop. I know you're mad, but that isn't fair, and you know it."

"You know what's not fair? My best friend lying to me about dating my brother. After you promised you never would."

"I made that promise when we were children! You can't seriously hold me to something I agreed to when I was barely a teenager!"

"Yeah well, I guess promises mean something different to me."

"I guess so, because when I promised to always support your decisions I meant it."

"Are we done here? I have a rehearsal to run." Jonathan turns on his heel and heads out the door.

If he thinks walking away from me is ending this conversation, he has another think coming. I storm out of the classroom to chase after him but end up running right into his back. I squeak in response to the impact. Before I can say anything I hear a voice I haven't heard since childhood, but it's a voice I know in an instant.

Jack Winters stands in the foyer of the auditorium dressed to the nines in an expensive looking three-piece suit with his hair perfectly coiffed. When I was younger his hair always reminded me of a cockatoo. Now that I'm older, it still does.

"What are you doing here, Dad?" Jonathan's tone is clipped and cautious.

"Can't a man come and visit his son?" Even his tone drips with a haughty air. A chill skates over my skin when I feel his eyes notice me. "Ah, Amelia. My, you have grown up."

Jonathan puts a protective arm out to shield me. "Leave her out of this."

Jack chuckles. "Always together. I guess some things never change."

"Why are you here, Dad?"

Jack takes a step closer. "You weren't answering any of my messages."

"Because I already told you I didn't know where Mark was. I didn't see any need to keep reiterating what was already said."

Another step closer. "I don't know what you think you're protecting your brother from. I just want to talk to him."

"If he wanted to talk to you then he would. I don't know why you think I could help you. We don't exactly talk." Whether he is referring to communication with Mark or Jack, Jonathan's words are accurate.

Jonathan grabs my hand and pulls me with him as he walks closer to the door leading to the theater. "Now, if you will excuse me, I have a job to do. I'm sure you understand."

Jack steps aside and lets us pass.

On impulse, I turn when we reach the door to face Jack. "Mr. Winters, I hope you know how amazing your children are. They're some of the most genuinely caring people I know, and I'm lucky to have them in my life. Maybe someday you'll actually want to know them."

I turn and let the door close behind me.

I run straight into Jonathan as I rush through the second doors into the house of the auditorium. He grabs my arm to steady me as he has thousands of times before.

"Are you okay?"

I nod. "Are you? Jack just showing up like that?"

Jonathan shrugs.

I nudge him in the arm. "You can't fool me, I know all your tells."

"I guess that makes one of us."

"I deserve that."

"Yeah, you do." A small smirk fighting at the corners of his mouth. It's not much, but I'll take what I can get. As if by muscle memory we walk in silence to the half-wall partition that separates the house into sections. Jonathan hops up first then gives me his arm helping me up.

"So, Jack?"

"He's been messaging me on and off for the last couple months trying to find Mark. I told him I didn't know where he was or what he was doing. When that didn't work, I just ignored his messages and calls."

"I'm sorry."

"For what? You're not the one who left your family and only recognize your children when you need or want something from them."

I pat Jonathan's arm, hoping it conveys even a smidge of the things I don't know how to say. We sit in silence. I want to speak, but I also don't want to interrupt whatever thoughts are racing through his mind.

Jonathan finally speaks. "I don't really think they are alike, Mark. He's nothing like our father." He lets out a puff of air. "He cares about people too much. Jack Winters doesn't care about anyone but himself."

I give his arm another squeeze. He continues, "Mark always tried to protect me, even when I didn't need it. Even when I didn't deserve it." He gives a humorless laugh. "Especially when I didn't."

"He's your brother. He loves you."

"Yeah. I know."

"Do you? Because I don't think he knows that."

"I've been a pretty crappy brother, haven't I?" Jonathan bumps my leg with his knuckle. "And friend."

I manage to hold back my full smile, but a smirk still escapes. "C+, but I hear there's extra credit available."

"Oh, good. I'd never hear the end of it from my students if it got out that I got a C+."

This time I can't hold back, and a snort escapes, causing us both into a fit of laughter. Tears are streaming down our faces as Jonathan's students start to filter in. I wipe my cheeks as I wave hello to them. Jonathan and I hop down from our perch, and he wraps me into one of his signature all-encompassing hugs. I don't know what the future holds, but I do know that somehow, some way, Jonathan and I will be okay.

CHAPTER 31

Mark

JHAVEN'T SEEN MILLIE all day, and it feels like an eternity. I was hoping I'd run into her at the high school when I was at practice because I knew she was going to try and talk to Jon, but no such luck. I came straight home to shower and change so I could head over to her place. I'm about to grab my keys when there is a knock on my door. I hope with all my being that it isn't Krystal. I don't have it in me to deal with her. Though those encounters have been almost non-existent since her encounter with Millie.

"Dan, what are you doing here?" I step aside to let Dan Jacobson in.

"I was in the neighborhood and realized I hadn't seen your place yet." I quirk an eyebrow, the movement making me wince after that fight. In the neighborhood? "Or maybe there was something I wanted to talk to you about." Here it is. The lecture about not telling everyone about me and Millie. "Jack is in town."

That was unexpected.

"How? When?" I can't seem to make any complete sentences. I knew my father would eventually come to Ridgeview. I haven't responded to his messages or calls, and Jack Winters doesn't give up easily. Especially if he thinks that makes him lose. Lose what? I don't know, but the number of times I have heard his mantra Winters never lose rings through the front of my memories.

"He came by the house earlier today. He said he's been trying to get a hold of you, but you haven't been responding."

"What did you tell him?"

"That if you weren't responding you were probably not ready to talk to him and that he should respect your boundaries."

"Thank you."

"Mark, I'm not sure why you moved back to Ridgeview, or why you don't want to talk to your dad, but I know you have your reasons and when you're ready to talk, you will. You were always an introspective child. I would suspect you are the same as an adult. Just know if you ever want to talk, I'm always here. You're not a kid anymore, but I still might have an ounce or two of advice. At the very least, I'm a pretty good listener."

In all this time, I've hardly thought about the why of my actions. I simply acted on impulse. Except it wasn't impulsive moving to Ridgeview. As much as I thought of it as running away from my father's control, I was coming back home. I was coming back to where I knew I was loved and valued. I've done a pretty terrible job at showing how much that means to me.

Dan stands and heads towards the door. "I won't keep you. I know you were heading out when I dropped by." He pauses and points at my face. "Your eye looks awful. You should probably ice it some more."

"HE JUST SHOWED up at the school?" I don't know why this surprises me. My father will do about anything to get what he wants even if that means going to harass my brother at school. This is all my fault.

"Hey," Millie grabs my face, forcing me to look at her, "none of this is your fault. Any and all action that Jack takes is on him. Not you. It's not your job to protect everyone."

I lean into her touch. "How do you do that?"

"Do what?"

"Know exactly what I need to hear."

Millie kisses me softly as she moves her hands from my face to around my neck. "You aren't as good of an actor as you think you are."

She kisses me again, but this time I pull her in closer and deepen the kiss.

"Or maybe you can just read me better than most people."

Millie shifts and sits on my lap. "Maybe that's because you let me."

I lean back further into the couch, pulling her body with mine. "I don't mean to be so closed off."

"I know," she says softly. "Letting people in is hard. It makes you vulnerable, and you don't like that, but, Mark," she sits up so she can look me directly in the eyes. "Being vulnerable doesn't make you weak. It makes you brave."

I let that sink in as we lay on the couch completely wrapped up in one another. We stay there in complete silence as I listen to Millie breathing softly as she lays her head on my chest, my hand rubbing her back absentmindedly.

I HAD TO step out of the office for a bit. It's been a long string of meetings with clients followed by long hours sitting in my office at my computer as I work on the contracts they need written up.

I'm exhausted. Mentally and physically. It's been nice having work distract me from all the things I can't fix. I don't know how to help Millie. I know she and Jonathan have talked things through now, but she's still been so upset about Ben, and I can't help but feel responsible, even when she continually assures me that it's not my fault. Now with my father in town, I know it's only a matter of time before he finds me. I know it sounds ridiculous, a grown man being afraid of his father finding him, but I am. Maybe afraid isn't the word. I've never feared for my safety, I just lost who I was as I became everything that I thought he wanted me to be. I don't know what to expect when I see him. When it comes down to it, I've always sought his approval, and knowing I don't have it after leaving Charleston like I did, I'm not sure I'm strong enough to withstand whatever he will lash out at me.

After my last meeting, Nancy invited me to go to lunch, and I couldn't say no. Not that I would want to. I laugh as

I think about how much I didn't want to get to know her when I first started at Lexington. Now I couldn't imagine my life without the crazy woman who has become somewhat of a surrogate aunt. Who has welcomed me into her family with open arms.

When we stepped off the elevator Nancy pulled my arm towards the pavilion of tables in the courtyard where Marty was waiting. He gives my shoulder a squeeze and Nancy a kiss on the cheek, then turns to the table and pulls out a chair for her to sit in.

"I don't want to intrude on your lunch plans. I can just go get something from the taco truck and head back into the office."

There's a knowing glance between the two of them as Marty starts to unpack the cooler he brought with him.

"No need for that. I brought sandwiches." Marty hands me a wrapped deli sandwich. "Nancy said you'd like a number six with no mayo."

I smile to myself. I should have known they had something planned.

I spend the next hour enjoying Nancy and Marty's company. I sit back and listen to stories of their travels and vacations they took when their children were young. As they go from story to story, Marty starts to take over as narrator and gets more and more lively as time goes on. Nancy once told me that I reminded her of Marty, I didn't know it then, but that was the biggest compliment she could have ever given me. Nancy adores Marty, almost as much as he adores her. They bring out the best in each other. I only hope that that can be me and Millie someday. The thought makes heat rise in my chest, but it's the good kind. The kind that makes a man want to get down on one knee and ask her to be mine forever.

MILES IS PACING by the front door of the office when Nancy and I walk off the elevator with an expression I can't quite read. I don't know what he's going to say, but the moment his eyes meet mine I know I'm not going to like whatever it is.

"Mark! There you are!" Miles says in a voice much louder than necessary for the small space. He looks behind him towards the partially open door. "Hope the meeting went well." Again, his voice is louder than it needs to be when I'm standing three feet in front of him.

"Uh, yeah. It went fine. Pretty standard."

Miles leans in speaking in a hushed tone this time, "A man claiming to be your father came in demanding to see you." My stomach drops. "I told him you were in a meeting and I wasn't sure when you would be back. I tried calling you, but it went straight to voicemail."

I look at my phone, and sure enough, there was a message from Miles. And the unopened one from my brother that I was too chicken to open last night. No matter how much Millie told me I should read it.

> **JONATHAN:** Dad's in town. He's looking for you. Thought you should know.

"I must have forgotten to take it off of do not disturb."

Miles nods.

Nancy rubs my back in a reassuringly maternal kind of way, and it's just what I need to know what I need to do. I'm not the same person I was back in Charleston, and I will never be that guy ever again. It's time to make that abundantly clear to the one person who never listens.

I smell my dad's cologne before I walk through my office door. The expensive kind that smells cheap. Or maybe it just smells soulless. Either way, Jack Winters has made himself at home at my desk reading through my files and contracts.

"I'd tell you those are confidential, but I doubt that would stop you from reading," I say dryly.

Dad's lips twitch as he closes the file he was reading. "I'd tell you that you did good work, but why lie to you? You're wasting your talents writing small time contracts."

There was a time not that long ago that those words would have destroyed me. All I wanted was to do good work to be seen as worthy, but I happen to like the work I do here at Lexington. I work with good people who want to help others. It's not all about the payout.

Dad's steely blue eyes meet mine. "What are you doing here, Mark? Ridgeview, really? Working in some small-time law office? You were about to be partner! The youngest in the history of the firm!" He lets out a frustrated breath. "I don't understand how you could give all that up. And for what?"

I take a deep breath to collect my thoughts. As much as I have been avoiding this conversation, I know it needs to happen. I need to say this. "I know you don't understand. And maybe I don't fully understand it either, but I like it here. I like working at Lexington. I like helping smaller independent companies, and I like writing contracts. And I like being back in Ridgeview. I like being able to see the people who matter most to me more than just on the occasional holiday. Not that you would care, but we actually had a family dinner the other night. Just the three of us kids and Mom. When's the last time you ever had time for that?"

"So that's it. Your mother finally got to you," Dad says cooly. It makes something inside of me snap.

"You don't get to talk about her that way." I seethe. "She's done nothing to you. Even after everything you put her—us—through, she still goes out of her way to not say anything negative about you. And trust me, there's plenty of negative things she could say that no one would contend."

"Now, Mark, there's no need to raise your voice. You aren't a child anymore."

"You're right, I'm not. I'm not the same kid who idolized you and would do anything to make you notice them. Or the one you abandoned the one and only time you invited me and Jonathan to your apartment after the divorce. I'm not the teenager who had to pretend he wasn't disappointed when you didn't show up to a game you promised you would come to or try and make a big show for my little brother so he didn't notice that you didn't come to yet another one of his plays. I'm not even the same broken mess I was when my knee injury ended my baseball career. I grew up, Dad. I changed. But you know who's never changed?" Dad gives me a humorless smile. "You."

"Are you done?"

I make a point of wiping my hands in front of me before putting them up in surrender. "Completely."

Dad stands up, buttons his suit jacket, adjusts his cuf-flinks, then strides towards me. He places his hand firmly on my shoulder and fixes me with a hard stare. "You think you know so much more than me, but you'll see. This place, it's too small for someone of your caliber. If you stay here, you'll drown. You won't reach your potential. You'll fail. You're just like me, Mark, we need bigger and better. We need to constantly be pushing ourselves for more."

A complete sense of peace washes over me as I realize that nothing he just said hurt me. None of it made my mind race or give a second thought. I'm free. His opinion of me doesn't matter. I don't need his approval.

"No, Dad, I'm nothing like you. I never was. I was just so desperate for you to notice me that I became what you wanted me to. But I'm done. I don't need your approval or your attention to know who I am. It's taken me a long time to realize that I have the ability to love and am worthy to be loved, but I am. So, I guess in a way I have to thank you, because if I wouldn't have left Charleston, I never would have come back to Ridgeview, and I would still be miserable."

I hear all-too-familiar voices coming from the lobby.

"Hi, sweetie, I don't know if now is a good time."

"Is he in a meeting?" The voice comes closer, then my door opens, revealing Millie. Dad watches her assessingly, and I don't like the look in his eyes.

"Oh!" Millie gasps. "Sorry, I'll come back later."

Before she can turn to leave Dad puts out a hand to stop her, and I swear if he lays one finger on her, I'll help him remove it. "No need, Amelia. I was just hearing all about how my son, here, loves being back in Ridgeview."

I step in front of her, blocking any access he might have to her. I've never known my father to lay a hand on anyone, but I'm not taking any chances.

"Have to admit it makes a whole lot more sense now." He looks at me gleefully. He's the Grinch deciding how he's going to steal Christmas. "Of course it comes down to the Jacobsons. It always has. For you, your mother, even your brother." He turns back towards Millie. "Now I will say, I didn't think you had it in you to wrap both of my sons around your finger."

"Leave her out of this," I grit out.

Millie wraps her arm around mine. "Don't," she whispers, "he's just trying to get a rise out of you. Just let it go. It isn't worth it."

I unclench my jaw and roll my shoulders.

With a satisfied smile, Dad strides out the door. "I do hope I didn't start a lovers quarrel."

I don't dignify the dig with a response. A moment later I hear the front door open then close. He's gone.

"Well, that was fun." Millie says, way more chipper than the situation calls for. I know she's just trying to break the tension, and I love her for it. I roll my shoulders as my breathing and heart rate begin to regulate.

Millie moves to face me, rubbing her hands up and down my arm. I'd say it made me feel like a puppy, but it's soothing, and I don't care. "How are you feeling?"

"Fine," I answer automatically.

Her hands leave my arms to grab my face, so I have no choice but to look at her. This is the second time in less than twenty-four hours that she's done this. "No. You don't get to shut down again. How are you really feeling?"

I take a deep breath. "I feel like I just had a run in with my dad. Like I was twelve years old again. I don't think I've told him off like that since then."

Millie wraps me in a hug, and it's the final straw. Everything I've thought and every feeling I've had bottled up for months, years even comes out. Millie listens to it all, even when I apologize over and over for rambling so much. She just rubs my back and listens.

She really is too good for me, but I'm grateful she doesn't think so. And I'll do anything I can to prove to her that I'm worth the cost.

"WHAT HAPPENED TO you?" Nick says as I walk into the locker room Saturday.

So much has happened the last few days I had almost forgotten the full-on brawl I had with Jonathan. I'm surprised more people haven't mentioned my still slightly bruised face. When I looked in the mirror this morning, I hardly registered the greenish-yellow tint along my jaw. My brother can undoubtedly pack a punch. Considering how sore my knuckles have been, I know he's most likely sporting similar battle scars. I still haven't talked to him since our fight, unless you count the warning text he sent me two days ago. I didn't even send a real reply, just a thumbs up emoji. Who even am I? This week has been far too draining. "It's nothing."

"None of my business, but it doesn't look like nothing."

"Just a misunderstanding." Millie says that she and Jon have talked about things, but since he and I haven't, it's the least complicated way to put it. The high school locker room is not the place to be talking about how I've been secretly dating my little brother's best friend and he didn't react well when he found out.

"That's some misunderstanding." Nick grimaces. "I at least hope Millie's been taking care of you." I furrow my eyebrows. "Don't look at me like that. I saw the way you two were looking at each other last week when you were coming to practice. Not to mention the rumors." A smile quirks up. "You two didn't think you could make out on a high school campus and no one notice, did you?"

"No. I guess not." I sigh. "So, basically, the whole town knows now?"

"Ridgeview has a pretty large population so I doubt it's the whole town, but since the Winterses and Jacobsons are basically Ridgeview High royalty, yeah, everyone here knows."

I sigh again.

AFTER A QUICK pregame warm up and an inspirational thought by Nick, the boys are out on the field. The stands are full. I scan the stands quickly for Millie, but she's not there. It's still early so I'm not worried. I know she'll be here.

Bottom of the fourth and it's our turn to bat. I scan the crowd but still no Millie. Maybe she went to go talk to Jon? She mentioned last night that she wanted to stop in on his rehearsal before coming to the game. She could have lost track of time.

Seventh inning stretch. Still no Millie. Something is wrong. She wouldn't just not show up. She's been talking about this game since I accepted the position. There is no way she would miss it. She knows how hard it was for me when Jack would miss a game. She was there when Natasha didn't show up to Ben's wedding. Millie shows up for things, she always has. She promised she would be here so she wouldn't just not show up.

Out of the corner of my eye, I see hands waving in my direction. I look and see Jon calling me over. I stare at him for a moment, but something's off. I jog over.

"It's about time. I've been waving my arms like a lunatic."

"Sorry. I'm a little busy at the moment," I say sarcastically.

"You don't have your phone on you, do you?"

I point to the field. "Again, I'm a little busy at the moment." I'm starting to get agitated. Not necessarily at him. I've just had way too many emotions come up to the surface this week and I don't have it in me to screen my tone of voice. Unless—something is wrong. Is it Mom or Rosie? Millie? My heart sinks at the thought. If something happened to her while she was on the way to my game, I'd never be able to forgive myself. I'm spiraling, and I know it, but Jon is taking way too long to say something, and I seem incapable of saying anything out loud.

"Millie called."

"Is she okay?" If she called, then she's okay, that means she's okay, right? She has to be okay. I need her to be okay.

"It's Dan. He's in the hospital."

Everything around me disappears. I zero in on Jon. "What happened?"

I'm already walking off the field. Jonathan races to catch up with me.

"The message said he and Norah were at the hardware store when he collapsed. All Millie said was that she was on her way here when she got the call and that she was trying to get ahold of you but that you were probably on the field already."

I pat my pants, but I don't have my phone or my keys. They are in the locker room way on the other side of the field. I need to get to the hospital, now. This is Dan. This is the man who taught me how to drive, how to shave. This is the man that dropped everything and flew all the way to Texas so that I wouldn't be alone when I had surgery. He might not be my biological father, but he's the only real dad I have ever known. I need to be there.

I look at Jon. "Do you have your keys? Mine are in the locker room."

He nods. "I'm right over here."

We don't say anything most of the drive. Torrance sent Jonathan the address for the hospital Dan was taken to and promised to let us know if anything changed before we got there. My mind is racing as I get lost in my memories. All the little things that Dan has done for me. From taking a punk twelve-year-old under his wing when he already had his hands full with his own children to coming over last night to check on me.

Above everything, one particular memory stands out.

Dan drives me to the hospital and talks with my surgeon. He's going to be keeping Mom and Norah in the loop on what's going on. When 10:30 comes around, it's time for them to wheel me back.

Surgery went well and the doctor says that there will be a scar, but nothing too noticeable. I will have recovery time and then it will be time to start PT. I'm not looking forward to PT at all. A couple years back when I hurt my arm, I had to do some PT, and it was brutal. I don't even want to know how much more it's going to hurt with an injury much more severe.

After getting released from the hospital, Dan drives me home. He hasn't left my side in two days. When we pull into my parking spot, he doesn't get out. He just stops and stares at me.

"What?"

His silence scares me. "Why are you staring at me?"

"You're not going to like what I'm going to tell you."

"You've been nothing but helpful since you showed up. I wouldn't have gotten through surgery without you. There isn't anything you could say that—"

"I called Jack."

Except that. I don't even know what to say. I haven't seen my dad since my high school graduation. We haven't even spoken in two years. "Why?"

"He's your father and had the right to know you were having surgery." He takes a deep breath then adds, "If one of my kids was having surgery, I would want to know."

"Yeah, but you're a dad."

"He's YOUR dad."

"No, he's my father. He didn't coach my little league teams or teach me how to drive. You did all of that."

"Yeah, I did, but being a dad is more than that."

"Being a dad is showing up." The words are bitter on my tongue. "He barely made it to my high school graduation. I was top of my class and a star athlete. I did everything, and he hardly came to any of it. But hey, I should be grateful right? At least he came to some of my stuff. When is the last time he showed up for any of Jon's stuff? What about Rosie? He hardly acknowledges her existence. He walked out on us when she was barely a year old. I'm surprised she even knows what he looks like."

I'm fuming, not at Dan, at Jack. It always comes down to me being angry at Jack. He's why I pushed myself so hard in school. He's why I pushed myself in athletics. Maybe, just maybe, if I was good enough, he'd show up and be there. Even after Dan called him, he didn't show up.

I look at Dan. "You showed up for the big stuff and the small stuff. You flew halfway across the country to sit in a hospital room for two days! You are more our dad than Jack will ever be."

I wish I could get out of the car, slam the door, and storm off, but I can't. I can't even get my leg turned to get out of the car without help. I just want to yell and scream. My eyes are stinging with emotion and I refuse to cry. He doesn't deserve my tears.

Dan drops the subject and helps me up the stairs into my apartment. He orders some pizza and turns on the TV to see if there is something on. We find an Astros game playing, but it's just too agonizing to watch knowing I will never play again so we turn it off leaving us in deafening silence.

Dan is finally the one to break the silence. "I'm sorry if I overstepped. I know it wasn't my place to call Jack."

"It's fine," I mutter. I'm acting like a child, and I don't even care. I do care, I don't want to, but I do. I sigh in resignation. "You *were probably right; he does deserve to know I had surgery. Did he actually pick up the phone?"*

"I left a message." Typical. "But he called me back." That's surprising. "He misses you. Did you know he's only an hour away?" I try not to make eye contact, but Dan can read me like a book. He nods. "That's why you chose to come out here, isn't it?"

I shrug. "I guess I figured that maybe if I was a good enough player maybe he'd actually come to my games. Even living an hour away he never came. Not that it matters now. I was injured and having surgery and he still didn't show up." I don't dare look at Dan. "I think that says more about him than any other time he didn't show up."

There is a storm of emotions rippling through Dan's eyes, but mostly they are filled with compassion. He knows more than any-one what Jack put us through. He clears his throat. "I'm allowing you one more day of self-pity and then you're done with all that negative talk. You understand?"

I'm so lost in my own thoughts that I jump when Jon speaks. "I'm sorry about the other night."

I look over at him. "Me too."

"Don't get me wrong, it felt kind of good to hit you." He gives a small chuckle, but there isn't any humor behind it. "But I never should have said what I did." He stops at the light and looks at me. "You're nothing like Dad."

Those four words are the greatest things he could have said to me. I don't want to be anything like our dad. I don't want to have anything to do with the man. I want as much space as possible between me and him. For years my biggest fear was not having his approval, then it became a fear of never measuring up to what he claimed to be my potential. It's only been the last couple of years that my biggest fear was becoming him. Up until Ben's wedding, I think I was well on my way to achieving that. I guess Natasha did me a favor when she reacted the way that she did when we broke up. Without her making my life miserable, I never would have even thought of coming back to Ridgeview. I never would have found what I have with Millie.

"I'm sorry, too. We wanted to tell you. We just didn't know how. We—me, I was a coward. And I'm sorry."

"You've always cared way too much about what other people think." My brother smirks as if he's remembering something, and I have no idea what he could possibly find amusing at a time like this.

"Um, I'm pretty sure you have accused me of the opposite. Multiple times in fact."

Jon shrugs. "I lied. Truth is, I didn't know how to measure up. You always had this presence about you. Even though you didn't speak often, when you did, people listened. And you were always so protective. One might argue overly so."

I smirk.

"I thought you hated me."

Jonathan looks at me with a furrowed brow. "You thought I hated you? Is that why you never came around much after you left? Why you cut ties?"

"I didn't cut ties."

"It sure felt like it. You would call Mom and talk to Rosie, but it's like you completely deserted me. It was like going through the divorce all over again, but worse."

Those words gut me. All these years I thought my brother hated me, and he thought I had written him off. All that wasted time we could have had the kind of relationship I wished we had. I'm such an idiot.

"Do you really care about her? Millie? Like really, really?" Jon's eyes flick to mine before going back to the road. "Because if you hurt her, I'll—I'll break you in half."

I can't help but laugh. "You'll break me in half?"

He shrugs. "It sounded like the right thing to say."

"Well, I have no intention of ever hurting her." I pause. "I love her."

"Wow," Jon gapes. "Did that hurt to say?"

I shove him. "Shut up."

He shoves me back with his free hand. "Just never thought I'd hear you say those words."

"I never had the need to say them before."

"Mom and Dad really did a number on us, didn't they?" It's a rhetorical question, but I answer anyway.

"One unintentionally and one carelessly, but yes."

"Are you happy?"

"I'm on my way to being very happy." I can't help the smile that comes as I picture Millie's face. The warmth and peace I feel when she's in my arms. I never knew what it was like to feel like this for someone. I never thought I was capable of it, but here we are.

"Then if you're happy, I'm happy." He looks over at me briefly before focusing back on the road. "And I wouldn't break you in half. I would think about it, but I wouldn't actually do it."

We find a parking spot and race inside. The elevator takes forever. The floor indicator shows it all the way at the top. I look over and see the stairs. Jon and I take them two at a time, making quick work to the fourth floor. When we arrive, we find the help desk and are shown the main waiting area that is filled with family and friends. I go hug Norah, who is sitting between my mom and Maeley.

"We got here as soon as we could."

Norah wipes at her eyes. "You're good boys."

"Any news?"

"Not yet."

I pat her knee. I scan the room for Millie. She's over by the window surrounded by her roommates and Jon. When I walk over, she all but sprints into my arms, holding on tight.

"I'm sorry I didn't make it to your game." She sniffles.

"I think you had a pretty good excuse," I soothe. Even in the midst of an emergency, she's worried about me. I really don't deserve her.

"I tried to call you, but you must have been on the field already." She starts to cry.

I shush her. "It's okay. It's going to be okay."

"You don't know that." Her voice cracks.

I pull her into a tighter embrace. She's right. I don't know what's going to happen.

"Whatever happens we'll get through it." I lean my forehead into hers and whisper. "Together."

I don't know how long we stand there like this when Matt breaks the silence. "So are we allowed to acknowledge that we all know about you two now, or is it still a secret?"

The whole room laughs. Millie and I separate, but I keep hold of her hand.

"How long did everyone know?"

Norah laughs. "I was suspicious at that first family dinner, but once you two were actively avoiding each other, I knew something had to be going on."

"The twins told Maddy that you and Aunt Millie were acting funny around each other weeks ago."

Story after story comes in on how everyone figured it out. It feels strange to be sitting in a hospital lobby laughing, but here we are. Everyone is laughing when Ben and Belinda arrive.

"What's going on?" Ben looks around the room.

Norah gets up and walks over to give them each a hug. "We were just distracting ourselves with stories of Millie and Mark."

There's a flash of something in his eyes, but I can't tell what.

Norah whispers something in his ear that Ben nods at. Then he straightens and leads Belinda to an open seat next to Ashleigh.

"Welcome to the pregnant corner." Ashleigh pats the seat next to her. Belinda gives her a curt nod then pulls out her phone. Ashleigh rolls her eyes and goes back to the conversation she and Kiersten were having.

I walk over to say something to Ben when the doctor comes in. We look at each other and just nod. We still need to have a full conversation, but I don't think he wants to kill me so at least there's that.

I only hear the end of what the doctor says. "He'll have to watch his diet and activity level, but his levels are looking good."

"Can we see him?" Norah asks.

The doctor nods. "Yes, of course." He looks around the room. "But maybe only a couple at a time. We don't want to overwhelm him."

Norah starts into planning mode, when Mom steps in. "Norah. Stop. We've got this. You go see Dan."

"Are you sure?"

"Go see your husband." She looks over at Maeley. "Why don't you go with your mom?"

When it's Millie's turn, I suggest Jon go with her. He gives me a nod of appreciation. I hold back and wait until the end before I go in and see him. As I walk into the hall towards his room, the nurse tells me that visiting hours will be ending shortly and to be quick. I nod.

"Knock, knock."

"Mark!" Dan looks tired and peaked in that hospital bed. He looks so...human.

"Dan the Man." My voice gets caught in my throat. I don't know what I would have done if things would have turned out differently. "Visiting hours are almost done, but I wanted to come say hi." I try to hold back the emotion in my voice, but I'm failing miserably.

Dan gives me a smirk, "Guess I only have a few minutes to ask if you've thought about our conversation yesterday?"

I nod. "I'm working through it."

"Good." He shifts in his bed trying to sit up. "Then I guess the only other question I have for you is, what are your intentions with my daughter?"

I laugh and wipe the moisture from my face. All of the emotions I've been holding in the last few days are threatening to come out all at once.

I clear my throat and stand up straight. "Nothing but the most admirable of intentions, sir."

"Do you make her happy?"

"I hope so. I try to."

"Will you do everything in your power to take care of her?"

"Yes, sir."

"Do you love her?"

"Yes, sir."

Dan smiles. "I'm proud of you."

Emotions catch in my throat. Those four words are everything I have ever wanted and needed to hear.

"Is there anything you need to ask me?" He gives me a knowing look.

I don't even have to think twice. "I'd like your permission to ask Millie to marry me."

CHAPTER 32

Millie

J'VE HARDLY LEFT my dad's side since he was released from the hospital. I'm pretty sure I'm annoying him, but I don't care. You can't scare someone like that and expect them to give you space. I've gone as far as sleeping in my childhood bedroom and bringing my laptop with me so I can work from the house.

"Mills, why don't you go get something to drink," Mom says from the opposite side of the couch.

I keep typing on my laptop. "I'm fine."

She clears her throat causing me to look up at her. "It wasn't really a suggestion."

I narrow my eyes at her and point to my tumbler sitting on the coffee table. "It's still more than half full. I'm fine."

"Amelia, go to the kitchen."

"Fine." I set my computer down and huff towards the kitchen like I'm some sullen teenager. When I walk in, all of my siblings are waiting for me. "What's going on?"

Danny slides next to me putting his arm around my shoulders. "Think of this as an intervention."

Matt copies the motion on the other side, sandwiching me in. "Mills, you're driving everyone nuts."

"You haven't left Dad's side since he got home," Maeley says gently.

"Neither have you," I retort.

"You've basically moved back in," Ben says.

"So have Jake and Drew!"

"Hey!" Jake complains. "We're only here until we start our next project."

"Yeah," Drew chimes in. "It just so happened that our break between projects fit in with when Dad was released and recovering from everything."

I roll my eyes. "So all of you can be worried and around all the time, but I can't?"

"Yes!" All six of them say in unison.

I wiggle out from under my brothers' arms. "That's hypocritical, and you know it."

"Millie, it's not that you aren't allowed to worry or be here, it's just that you—"

Danny stops mid-sentence as Ben takes over. "You tend to take over."

"I do not!"

Matt tries to hold back a smirk, "Yeah. You kind of do. You're Mom. And Mom tends to take over things. So you can imagine how annoyed Mom is that she is being out-mom-ed."

"So all of this is to say that I'm not letting Mom take care of Dad like she wants to because I'm in the way?"

"I think she's got it!" Danny cheers, and I smack him in the stomach.

"Okay, fine. I'll go back to my place."

"Good. Go hang out with your roommates. Go hangout with Jonathan. Go do something with Mark."

I nod. I guess I have been a little too preoccupied with Dad to pay attention to anything or anyone else the last few days.

"Fine."

Mom walks into the kitchen behind us. "Did she agree?"

I turn to face her. "You do know you could have said something to me yourself, right?"

Mom smiles at me. "Where's the fun in that?"

I laugh as I give her a big hug.

"I'm sorry I took over. I was just so worried."

"I know, sweetie. But it's not your job to take care of us." She leans back. "At least not yet. Maybe someday we will need that, but for right now, just keep being the child and let us be the parents?"

I nod.

As everyone starts to leave the kitchen after my, not so subtle intervention, Ben hangs back. He's silent until we're the last two in the room.

"I talked with Mark last night."

"You did?"

"Yeah."

"And how did that go?"

"Fine. We had some words, but he's still my bro."

Since Ben is openly talking to me, I refrain from rolling my eyes at his use of "bro".

"We talked a lot about you."

"And what did you say?"

Ben's head hangs low, "At first, I was mad. That you two were spending time together. That you started dating. That you lied about it. Then I felt bad that I was mad, when I was probably proving exactly why you didn't tell me. I guess I can get a little territorial."

"You think?" I say dryly. I've held back from saying a lot of what has been swimming through my head. Something was bound to slip through.

Ben sheepishly looks me in the eye. "I deserve that."

"Look, I know you think I'm not good enough for him, but I really care about Mark. This isn't something casual for me."

His eyes sharpen. "I never said you weren't good enough."

"It was just implied."

"No. No, it wasn't. Millie, Mark is my best friend in the entire world. I would do anything for him, but you're my little sister." There's a slight wobble to his voice. "There isn't a person alive that is good enough for you. You have to know that."

My eyes are stinging with unshed tears. "I had no idea you felt like that."

Ben wraps me in a hug, "I'm sorry I ever made you feel like I didn't care. You deserve the world. And if what you want is Mark, then he's lucky to have you."

AS SOON AS I walked through the door of the house, my roommates pounced on me. I was given fifteen minutes to get ready. They even had an outfit laid out on my bed. I barely got dressed before Kiersten and Tori were all in my business doing my hair and makeup, which now that I'm sitting in the back of a car with a blindfold on feels extra ridiculous.

"Where are you guys taking me, and why do I have a blindfold on?" I protest.

"So you don't know where we are going." Jonathan's voice sounds from the driver's seat. Oh, he's in on this too, great.

"This is kidnapping!"

"Only if you were restrained. And you aren't," Tori calls back.

I might not be restrained by cuffs or cords, but it's not like I can move. I'm firmly squished between Amara and Kiersten in the back seat of what I'm assuming is Jonathan's tiny compact. You know, a guy as big as Jonathan should have a bigger car. I mean I know he's not as tall as Mark, but it's not like he's short.

The car comes to a stop and I lurch forward a little.

"Can I take this thing off now?"

"No!" Tori calls, but she sounds further away now. Did she get out of the car? What on earth is going on? I hate surprises, and all of them know this.

Amara helps me get out of the car and turns me around. Kiersten comes to my other side, and the two of them continue to guide me to wherever my former friends have decided to sacrifice me, because that's the only thing I've come up with that makes any sense.

This morning my family plotted to get rid of me, and now my friends are finishing the job.

We come to a stop. I feel someone step in front of me and start to undo the blindfold. It takes a minute for my eyes to adjust to the light. When I do, I see that it's Mark who is standing in front of me.

"What's going on?" I ask him, confused.

"I asked if they could help me with a surprise, and I guess this is what they came up with." He shrugs, motioning to Jonathan and Tori.

"That's it, no more crime shows!" I call over to them, but I'm pretty sure I'm starting to figure out what's going on, and I'm already starting to cry.

"Don't." Mark points at me. "Don't ruin the surprise. I worked too hard to pull this off only to have you figure it out."

I laugh, but the tears are already streaming down my cheeks.

He pulls me with him, not that I'm resisting. As we walk through the empty market, past the food truck parking, and towards the makeshift dance floor, the twinkle lights start to come on overhead. Through my tears, I spot Duncan with his whole set up on the stage, and he starts to play music through the speakers. It takes a moment to realize what's playing.

"REO Speedwagon?" I look up at Mark, who is also starting to tear up.

"Of course." He stops, putting both of my hands in his. "Millie, I never could have imagined how much my life was going to change when I moved back to Ridgeview. You're everything I never thought I could deserve." Oh gosh. The tears. "You've taught me how to love. And more importantly, you've taught me that I'm worthy to be loved." Oh, he needs to hurry up with this, I'm about to burst.

Mark lets go of my hands and I'm reluctant to let go, but then he gets down on one knee and pulls out a box I would recognize anywhere. Only when he opens it up, it isn't my mother's ring. Or rather it is, but there is something added to it. There are two small diamonds on either side of the solitaire.

"This ring, like us, has history. Some of it good, some of it bad, but all of it is what helped lead me to you." That's when it hits me. Helen's ring. He's combined both our mother's rings together. A fresh jolt of emotion hits me. "Amelia Jean Jacobson, will you marry me?"

I crash into Mark, full of emotion. Flinging my arms around him, I kiss him like I need oxygen and he's the only way to get it. We're smiling. We're laughing. We're crying. I'm all enveloped in the moments until a catcall tears us apart. I look up to see that not only are my friends here, but the entirety of our families. I hadn't even noticed them before.

"So, is that a yes?" Ben calls.

I look at Mark, and we start to laugh again. He leans down to whisper in my ear, "You know, you didn't actually answer the question."

I smile up at him. "Yes. The answer is yes."

He smiles and gives me a quick kiss then turns towards our family and friends and yells, "She said yes!"

Millie

Four Months Later

MARK AND I have opted for a small ceremony, just close friends and family in my parents' backyard. We initially didn't want to wait, but once Rosie was offered a dream internship with a designer in Paris thanks to one of her mentors, we decided to wait until she would be able to be there. The whole property is gorgeous. Simple yet elegant as only my mother can plan.

Some might say getting married after only dating such a short amount of time is crazy, but for us, it's been twenty years in the making. Why waste another moment? As cliché as it sounds, when you know you know. I dreamed from the time I was twelve, hoped from the time I was seventeen, prayed from the time I was twenty-two, and knew with absolute certainty the moment I saw Mark in the lobby of Lexington that there would never be anyone else for me. Thankfully he came to the same conclusion. (Just maybe not quite as early as I did.)

I look around my childhood bedroom at my best friends who have been by my side. Kiersten wipes a tear running down her face as Amara tries to busy herself with the bouquets. (She has no idea that Duncan is planning to propose next week.) Tori and Jonathan are over in the corner in deep discussion. Five months ago this would have worried me, but since the run in with Jack at the high school, Jonathan and I have had a lot of heart to hearts. He and Mark are in the best place they have ever been, and he's been nothing but supportive.

I've also gotten a lot better at speaking up for myself when we are together. I still want to see Jonathan and Tori happy and will usually concede to what they want to do when we hang out, but I also don't force myself to do anything I really don't want to do. I'm happy to report I haven't had to go running once. Jonathan and Tori were the biggest helpers in Mark pulling off that magical proposal. After all, who knows you better than your best friends? Though I really could have done without the kidnapping. Just wait until it's their turn!

I face the mirror again, running my hands up and down the delicate lace. Rosie really outdid herself with this gown. It's a fitted lace gown with light and flowing sleeves that come down just past my shoulders. The heart shaped open back is the perfect touch, with its pearl buttons extending the rest of the way down my waist. I have no idea how she found the time, but I'm eternally grateful. I couldn't imagine a more perfect dress to get married in.

"You look beautiful," Jonathan says as he slips his arm around me and stands beside me.

"You really think so?" I look at him through the mirror.

"I know so. You sure you really want to marry my brother? It's still not too late to change your mind."

I laugh and nod, "I'm sure."

"Your mom has your something blue, but I thought you could use these as your something borrowed." Tori walks up holding a box. When I look at her in confusion, she opens the box to reveal a pair of bubble gum pink stilettos. I can't help but laugh.

"Just don't throw them at anyone's head this time," she says with a twinkle in her eye.

"But it worked out so well last time," I joke.

Tori wraps her arm around my other side, and the three of us stand there looking in the mirror. My eyes start to brim with tears.

"No crying!" Torrance chokes out. "We don't have time for me to re-do your makeup."

"You two are ridiculous." Jonathan hip-checks me, making me hip-check Tori in return. His eyes glisten as he pretends to scold us.

"It's time." I turn to see Danny standing in the doorway. "Wow. Look at you." The pride in my big brother's eyes makes my eyes sting all over again. If I'm crying this much seeing everyone else, what am I going to do when I see Mark? "You're radiant, Mills."

"Thank you," I say as he pulls me into a bear hug then lets go.

"I better not mess up your hair and makeup. Pretty sure every woman in this place would have my head."

I scrunch up my nose, and he bops it lightly. "Mom wouldn't, but the rest might. Ashleigh definitely would."

Danny snickers, "Truth."

Dad clears his throat from behind us. "Why doesn't everyone get lined up while I get a moment alone with my daughter?"

Everyone starts to clear the room and head to the designated spot on the patio out back. I try to hold in my tears, but the look on my dad's face makes it almost impossible. He's beaming with pride, and his eyes are shining with tears (who knew we were such an emotional family?). I can't help but think of how things could have ended so differently that horrible day four months ago. I shake the thought from my head. This is my wedding day; no need to think about things that didn't happen.

"You're a vision in white." His voice is thick with emotion.

"Thank you, Daddy."

Dad gives my hand a squeeze, "Mark is a lucky man." His voice takes on a serious tone. "I wouldn't have been able to give my blessing to a lesser man. You be good to each other." I nod. "Love each other. Support each other."

"Yes, Daddy." If he's trying to stop me from crying, he's doing a terrible job. "All I've ever wanted is to love someone and be loved as much as you and Mom love each other. In case you haven't figured it out, you guys are kind of relationship goals."

"You're never going to have a marriage like your mom and I have." His words take me aback, but he continues, "Because you and Mark aren't us. Just like you aren't Helen and Jack. It's up to you what kind of relationship you build. There isn't a secret formula that you can calculate. It's like your ring." I look down at the ring consisting of both our mother's diamonds. "For better or for worse, the marriages that those came from made you and Mark. They helped shape how you see the world and how you respond to it, but they aren't you. It's up to you and Mark what type of legacy you will leave for your children. Some of it will be good, and some of it won't be as good, but it will all be worth it if you put the effort into it."

I nod, not knowing what else to say.

Dad gives my cheek a kiss and settles my arm into his. "Now how about we head outside and get you married."

I squeeze his hand and follow his lead out to the patio.

As we make our way to the top of the aisle, I look at all our friends and family who are here. All my brothers, including Ben who is standing up by Mark, and my sister and my sisters-in-law (including my sister-to-be, Rosie) who are standing with me. Helen and my mom are sitting together with bright smiles and shining cheeks. A majority of Quimby is here, as are members of Lexington. There are even members of the Ridgeview Hawks baseball team here, all to support their now officially official assistant coach.

My nieces do a beautiful job as flower girls, even if Ashtyn had been disappointed she couldn't be a grooms-man. I look and see my best friends take their places with Jonathan right by my side. He gives me a wink then turns to face his brother and gives him a thumbs up. The small gesture makes all the emotions I'm feeling that much more intense. They are still far from the close relationship that I have with my siblings, but they're trying.

I don't dare look at Mark until I am almost right in front of him, I know I'll be completely undone as soon as I do. As soon as I look at him our eyes lock. The rest of the world disappears; we are the only things that exist.

As he takes my hand, he gives it a squeeze and leans down to whisper in my ear, "I'm all in."

I smile up at him.

"I'm all in."

Mark

18 Months Later

I NEVER REALLY THOUGHT about what married life would look like. For most of my life, I was convinced I never would get married, but Millie changed everything. Well, once I allowed myself to let Millie change everything.

I never knew it was possible to love someone so deeply that you'd want to put their wants and needs above your own. I never saw that with my parents. Dan and Norah just seemed too ideal, and they still kind of are, but theirs is a love that Millie and I strive to emulate in our own way.

We didn't send Jack an invitation to the wedding—well, technically we sent one, but it arrived purposefully late. I wasn't ready to face him after all that had happened, and Millie respected my decision. We did end up going to see him when we were back in Charleston helping Todd move to Ridgeview a few months after the wedding.

Millie's got it in her head that he moved to be closer to Trina, but I think she's got love on the brain, and since most of her friends have already made their own matches she's moving on to mine. Todd and Trina met for the first time at our wedding. Pretty sure Millie is trying to orchestrate a real-life Hallmark movie. I really need to cut her off from watching them, but then again, I'd lose my excuse to watch them, so maybe we can just limit it to a few a week.

Mom and Norah have been more than thrilled that they're finally related. It's their dream come true. The only thing better (which they remind us repeatedly) would be to have a shared grandchild. Dan is constantly telling them how ridiculous they are, but I'm pretty sure he's hoping for the same thing.

Shortly after we got engaged, I started the updates on my townhouse. What started as a way to spend time with Millie turned into starting our lives together. Thanks to Jake and Drew's latest business venture, Jacobson Bros Construction Company, we were able to pretty much finish everything before the wedding with a few last-minute touches after Millie moved in. A year and a half later and we still haven't decided what to do with the spare room but are using it as a home office for the time being.

I WALK INTO the door after a long and grueling session in the gym with some of my players. I have a few who are being looked at by scouts, and it's important to keep them in tip-top shape. When I signed the official contract to be a coach, I promised the whole team that I would be with them every step of the way, just like my coaches were with me. That means training even in the off seasons.

The house is strangely quiet, which if you've met my wife is highly suspicious. I suddenly get the urge to check behind corners and look above doors. She's been home all day, so there's no saying what mayhem she could have concocted. If there's one thing I have learned about the entire Jacobson family since becoming a member, it's that the whole lot of them love pranks. The bigger the better. Idle hands and all that.

After a few minutes of searching, I call out, "Mills?"

"In the second bedroom!"

I follow her voice and find her pinning paint swatches to the walls.

"What are you doing?" I ask, equal parts amused and confused.

"Trying to decide what colors to paint the walls," she says matter-of-factly.

"I can see that, but why? I thought we decided to wait on paint until we decide what we want to do with the space?"

Millie turns to look at me. "But I did decide."

I can't hold back my grin because it's such a Millie move. As soon as you think you have her figured out, she goes and changes it up. "Oh, did you now?"

"Yep." She turns back to the wall and continues to pin up color swatches.

I walk behind her and wrap my arms around her. Leaning down, I give her shoulder a quick kiss before moving my way up her neck. Stopping right below her ear, I whisper, "And what did you decide?"

She gives a slight shiver as she leans into me.

"I was thinking we could use it as a nursery." As she says the words, she takes my hands and moves them to her stomach.

My eyes go wide as understanding dawns on me, I twist her around to look at me. "You mean—"

Millie looks at me with tear-brimmed eyes and a wide smile. "Doctor confirmed this morning."

I yip and yell, picking her up and spinning in a circle. Millie laughs and squeals as she holds on to my shoulders.

When I stop and finally put her back down on the ground, she interlocks her fingers behind my neck. "Are you sure you're okay with this? We've hardly even talked about having kids yet."

I look down at my beautiful wife and give her a kiss that I hope tells her just how okay I am. When I pull away, our breaths are ragged.

I put my forehead to hers and whisper, "I'm all in."

The End.

CHARACTER GLOSSARY

AMELIA (MILLIE) JACOBSON – fourth Jacobson child, best friends with Jonathan Winters since birth, book editor

MARK WINTERS – oldest Winters child, best friends with Ben Jacobson since birth, lawyer

DANNY JACOBSON – Millie's oldest brother, married to Ashleigh, father of Ashtyn and Austyn, expecting third child

BEN JACOBSON – Millie's second oldest brother, married to Belinda, expecting first child, best friends with Mark

MATT JACOBSON – Millie's older brother, single father to Madelyn (Maddie)

JAKE JACOBSON – Millie's younger brother, twins with Drew

DREW JACOBSON – Millie's younger brother, twins with Jake

MAELEY JACOBSON – Millie's younger sister, youngest Jacobson child

JONATHAN WINTERS – Mark's little brother, Millie's best friend, high school theater and choir teacher

ROSALYN (ROSIE) WINTERS – Mark's little sister, in fashion school

TORRANCE (TORI) RODRIGUEZ – Millie's roommate, best friends with Millie and Jonathan since middle school

KIERSTEN DAVIES – Millie's roommate, friends with Millie since college

AMARA LAHIRI – Millie's roommate, friends with Millie since college

TODD BISHOP – Mark's college roommate and friend since college

DUNCAN SULLIVAN – Amara's long-time boyfriend

DAN JACOBSON – Millie's father

NORAH JACOBSON – Millie's mother, best friends with Hellen Winters since childhood

HELLEN WINTERS – Mark's mother, best friends with Norah Winters since childhood

JACK WINTERS – Mark's estranged father

ASHLEIGH JACOBSON – Millie's sister-in-law, married to Danny, mother to Ashtyn and Austyn, expecting third child

BELINDA JACOBSON – Millie's sister-in-law, married to Ben, expecting first child

ASHTYN JACOBSON – Millie's three-year-old niece, one of Danny and Ashleigh's twins

AUSTYN JACOBSON – Millie's three-year-old niece, one of Danny and Ashleigh's twins

MADELYN (MADDIE) JACOBSON – Millie's five-year-old niece, Matt's daughter

ACKNOWLEDGMENTS

Thank you to my parents for always fostering my love of books and encouraged my creativity. To all those who told me I should write a book. Becca Watkins for being my sounding board throughout the entire process and reading every single early draft. Sara Beth Schneider for all of her encouragement throughout the editing process. And Stephanie Anderson at Alt19 Creative for the amazing cover and formatting.

A special thank you to all those who have read and will read this book. Who could have ever thought a kid who struggled with dyslexia would end up here. Thank you for making a dream I didn't know I had come true.

MEET THE AUTHOR

California born and raised, current Texas resident. Amy studied Early Childhood and Special Education at Snow College and Brigham Young University Idaho. Amy is an early childhood teacher, an avid reader, and is a trained choral singer. When she isn't writing, Amy enjoys cooking, baking, and spending time with her golden doodle, Bennet.